JEZEBEL

Tae Thomas

CONTENTS

CHAPTER ONE

Jezebel

"Jezebel, where are you?!" The strike of a whip on empty air. "Come out, come out." Another strike. The door creaks open. "Found you!" Devil's face. "Turn around. Be a nice little girl." Cruel eyes, twisted mouth. "Don't want to end up like your mother, do you?" Tears — mine, not his. "I said, turn around!" The loss of patience. **Never** anger the Devil. "Now!" Don't stare defiantly; keep your head down. *Slap!* The back of a hand. The sting of a blow to the face. I turn. *Crack!* The whip comes down again and again on my back. Never in the same spot. "Now say you're sorry." Don't say a word; it'll only make it worse. "That's right. Know who the one in control is. Me!" Through clenched teeth, I hold back a whimper brought upon by the pain. "No more space left. That's enough for now. I'll be back later. Might want to get your back checked — it's in ribbons." Cruel laughter.

"Ugh!" I mumble with mixed emotions of despair, anger, and sadness. I hate my life! Footsteps retreating echo in the silence. I feel the pain, but it's not as strong as it used to be. My vision begins to blur as unshed tears rise to the surface.

"Get changed," comes another voice. "We have guests. Make dinner ready for 5:30." Devil's sidekick. Never far behind. Never alone. Don't let your guard down ever again. Or you're dead.

I change. I've no choice but to throw this top away; it's ruined now. It was one of mother's. I took it from the burn pile when they weren't looking. The lashes always with shirt on — so they don't cut too deep. Always on back — so no one sees. The scars don't stick out.

Blood's everywhere, but only in my mind. The whip hasn't brought blood for years. Not since they first started after the Devil finally broke mother. Until then, all I got were slaps and hits, not the whip. That was the only good thing mother did for me before she died — she took the whip instead of me. Thank you, mother. But no thanks for leaving me all alone.

I was never allowed to see her — according to her will or out of her control? It's highly likely that it was her decision...I mean, she never even screamed my name, just to see if I could hear her. Then, she died; I never got to say goodbye.

I'm not allowed to see her, where she lives in the ground. I've actually never seen the outside. I'm not allowed to go anywhere — I only leave this tiny room to make meals. I get tutored through the slat in the door by the Devil's friend.

I leave my room. Next, comes the hall, all doors — but one — locked. Trust me, I've tried them. Many times.

I go to the kitchen. Devil's friend — my tutor — is waiting. They must always watch — especially in the kitchen, where there are knives. Yeah, right, like I'd try anything; they'd have control of the weapon, and my throat slit in under a second.

"Boss wants soup, bread, and beef. The best and no less. Not for these guests." I wonder who could be so important. "Show them a nice home-cooked meal worthy of Brilla." So, that must mean they're from a different country. Interesting. "Don't screw up!" As he leaves, he bumps into me. "And watch where you're going!"

I go to the counter, where all my tools are. But why did he leave? I'm not allowed to be alone, without supervision. Out of the corner of my eye, I notice something different about the counter. There's a small vial.

And there's something in my hand. My tutor put it there when he bumped into me. I look around, making sure I'm alone before opening up the folded note. *It will only last for 6 hours. Guests will help you leave. Act normally.*

What's this? Me, leave the only place I've ever been since I was born? I grab carrots; celery; tomatoes; green beans; and peas from the fridge and start to chop them. I mean, yeah, I want to get out of the Devil's place more than anything in the world. But, for someone like me, there's no freedom; I deserve what punishments I get. I push the chopped vegetables from the cutting board into the pan on the stove. He'd catch me, and my life would be way worse than it is now.

I get started on the beef. The Devil might even just kill me — less of a trouble with me gone. I guess it's worth it. Because I'd rather be dead than live the rest of my life like this. It'll be never-ending torture until I break, like mother.

I finish with the beef and put it into the soup pot. Now, it's time for the bread. Good thing I prepared a loaf this morning, at the crack of dawn — when the sun rises. I never see it; there are no windows in the rooms that I'm allowed in. All that needs to be done now is to let the bread bake. I've 1 hour, should be enough time.

I've got nothing to lose, I'm going to do it. I'll run away. But why's my tutor helping me? It's probably a trap.

I put the bread in the oven and set it. But...it's a risk worth taking. I'm actually going to do it. I'm not going to end up like mother. I'm going to get out of here, and live my life with rights and freedom!

I get started on the cream for the soup. I should add fish so that the Devil can't detect anything weird. I pick up the vial and look at it — it's got a clear liquid, but is that good or bad? Is it toxic?

I go to the other side of the kitchen to see what we have. The fish section's mostly empty. But I see a squid. Skinned, not whole. And not a fish either — I think. Or is squid a fish? I don't know. Hopefully, it'll do the job. But if this is to go off without a hitch, shouldn't everybody — the Devil, guards, and Devil's friends — all be affected?

I continue to work on the soup, adding the squid cream to the beef and vegetables and stirring it all together. I'll have to add the vial at the end, in almost all the bowls. But not into the ones for the visitors — I don't want them to be affected.

I let the soup cook the rest of the way. I check on the bread — almost ready. The beef, vegetable, squid soup actually smells pretty good. I wonder if it tastes good too. But I'm not gonna try it. For one: it's too disgusting of a thought. And second, I'm not allowed to eat until the barest of crumbs are left.

Finally, the soup's done. I turn off the stove and grab the cleanest bowls from the cupboard — 20 in all; about 17 of them will be the Devil and his people. I start filling each bowl with soup, slice the bread after it has cooled, put the bread slices into baskets, and place everything on a giant serving trolley. Then, I go to the fridge to grab tonight's drink. Looks like it's lemonade. Lucky jerks!

I love lemonade. I've only had it once, but it was enough to know how good it tastes.

When I was 6, mother snuck it to me. One night, someone left her door unlocked, and she came in search of me. This was before I slept in my small, very tiny room. And I had a door that locked only during the day — why would anyone escape during the night? Especially if they've no one and no place to go? They want to sleep, the only escape from their terrible reality.

She took me to the kitchen and gave me a drink — it was lemonade. It was the first time I actually saw her. When I was 5, I only caught a glimpse of her before I was beaten. She looked completely different then than she did when I was 6 — she looked more alive this time. And when she came to me, I had an inkling that she wasn't the one who didn't want us to be together.

When my door creaked open, I startled awake. Thinking it was the Devil, come to do what he did to me when I was 5. He doesn't bother with me until daytime, only that one night was an exception. So I ran to the corner of my room and scrunched into the tiniest ball I could.

Mother started crying; she ran to me. She picked me up and started comforting me. Saying things like "Jezebel, don't be scared. I'm your mummy. I am here for you; I love you. I'll protect you. Nothing and no one has a right to hurt you. My strong little girl, I am so sorry." Her voice broke at the end.

Then she started to really cry while whispering my name over and over. I think it was because she had never really seen me — or held me — before. She finally realized who she had in her arms.

She started to get a grip on herself. She knew we didn't have long before somebody found her. She set me down, stood up, turned around, and pulled me up. Then she put her hand in mine, and we walked through the door, and all the way to the kitchen. She never let go of my hand. She went to the fridge, and got out a pitcher containing a liquid I had never seen before. She poured a glass, gave it to me, and told me it was lemonade. She said it was the best drink ever made. I took a sip. My mouth exploded with taste. Delicious was the only thought in my mind. In 5 seconds, I finished off the whole glass full. I felt very sleepy. I gave the glass back to mother, and my eyes started to close. As my eyes closed, the last thing I saw was mother putting the glass in the sink and turning back around to pick me up. She leaned my head on her shoulder, whispered nice things, and sung a little lullaby. Then I fell asleep; I don't know what happened after that.

But the next day, I woke up in a different room. The one I have now. My clothes — made up of rags, only 2 sets of tops and bottoms, plus underthings — were in the room too. I got out of the teeny bed and checked the door. It was locked, even though the time to lock the door was still at least an hour away.

I could hear someone screaming — that's what woke me. I remembered the night before. "Mummy," I whispered. She came to me, she gave me lemonade. But she hates me. I've never seen her...except for when she had the Devil beat me. But that night, when she came to me, I knew the truth. My mother never gave me up. She never told the Devil to beat me. It wasn't her choice not to see me because she had no choices. My mother loved me.

That's what got me through my life to here. The fact that someone loved me so much that she'd risk whatever the consequences. That scream that woke me, it was hers. She was caught out in the kitchen with me on her lap. Afraid that I'd

escape now that I knew the truth, I was put into a tiny room —
that only had room for my bed — and the door was kept locked at
all times. I never saw mother after that.

*I spent the whole day saying "mummy" over and over, rocking
back and forth, while crying. Knowing that she was getting hurt
because of me.*

That's the reason why I went mute. Why I now never let
my guard down. I'll get my life back and avenge my mother.
She didn't deserve what happened to her. I deserved it because
it was my fault. Everything's my fault. My fault that mother got
punished — she came to find me.

My fault that she was tortured to the breaking point. So,
I'll get out of this hell for her. I deserve what happens to me here.
But to save what is left of her — me, her spirit — I will leave this
place and never return. I'll find a way to give the Devil what he
deserves: his own hell.

I pour the lemonade into glasses, and place the glasses on
the serving trolley. I hear footsteps heading towards the kitchen.

I pour the vial into all the bowls except 3. I must
remember what 3 don't have it. Quickly, I shove the vial into the
oven.

"Dinner now!" The Devil's sidekick comes through the
door. I get behind the trolley, begin to push it — my arms
straining with the weight — and follow him through the door
and onto the path to the dining room.

CHAPTER TWO

Bryce

The Prince got an invitation to dine with the Devil. He didn't want to accept; even though he's not a spy, he knows evil. But I convinced him to accept; I have evidence that the Devil was the one who captured Linris. The letter had the usual villain cockiness — the point where they want to boast about accomplishing a task that was supposedly impossible. He has a surprise to show the Prince — I suspect that he wants to taunt The Circle that he could defeat their best spy.

We never leave a person — spy — behind. If we lose one, we lose the whole thing. We are a team, a small circle of spies who ensure that the royal family is safe at all times.

When just one goes missing, it could be very dire for the royal they were assigned to protect. Linris was in charge of protecting the Prince's father. A little while after she got captured, the king was killed, leaving the kingdom in the hands of his infant son. So, once I find Linris, she can protect the Prince. Then, I can finally be promoted to protecting the whole palace instead of just one person.

Linris disappeared 19 years ago. I may have been only 6 at the time, but I was still a trainee — I saw her around a couple of times before she got captured. She was very strong for a woman. She was one of the best, still is, and will be, once I find her. I don't see how I will be able to find her if The Circle has been searching all this time.

I remember precisely what Linris looked like. That's why when the evidence was uncovered, The Circle sent me. And, of course, I had to find a way to include the Prince, seeing as it's my job to protect him until I can get someone else to do it. Don't get me wrong, Theo's my friend, and he's not the worst royal to be assigned to, but it's always been my dream to protect the whole palace. And I can't do that while worrying about a specific person not getting their back stabbed. The invite was the perfect excuse I needed to go after Linris...and keep an eye on the Prince. Hopefully, I can find Linris, and head back to Musalin before anything happens.

Linris had neat waves of black hair; blueish-green eyes; a uniquely shaped, pale face; and the smallest nose I ever did see.

So that's how we all ended up here: me; Prince Theo; his mother; and another loyal spy who is a very close friend of mine, Guvnor Trus.

I was told that dinner is at 17:30. My watch says 17:20. Shoot, I should probably get ready. I grab a suit from my suitcase, my blackest dress shoes, and a stylish black tie. As I'm finishing with my button top, there is a knock at the door.

I make sure that my trousers are on right before I go to answer it. I sure do hope it's not the Devil — I'm not ready to face him just yet. Whew, thankfully, it's not the Devil. But it is the most unexpected person you could give me right now: Commander Drew Arch, a spy who went off the grid after Linris got captured. He comes in and closes the door behind him.

Drew looks suspiciously around before he turns his weary eyes on me.

"I'm sorry for leaving without a word, but I had to stay and protect Linris."

"You're going to have to say more than that for me to heed your words."

I am barely ever shocked — when you are in this line of work, you're always prepared for the unexpected — but what Arch says next, blows the roof off of my head.

"I had to protect Linris because she was pregnant. I don't know who the father was. But she had a close call to being caught trying to kill the agent on The Red List who was after the king. You know how The Red List has the Devil on their side. She was afraid for her unborn child. If she were to actually get caught, the Devil would most probably kill her baby. She didn't want that, so she called me and I killed The Red List agent." He says in a rush, seemingly not even to breathe once. It takes me a moment to decipher all of his words.

"That doesn't explain how she got captured — if it was you who did the kill. And where Linris is now, and this unborn child — that nobody but you knows of."

"I did kill the agent. And I was caught doing it. Linris tried to help me and explained that she killed the agent. I was torn, I could either agree with her, and lose her and the child. Or disagree, and get us both killed. Problem was that the person who caught me was the Devil himself. He saw how I did the kill, and he appreciated my handiwork. So, he offered me a job as one of his hitmen, his friend."

"But why did you accept? You're evil, aren't you? The fact that Julian took out your family still haunts you, doesn't it? Why would you, of all people, join the other side!?" My voice starts to fill with despair, but I can't help it. The Circle evokes a lot of emotion in me; it is my life and has saved me from the brink many times. "You were a legend," I am able to rasp.

"I had no choice! H—"

"No choice, everyone has a choice. And you chose wrong!"

"If you would just let me finish."

I sigh. I'm getting ahead of myself. I just need to take a breather and not let my emotions dictate my actions; the Devil might be watching. "Ok. Continue."

"Linris was right there. She was very beautiful. You couldn't tell that she was with child yet. So, the Devil took her for himself. I had to agree to become one of his hitmen in order to protect Linris and her child." Arch pauses for a breath, despair clouding his gaze. He rakes his hand through his hair in frustration. "The Devil brought Linris back here. He started doing horrible things to her. Such horrible things, that by the time the child came, he believed it to be his. So, he took it and has kept it locked up."

"Who is this child? What is its name?"

"Her name is Jez; she hasn't seen the outside her whole life. She's kept in a tiny room, only let out to make the meals. Linris never got to see her baby after she gave birth. Linris despaired away, so much so that **you** couldn't even recognize her. Losing her freedom, then her child, it was too much for her. She couldn't bear it."

"But...why did she just give up? She was a warrior; she could have grabbed her daughter and escaped. So why didn't she?"

"She **was** a warrior. But she just couldn't take it. She lost everything that mattered to her. There was no way out. The Devil is both the worst and the best. Nobody — not even Linris — could escape him, at least not on her own."

"Where is the father of her child? Couldn't he have saved them? Why did he just let them get captured and leave them to die? And what part do you play in all of this? Why does it have to be **you** who protects them?"

What Arch says next, really surprises me. All of a sudden he explodes.

"I was her love! Ok?! I stayed because the child was mine. Linris and I loved each other. We were going to ask if we could leave the business for a little while so that we could have the child and spend time together. But I wasn't able to save her from the Devil. Not if I didn't want him to kill both us and our child."

Arch begins to crumble.

"I couldn't save her. I couldn't save either of them."

"So, does this mean that Linris and the child are dead?"

"Linris is, but our child isn't." I have a mental snap; so, that's what the Devil wants to boast about. The fact that he was able to kill Linris, and he probably has her child working for him. I bet you that he's turned her evil.

Arch is still talking. "But Linris didn't die that day, she died 11 years after we were captured — 8 years ago. When Jez was 5 years, the Devil noticed that Linris was killing herself. So he took little 5-year-old Jez to her mother's room and beat her until her mother came back. From that day, Linris took every blow, every strike of the whip, just so Jez wouldn't have to. But after a while, her body just couldn't take it anymore. And it broke. She broke. At this point, Jez was 10 years. The Devil then started to whip Jez. One of the worst parts was that she didn't even know her mother had passed until she was 13 — when she tried to escape. She went to her mother's room to take her with her. And all she found was her mother's stuff in boxes, ready to be burned."

"Poor girl. What happened to her?"

"She's still here. She took some of her mother's stuff, but hasn't tried to escape since. I told her that you would rescue her."

"But I'm no knight in shining armor. What if she doesn't even want to be saved?"

"It doesn't matter what she wants. What matters is I want her out of here; I want her suffering to end."

"I can't save her."

"You came to save Linris."

"That's different. She was one of us. There was a warrior in her." Jez has probably never been taught a useful thing in her life to be a spy and protect someone.

"Just give her a chance. Please? I will even get down on my knees. I am begging you to free her. I can't bear the sound of her screams, her sadness anymore. I want her to have a life. One she has never known, a normal life. One with choices and crossroads."

"I'll think about it."

A gong sounds. It's already 17:40. And I don't even have my shoes or tie on yet. Luckily, my suit is on and all buttoned.

When I look back up, Arch is nowhere to be seen. Huh, I didn't even hear the door open or shut.

CHAPTER THREE

Jezebel

My arms are so weak. They buckle under the pressure of pushing the trolley. Usually, I don't have to take in a lot of food all at once. On a normal day, the Devil's friends eat only when they're free — which is at many different times. Usually, the Devil only eats with his sidekick and 7 guards. So instead of 20 meals, I only have to carry 9. This is the first time a visitor has come whom I'm allowed to serve. When we get visitors, I can't serve them because the Devil is afraid that they'd try and help me to escape. These visitors must be special.

The Devil's sidekick always comes to get me when everyone is sitting down at the table. The Devil has 2 dining rooms: a huge one where he entertains guests, and a small one that's just for him; his guards; and his sidekick. I've never seen the huge one. I assume that it's hideously decorated; all the rooms I've seen are. Whoever designed this place has bad taste.

The walk from the kitchen to the big dining room takes way more time than it does to get to the small one. When we finally get near the door, I hear the Devil talking.

"Shouldn't be long now. I have my servant deliver the food. Try to scarf it down for her benefit — no matter how bad it tastes — she's also the chef. If you anger her, she will throw a tantrum. And I would never hear the end of it."

"Oh, well, I don't think it's going to taste that bad. For someone who is — how old did you say she was?" Comes another voice, one that I've never heard before.

"She's 18."

"Well for someone who is that old, she can't be that bad of

a cook. Not if she has experience."

We come around the corner and enter the dining room. The Devil's sidekick holds open the door for me, only after I bumped into it with the trolley. As I pass him to go in, he whispers, "Don't talk to them. Don't even look at them. Or you will pay dearly for it later. Good luck". He laughs cruelly and walks away. I wonder where he's going. Why isn't he eating with the Devil? He always does.

I prepare to enter the dining room. I'll keep my head up, staring into space in front of me. Only look to set meals down. Then I'll keep my head down until I'm needed again. I won't look at anyone in particular. If I do, I'll get punished. He has reminded me so many times during our torturing sessions when the whip makes its mark upon my back.

As I step into the dining room, all conversations end. Everyone looks at me; I can feel it, even though I can't see it or them with my hair blocking my eyes. I go to the first person I see out of the corner of my eye. It's a guard. I give him a bowl of soup with the stuff from the vial in it; a piece of bread; and a glass of lemonade. I do the same for the next one, who's another guard, and the guard next to him. Then I come to the first one of the Devil's friends. All of the people of the household are on this side of the table.

I finish with them and finally get to the Devil at the head. When I give him his meal, he starts to talk again. "So this is the servant I was talking about. She's not the best I could get. But she's the only one that stayed." Now to me. "Girl, say hello to the guests and be sure not...to...spill...anything." As he talks, he's doing it with his hand and purposefully spills his glass of lemonade on my dress. "Oh. You should get that cleaned. Oops. Try not to do that to the guests." He shines a fake smile in my direction.

I feel so humiliated. My face wants to redden...but I don't let it. I keep up my mask of indifference. I can't let my guard down. I don't say anything, I even try very hard to hold back the tears that want to fall. This was the last thing that I have of my mother. Well, the last piece of clothing. I always have on the necklace with the spyglass pendant that my tutor gave me. He's always been the nicest to me. He said it was my mother's before she died. He also said the pendant is a spyglass — which is used to see things in the distance; it's mainly used on ships.

I quickly put the rest of the meals — I've 4 left — at the guests 'places. Oh no! One guest will have the stuff from the vial and they'll be affected. I can't change that. I hope that they still take me away — for my mother's sake. I give the vial-affected bowl to the last one at the table.

Once I finish passing out all the plates, I put the tray on a small table in the corner, and stand next to it. I look over the guests quickly and then put my head down.

There are 4 in total. Three are guys, and one is a woman. The woman is very pretty. She has blonde hair; brown eyes; fair skin; a medium-sized nose; and small lips. She's wearing the best jewelry I've ever seen: ruby earrings, modest layers of pearl necklaces, and something breathtaking on her finger that shines like nothing I've ever seen before when struck by the light from the chandelier. Not that I've seen much. But mother was wearing some all those years ago when she gave me lemonade.

The woman is sitting next to a young man, who looks about my age. He looks a lot like the woman — he must be her son. He has the same blonde hair and nose. The only differences are his eye color and shade of skin.

My mind completely blanks. Come on, mind: every detail counts. Ummmm, he's a little bit tanner than the woman. Oh! And his eyes are green. He's the last one of them, farthest from the Devil. Oh no. He's the one who'll be affected. I hope he doesn't hate me when he finds out that it was me who put the poison in the soup.

On the other side of the woman, there's a man who looks about in his 40s. He doesn't look at the woman with affection — mustn't be her husband. The blonde, green-eyed young man doesn't look anything like him. So, it's not his father. I wonder who he is though. He looks like he has secrets. I know what it's like to have secrets. They can hurt; they can destroy.

The final guest is sitting close to the Devil. He seems to be watching the Devil's every move and keeps looking at the other young man. If I didn't know any better, I'd say he's looking out for the young man. And he seems to believe that the Devil's a threat. He's smart.

I feel someone looking at me. I don't look up, though. I know it's not the Devil — I know how his look feels by now. His makes goose pimples form on my arms and makes me feel like I'm doing something wrong. This look doesn't feel like that at all. It feels like a friend, like someone who wants to know more.

I hate having new people here, looking at me. I don't know what they think. I'm hideous and not anything nice to look at. So, I think the worst of what they might be thinking. I start to fiddle with my hands — but not noticeable enough that I get yelled at.

CHAPTER FOUR

Bryce

Finally, it's dinner time; I'm starving. I haven't eaten all day, I've been too nervous about actually facing the Devil. Nobody gets that nickname by being friendly. I don't even know what his real name is, I don't think anybody does. He's just…the Devil.

I start down to where I have been told the dining room is.

What Arch exposed has shocked me to the core. How could Linris have a child, and no one in The Circle knows? Not even her sister knows; she hasn't been the same since Linris was captured, I bet bringing Jez to her would cheer her up. But then there's the fact that now I have to save somebody who can't even defend herself.

As I told Arch, it's completely different than saving Linris. I actually wouldn't have been saving her, I would have just helped her to escape. Once I had a way out, she could have fought alongside me. Whereas Jez probably has no way to defend herself; she can't fight her way out. Instead of helping her escape, I would have to save her. I would fight for her and me, all the while protecting Theo.

I know that I've been training my whole life, that I keep watch over an entire kingdom — and its Prince. But it's way harder to save someone, especially if you're going against the Devil.

I can't believe that I promised her dad, Arch. That is so weird a thought, even in my head: Arch, a father. He's not really the type, he put his everything into the job. But I guess that would also make it easy to protect your daughter. I can't just leave her here, now that he knows I said I would.

I don't know how I'm going to pull it off. It will have to be tonight.

We're leaving tomorrow. I'll see what I can do. I have rescued people before. All I have to do is find an escape route and make sure I can get 4 people out of the Devil's place safe and sound. Even though Trus is just as good of a spy, he's getting on in years. Plus, I have a higher rank, making me responsible for all of them — even Trus. It's a lot of pressure, but I will not buckle under it.

After many stairs, I reach my destination: a dark brown door with a gargoyle knocker. That's weird and creepy. Only front doors have knockers. The doorknob is a spider. What, did Halloween throw up here?

When I enter the dining room, its size causes my mind to blank. I've never seen a bigger or more exquisite room for dining, and I've been to a lot of the royal family's palaces with Theo. The table looks to seat at least 30. Why anyone in the world would need to seat that many, I have no idea. The Devil may have henchmen and guards, but to have them all sit down at once — even the Devil would see the fault in all of that.

One side of the table has the evilest, most vicious-looking people. At the head is the most horrid person in the world; he just radiates evil. There's definitely no doubt as to who the Devil is. Think of the worst, most evil thing in the world, then times it by a thousand. And that still doesn't reach the height of the Devil.

They even say that he is immortal. Who knows? I definitely don't want to find out. I just want to grab Jez and go.

On the other side, there are three chairs between the Devil and my group. In the 4th seat down, is Trus. Next to him — in the 5th seat down — is Atria. And next to her, her son Theo. Guess I'll have to sit in the third seat down. That's the best position to keep the Prince safe, with me between him and the Devil. Plus, the closer I am to the Devil, the better I can keep an eye on him, without it looking too suspicious.

As I go to sit down, everyone seems to hold their breath. A man peels away from the wall and goes down a hallway leading from the opposite side of the room from which I came. Where is he going?

The Devil looks at me; I look right back at him. Neither of us blinks. His place, his dominance. But I'm not going to back down that easily, not to the person who broke our best spy. He deserves a place worse than hell. He doesn't deserve to get his evil way in the end, but he does, every time. I break the staring contest; I can't have him watching me, I'll get caught and Jez won't be saved.

Everyone lets out a breath.

The Devil won't be getting his way this time. I'll make sure of it. I will rescue Jez and destroy him. But I won't be destroying him today. No, today is all about rescuing Jez and getting the hell out of here.

The Devil starts talking. I listen, all the while wondering about the identity of the servant who he's talking about. Is it Jez?

Just then there's a bang on the closed door leading to the hallway that the man went down. Guess that man is back now.

After the bang, the man opens the door; in comes a small, scrawny girl pushing a trolley at least three times her weight. Her very long hair covers her face.

The man pulls her aside and whispers to her harshly before leaving. The girl fully enters the room and starts delivering the dishes to each person on the evil side. When I can finally see what she looks like, I gasp silently. She looks exactly like Linris. But Arch said she died. How can she be dead, if she's right here?

Oh! It's not Linris. This must be Jez. She looks exactly like Linris, with the same face and hair color. The only difference in her appearance is that her hair looks a mess — like it has never seen a brush. She has brown eyes, like Arch. She has a little bit of a dark hue to her skin, also like Arch. But she mostly looks like Linris.

I wonder if Atria notices; she was very good friends with

Linris. I look over at her. By the look on her face, you would think she has seen a ghost.

While the Devil talks to the girl, he spills his lemonade on her — you can tell he did it on purpose. Everyone on the evil side starts laughing. Until now, her face has been a mask. But when the lemonade is spilled on her, for a quick second, you can see hatred and embarrassment flicker. But in another second, that mask is back in place; if you weren't looking, then you wouldn't have noticed.

There are tears in her eyes, but none fall. The Devil asked her to talk. Yet, she doesn't say a word. Why not? Arch had said that he was sick of hearing her screams, so she must talk — maybe she just doesn't do it in front of the Devil.

She doesn't react besides from what I saw after the lemonade fiasco. She just continues serving the rest of us and when she is finished, she goes to a corner of the room that contains an alcove. She pushes the trolley perfectly into it, stands aside, and seems to quickly scan my side of the table — why does she do that? Did she do it to see who we are, or is it just a thing she does every time that she serves people? She then tilts her head down and doesn't look back up.

I look at Theo, he seems all right; he didn't notice anything that just happened. He doesn't like being in a room with a lot of people — especially when they are as evil as this bunch, so he has shut everyone out and started to eat. I look back at the Devil to see if he's eating; maybe poison was put into the soup, a perfect way to get rid of the ruler of Musalin. He took out Theo's father, so why not kill Theo too? Nope, no poison, he's eating his soup very heartily. I look in Jez's direction; she's in the same position, but she's fiddling with her finger. What did she do?

Everyone is eating; I sniff my bowl when no one is looking. I don't smell anything other than the soup. I start to eat it. This tastes really good. The beef is just right, the vegetables are good-sized, and the squid really brings the flavor together. The Devil lied about her cooking. So, he must have been lying about how Jez acts. That's good, one less thing to deal with. I take a nibble of the bread — can't be too cautious, it might be poisoned. The bread is really good so I take a bigger bite, it is cooked at just the right temperature and time. Crispy but not burnt, and not too doughy. I wash it down with some of the drink — I don't test that for poison, there was none in the rest of my meal, and who the heck would put poison in a drink? It's better to conceal it in the soup with the weird taste of squid. Tastes like lemonade, but unlike everything else, it actually does have a funny taste. It's not poison, it just doesn't taste right. Must be the lemons; the ones in Musalin taste better.

After 6 minutes, people start acting weird — Theo being one of them. I look at Trus, who is also looking around. After seeing everything that is happening to everyone, Trus pushes his soup aside. So there was something in the soup, I knew it! But, I didn't smell anything in mine. Atria isn't having a reaction either, but she is looking worriedly at Theo. He's the only one in our group who seems to be affected by whatever was in the soup.

Everyone is choking and starting to lose their breath. They all slump after one minute of struggling and appear to be unconscious. I look at Jez, she has a worried look about her...no, not worried, a very scared look — like she did something wrong and is going to get in trouble.

She's rooted to her spot but looks at me; she's begging me for something with her eyes. Arch told me that he told her I would save her, THAT'S WHAT'S GOING ON! She must have poisoned everyone so that she could escape with us. But she has poisoned Theo. She's not going to get away with this. I'm not saving her anymore. I'm going to drag her back to Musalin with me and force her to give me the antidote to save Theo. Then, I'll decide what her fate will be. But I can assure you, it won't be nice.

I get up; Trus looks at me. "What are we going to do?" He asks me, but I ignore him and start to walk over to Jez. Trus stops me with a hand on my arm, "What are you doing? Where are you going?"

I shake Trus 'hand off and storm over to Jez. Once I reach

her, I start to shake her.

"How do you fix it?! What's the antidote!?" I shout in her face.

She doesn't say anything; she just keeps staring at me with eyes full of fear. "Well, answer me!" I shake her a few more times; she opens her mouth and tries to talk, but nothing comes out. I drag her over to where Theo is knocked out, point at him, and turn to her. "How... do... you... stop... this?" I say slowly, in case she can't understand what it is that I am saying. Atria looks up then, focuses her gaze on Jez, whispers Linris 'name, and freezes.

Jez just shakes her head and points to the rest of the people who were poisoned. She tries to convey something with her eyes. She meant to poison the Devil and everyone but us. That's why Trus, Atria, and I weren't affected. She miscounted when she poisoned the soup.

Jez seems to come to her senses. She forces my tight grip off and runs from the room. I go to follow her, but Trus stops me.

"Let her go. We need to help Theo."

"But she knows how to fix him. We're going right now. And we are taking her with us."

"We can't, she belongs to the Devil. We are here for Linris, not whoever that is."

"Linris..... She looks exactly like Linris." Atria finally says something.

"I can't leave her. I promised Arch. S—"

"Arch? But nobody has heard from him for 19 years," says Trus.

"What I was trying to say was, she's Linris 'and Arch's daughter."

"Linris had a daughter?" Atria whispers.

"Yes and that's her. I promised Arch we would take her with us. He wants her to be free. I'll take her with us, but I'm not going to let her go until she saves Theo."

"Where's Linris?" Asks Trus.

"She's dead," I mumble, shamefully as if it's my fault that

she's dead. If only I had come earlier, I could have saved her. But no, Arch said that she's been dead for a few years now — I would never have gotten here on time. "Now will you help me with Theo? We need to go. Right now!"

They both look very shocked and stricken. They knew that we came here to rescue Linris. Atria had her hopes up that we would find Linris and that everything would be good, that life would go back to the way it once was. She looks very pale, as if all hope has been drained from her soul.

Trus helps me with Theo; I get on his right side, while Trus goes to his left. We lift him out of his chair and carry him between us. We head out the same door Jez used; we're going to find her and get the hell out of the Devil's house. Atria falls into line behind us while anxiously eating a piece of bread.

CHAPTER FIVE

Jezebel

I stand in the corner with my head down for a little while. When I start to hear strange noises, I look up. Almost everyone at the table's choking and finding it hard to breathe. Their faces turn a strange hue of green until they lose their inevitable struggle to unconsciousness. Oh, My God! Did I do this? I couldn't have. I'm not evil. I don't do anything bad. On the outside, I'm frozen. But on the inside, everything's chaos: my world's crumbling around me. I need to get out of here, but my feet won't work.

It's not as bad as it could be, 3 of the 4 guests are fine. But the fourth — the 1 my age — is down. Oh, no! I hope what was in that vial doesn't kill him. I wanted to get to know who he was. I wanted to at least say "hullo" before he died.

The woman tries to see what's wrong with the young man. The older man pushes his food away and looks worried. The other young man, his face is completely transformed. He looks so angry. He looks like the Devil does when he's about to torture me. My limbs begin to shake and quiver. I was told they'd save me, not beat me. What if he takes his anger out on me? He must be angry that his friend's down. He must also know that I'm to blame.

He starts to come over here but gets stopped by the older man. They have heated words. He blows off the other guy and storms over to me.

This is it. He's going to hit me. He's going to end me, not save me. I try to cower, but nothing moves: I'm still frozen. He starts to shake me and asks a bunch of questions. I can barely focus on what he's saying, I'm so scared. But at least he hasn't hit me yet. I think he's demanding I help fix his friend?

I try to tell him that his friend will be fine in 6 hours. My mouth opens, but no words come out.

He drags me over to the other guests, asking me how to save his friend. He talks to me like I don't understand his language. His grip's tight; he's hurting me. I look into his eyes to get his attention, to get him to listen to me. I turn to the rest of the table and motion with my hand to everyone who's affected. I want him to know that I didn't mean for his friend to be affected, but my voice still won't work. I'm not sure if he gets what I mean, he continues to be mad and demands that I fix his friend.

I break away from his grip and run. I need to collect what little I have so that I'm ready to leave. I also need to find a piece of paper and a pen.

I make it to my room very fast; I ran all the way. I stuff my mother's perfume bottle into my dress pocket. Along with my baby blanket and the other gifts from my tutor. I stuff all that I can into my dress pockets. I can't fit my book and I put on my hat. I leave out my notebook and pen.

I open up the notebook to the first page; I've been working from the back to the front, so as not to ruin the perfect beginning. I click the pen so that the ink point's out. I write as quickly as I can. I end up with: *My name's Jez. I'm very sorry about your friend. It wasn't meant to affect him, but it did. It only lasts 6 hours. I don't know what it is. Hopefully, it has no bad effects. Please don't hit me. Please save me, not kill me. I'm not bad. I'm not bad! I'm not bad?!*

The "not bad" part's scribbled. I'm very angry and disappointed in myself for poisoning those people. They definitely aren't good or innocent, but what I did was very bad; I try so hard not to be like them.

As I finish writing the note, I sit on my bed and start to rock back and forth. This is it, I'm officially losing it; they aren't going to save me now. I did the 1 thing I said I'd never do: be bad.

The door's slammed into and opened. I jump. I can't stop

the shaking.

In comes the young man — still angry — and the older man holding the affected young man between them. The woman comes in behind them.

I try to give the young man my note to read, but he won't take it. All he wants to do is yell at me. He's demanding that I give him something called an antidote for his friend on the way to the airport. I don't have a clue as to what an airport is — is it the way out of Brilla? If so, I'd be all happy and excited, but the way that he says it, makes me feel like I shouldn't be. I don't let my emotions show. The confusion; anger at myself; happiness; and anything else that I'm feeling right now, doesn't show. It's all hidden behind the mask I've worked 10 years to perfect.

I write something else down on the note. *Please stop yelling. I'm very sorry. Please, please, please. I shouldn't have poisoned your friend. I hate myself. Please don't hate me too. I am at fault for my mother's death and her suffering. I've already come to terms with its heavy weight, and I've been punished over and over. Please don't punish me too. Who's Linris?*

He still doesn't take my notebook to read. But the woman does. She reads it all. Tears come to her eyes; she hugs me and says it's going to be all right now. That they're going to save me. That nothing was my fault.

What the woman has done, makes the young man stop yelling and finally read my note. He doesn't apologize for everything he has said or done. But he does stop looking angry. He tells me to pack a bag and that we're leaving. They just have to grab all of their packs and call something called an uber. What's an uber? What does it do?

I write down that I already have everything; I'm ready to go. He reads what I wrote. Based on his judgemental look, he must think I'm lying. I don't care if he thinks that I'm a liar; I know that I'm not.

The woman takes the notebook from the young man and reads what I just wrote, she hugs me even tighter. I think she's trying to comfort me. I've never had anyone touch me like this, except for that 1 night all those years ago. My vision begins to blur. No, don't think about mother. You're being saved and taking her spirit with you — where she can finally be free.

I double-check to make sure that I have everything and my hand brushes against a slip of paper. I pull it out, unfold it, and read it. Oh! It's the note from my tutor. I hand the opened note to the young man. As he reads it, his eyes go wide.

"Your tutor?" He asks me.

I nod my head.

"Your tutor's Commander Drew Arch. This is his handwriting. He's a person I know."

I allow shock to disrupt my mask, then curiosity. If I want them to trust me, I have to start letting them see who I am and that I mean no harm. I hate the idea of opening myself up — you need to guard yourself against everybody — but I need them to trust me.

The young man understands the question I ask with my eyes.

"He's on our side. He told me to save you."

My mouth forms a word: "Oh". Well, no wonder he has always been nicer to me than the others. He's always been on my side. I knew he couldn't have been evil like the Devil. My tutor was never mean to me; he never even raised his voice when I didn't get something right. And he's the only 1 in the Devil's house who hasn't hurt me in any way.

CHAPTER SIX

Bryce

I lead the way down the long hallway; all the doors on either side that we pass are locked. At the very end of the hall, we find an unlocked door. I ram into it with my shoulder.

I find Jez on the bed, with a book next to her, a hat on her head, a notebook on her lap, and a pen in her hand. She's just sitting there being useless; so, what other choice do I have than to start yelling at her? "Help me save Theo! He ate your poison! It's all your fault! Bring him back!" She tries to hand me her notebook while I am shouting at her. I don't take it, but Atria does. When she's done reading what it says, she goes to soothe and comfort Jez. She hasn't done that to anyone for years; she hasn't gotten that close to someone who's not Theo since Linris got captured and her husband was killed.

Well, now I have no choice but to read what she wrote — just to see what made Atria act this way.

My name's Jez. I'm very sorry about your friend. It wasn't meant to affect him, but it did. It only lasts 6 hours. I don't know what it is. Hopefully, it has no bad effects. Please don't hit me. Please save me, not kill me. I'm not bad. I'm not bad! I'm not bad?!

Please stop yelling. I'm very sorry. Please, please, please. I shouldn't have poisoned your friend. I hate myself. Please don't hate me too. I am at fault for my mother's death and her suffering. I've already come to terms with its heavy weight, and I've been punished over and over. Please don't punish me too. Who's Linris?

At the end of the first part, it becomes kind of crazy sounding. I can't even imagine what has happened to her; she has survived 18 years in the Devil's house. The Circle's best spy didn't even last that long, Linris only lasted 11 years. We are lucky that Jez is still sane. You'd think she'd be crazy by now, but she's not completely out of her senses. I don't regret what I said to her. I meant it and there is some truth to my words. I just feel bad now for shaking her and stuff. She thought that I was going to hit her. Poor girl. What has happened to her that would make her believe that a nice person who was said would save her, would actually kill her? I'm not even sure that I would have lasted.

"Where's all of your stuff?" She's gotta have stuff, right? Arch would not let her go without a few gifts — especially on her birthday. I look around her room. Man, is it tiny or what? I'm surprised she has done so well here. She must not be claustrophobic. I'll admit, she has some good qualities for being a spy, one of our circle.

She hands me her notebook again, why doesn't she just speak to me? This would go way faster if she would just talk. She does have all of her stuff? She's got no bag...nothing but a book, notebook, hat, and pen — that can't be everything.

Whatever, we need to go. I need to get her to The Circle. Now that I know that her mother can't guard the Prince, maybe Jez can. She's very observant; with just a little training, we can have her working in no time. She would be appreciated, loved, and a part of something. And I don't think that Theo would mind: she's quiet, so she won't tell anyone about him. And she could be very loyal — who knows what other good qualities she already has.

She hands me a small piece of paper. I read it, *"It will only last for 6 hours. Guests will help you leave. Act normally".*

It all makes perfect sense now. Before he went off the grid, Arch was one of the best potion makers. He was a double threat: espionage and potions. Every one bought from him. Of course, he made the potion that would give Jez enough time to escape.

Ok, so it will only last for 6 hours. Good news for Theo, bad news for us. We have about 5 hours left now and we still have to get to the airport. I tell everyone the plan; they have varied reactions: Jez looks both curious and shocked — I just remembered that she's never been outside before. Well, this will just go great, won't it? Of course, it won't! She'll be excited at everything she sees and will want to know how it all works. She'll waste our time and make it easy for the Devil to catch us! Ugh, I'll worry about it when the time comes. Trus 'look says that he's ready for anything; Atria looks very shaken and emotional.

We all head into the hallway, and back to the dining room. We walk through it and to the door on the opposite wall that goes to the rest of the house. Once exiting the room, we all split up. Trus takes Theo to his and Theo's rooms, where they will collect their bags. Jez goes with Atria, and I turn around and go back into the dining room. Some loose ends need tying up, literally. I pull rope out of the hidden pocket in my suit coat.

I start with the Devil: I tie his arms together to his legs, ending with him tied in a ball. I then do the same to all the others. It only takes me about 10 minutes. Now, it's up to my room to collect my case and bag — good thing that I kept everything packed.

When I get up to my room, the door is slightly ajar. I left it closed. Either someone's in there right now, or someone was. I grab my pistol from my pocket and open the door so that it won't creak. When the door is fully open, I take in the scene. My stuff is strewn all over the floor. My room has been ransacked! I enter quietly, just in case whoever did this is still here. I listen but don't hear anything — not even someone breathing. The coast is clear. I start to pack all my stuff back together. As I finish, someone whispers in my ear. It sounds like the wind would if it had a voice. The voice tells me that I need to leave because someone is coming.

That's it, we need to leave RIGHT NOW!

I grab my suitcase, open the door, and walk down the

stairs as fast as I can — without giving away that I am running. My room was on the 1st floor, whereas everyone else is close together on the ground floor. I run through the halls that take me to the dining room, I then take a hallway next to the door to it that will take me to Atria's room. Her door comes up on my right; I knock on the door, then step inside. I find Atria sitting on the bed with Jez next to her — she's attempting to brush through Jez's hair. They both jump as I enter. I close the door behind me.

I take out my phone and turn on an app that someone from The Circle created — it takes away what we are really saying and replaces it with nonsense, like the weather.

"Ok. Don't react. But I think somebody knows of our plans. My room was ransacked. They didn't get anything, but they might be onto us."

Jez looks really worried and scared, for in Atria's company, she had completely shut her mask off. The color Atria had regained again drains from her face.

"Are you all packed? Do you guys have everything?"

Jez nods. Atria says "Yeah. My rucksack is by the door."

"Do either of you know which room Trus and Theo are in?"

"They are bound to be in Theo's room by now."

"Ok. Grab your bag, we'll find them, and then leave. Atria, you may want to grab your gun, there's a possibility that we'll have to fight our way out. We'll shield Jez."

Atria goes to her bag and pulls out two pistols and a knife. She hands the knife to Jez. "You know how to use this, right?" Jez answers her with a nod.

CHAPTER SEVEN

Jezebel

When we leave my room — forever, bye room, never gonna miss you — I stay right by the woman. When we decide where we're all going, I go with her to her room to help her pack. We go to a nice, light wood door — the most normal-looking thing in this house of horrors. She opens the door and lets me go in first. Her room's so much bigger than mine, even bigger than the one I had until I was 6. There's a canopy bed, a wooden dresser, a desk, and 2 bedside tables! My old room only had a single bed and a small bedside table. Even guests get treated better than me. What did I ever do?

The woman goes over to something on the bed, a storage thing, but it can be carried. That must be what the young man called a "bag". She checks it over and seems to be satisfied with what she finds. She turns back to me and beckons me over. She sits on the bed and invites me to sit next to her. There's something in her hand. It looks like the hand mirror that's in my fairytale book, but instead of having a reflective side, there are bristles sticking out of it.

I cock my head questioningly. What does it do? What is it? What if it's something that hurts? I've never seen anything exactly like it in my whole life. Some fear must've shown in my eyes, for she explains to me what the object is. It's a hairbrush, and by what the title suggests, it's used to brush your hair. I've wondered how her hair looks so nice, and why mine feels rough and icky. She must brush her hair every day. I've never had mine brushed before. Does it hurt? I hope that it doesn't. I want my hair to look just like hers. She turns me so that my back's facing her. I flinch, thinking that she's going to see my ruined back, or that she'll hit me. But all she does is say, "I just want to brush your hair. It's very messy and tangled-looking. I bet you that it would look very pretty if it was brushed."

I feel my face redden, it's a good thing that she can't see it…then I'd be embarrassed. That's the nicest thing anyone has ever said about me. She called me pretty — well, a potential of pretty — and it brings tears to my eyes. Nobody, not even my tutor, ever complimented me.

She starts to pull the brush through my hair, it hurts and feels as if she's pulling hair out. The brush stops. "This is the toughest hair I've ever had to brush. Hang on a sec; I think I have a detangler spray." I turn to watch her as she digs around in her bag. After a minute, she comes out with a weird-looking bottle. "Well, turn back around. I'll make you so pretty, that the boys will swoon — and I'm only working with your hair."

I turn back around, and she sprays the stuff in my hair, before going back to brushing it. It still hurts, but not as much, and it doesn't feel like she's pulling it out anymore.

When the woman's almost done with all my hair, there's a knock at the door. A second later, the young man comes in. He has a thing on wheels trailing him. There's an urgency to his face.

Oh no! Somebody went through his stuff. Oh, never mind, they didn't take anything. But still, how horrible. I hope he's ok with the invasion of privacy — I don't want to see him get angry again tonight. I don't think that I could handle it. And this time, he might even hit me.

The woman and young man talk as if they've forgotten my presence. Then, the woman pulls 2 weird, but cool-looking things out of her bag, along with a knife. She hands me the knife. The feel of it is so familiar.

It transports me back to when my tutor would take me out of my room on nights when the Devil was away. He'd take me to a room containing targets. He said I'd need to defend myself. And so he taught me. How to punch, use my elbows, kick a man in his special spot, and how to aim accurately with knives. My favorite were the knives. I excelled at it. I hit the bullseye every time.

I'm so lost in memory, that I don't hear what the woman asked of me. So I just nod. They head out the door and I follow them. I assume that we're going to get the other 2, then we can leave! I can taste the freedom already. Wind in my hair, sunlight in my eyes, birds singing, water rushing, people — I…I don't like people; the only bad thing about freedom: so many people.

As we near the first room, the young man tells us to stay back. He goes to see if it's clear. If someone was snooping around in his room, he has a right to be suspicious. I hope nobody gets in their way. I can't last much longer here; I need to get out. And I can't do that without the help of these people.

The young man enters the room and comes right back out. He shakes his head: no one was in there. The men should've been in there.

He takes us further along the hallway, farther from the exit. Before we even turn the corner to go into the 2nd room, he motions for us to stay back. Silently, he moves around the corner and to the door.

He sure is taking his time. I creep forward, while the woman stays back. Quickly, I peek around the corner. The door's wide open; the young man's standing in the room, a little in front of the door.

He doesn't move, he just stands there. He looks prepared but also held back. I need to see why he's not doing anything. As I get closer, I hear a voice. Not the young man's voice or that of the older one, but somebody else's. Somebody familiar.

While the young man's not looking, I position my body so that I can see into the room, without whoever's in there being able to spot me. I rush back to the woman.

What I saw's not good at all. Now, we can't escape. The older man's tied to a chair, trying to say something to the young man. The other young man — the affected one — is face down on the bed.

33

But the worst part is, there was a man holding an object similar to what the young man and lady have. The man's the one whose voice seemed familiar: it's the Devil's sidekick. That's why he didn't eat with the Devil, he was told to capture the guests.

I'm not going to let *him* stand in my way to freedom. I get the knife into position. The woman looks at me worriedly. Silently, I creep to the door. I can't screw this up, I've 1 chance. *Aim for the bullseye, Jezebel,* whispers the wind. I will. I'll aim for the bullseye and not think about anything else.

While the young man has the Devil's sidekick distracted, I throw the knife. It whizzes past the young man's ear — close, but not close enough to do anything except nick him; over the older man's shoulder; and right into the bullseye, the Devil's sidekick's heart.

As the Devil's sidekick collapses onto the floor, what I've done sinks in. I've killed someone just so I could get free. I've done the most horrible thing I could ever do. I'm officially evil. NO!

I shouldn't have, there must've been another way. I did what I was never ever going to do in my life. I killed someone. I've never done a bad thing in my life. My life's turning upside down! In less than a day, I've: poisoned people, killed a man, and am escaping from the Devil.

I'm so bad. I deserve to rot in hell. I shouldn't be allowed to escape now; I don't deserve my freedom. I can't let these people save me, they're nice and innocent, but I'm not.

When I get back to reality, the young man's staring at me. I see that the woman has freed the older man and has saved the younger one from suffocation. The young man just keeps staring at me, he too knows I've done something bad. *Nice job Jez, you've made the people who came to rescue you hate you.* Oh, shut up mind! I didn't mean to kill anyone. I try to tell the young man "sorry"...but nothing comes out. Stupid silence, I actually want to talk now. It should be safe enough with the Devil poisoned for me to talk and not get punished.

The young man stops staring at me but doesn't become

angry again. He just tells me "Nice aim" and goes to talk with the woman and older man. While they're discussing whatever it is that they need to talk about, once in a while, one of them looks over at me. Perhaps I shouldn't be hearing whatever it is they're saying? Or maybe, they're talking about me? No, they won't be talking about me, because they aren't going to save me anymore — not now that I've killed people. I need to give them some privacy and give myself some time to think without them distracting me. I back out of the room and silently close the door behind me.

CHAPTER EIGHT

Bryce

Our first stop is Theo's room. His bags are still there, but he and Trus are not. They must still be in Trus 'room. But what's holding them up? As we near Trus 'room, my ears pick up muffled grunting. I tell Atria and Jez to stay back, against the wall. I'll look and see if the coast is clear. As soon as they do that, I creep silently to the door and open it as quietly as I can. The first thing that I see is Trus tied to a chair, tight ropes binding him, and a rag in his mouth. He's trying to shout for help. Theo isn't tied up, but he is face down on the bed with his hands bound together.

And behind them is that man from earlier, the one who had brought Jez to the dining room. He must have left so that he could lie in wait — allowing him to capture us after dinner. So, this dinner was really about taking the Prince hostage, huh? Well, his plans are about to be ruined.

As I step into the room, a floorboard creaks under the weight of my foot. The man looks up. He jumps behind Trus — to use him as a shield. He starts to taunt me. He has a gun too, he will shoot Trus if I come any closer, blah, blah, blah. But I can't get a clear shot from where I am — Trus is in the way. If I want to kill the man, I will have no choice but to go further in, but I can't. The man will kill Trus, and Trus is my friend.

As I am debating what to do, an object whizzes past my ear. It goes over Trus and into the heart of the man. I turn around; Jez and Atria are right behind me. Jez was the one who had the knife, but it had to be Atria who threw it because Jez was never taught anything. But Atria wouldn't have had time, and Jez looks like she did something wrong. She tries to say something, but nothing comes out. Atria runs into the room, cuts Trus free, goes to Theo, and flips him over so that he's no longer suffocating.

Jez still looks really bad. She's just so distraught. She looks even closer to going over the edge of insanity. She must not have killed anyone before. I have killed a few people, it comes with the job. I don't remember what my first kill was like, how it left me feeling — it's been that long. I believe that I was 11, so I can't imagine what Jez must be going through. Because even though it seems Arch was leaving out a few details — like how Jez is good with a knife — she hasn't been trained to actually kill someone. I was, so my first time was different.

But Jez really does have good aim, and I tell her so. It's the only thing that I can think of to say to her. My mind is still a little shocked by how accurately she threw the knife; she knew just where to hit the man in order to kill him.

I walk over to the man, needing to make sure he's dead. I feel for a pulse — none. We're going to have to get rid of the body. I'll worry about that later, right now I just need to focus on getting us out of here. I promised Arch that I would rescue Jez.

But first, Atria, Trus, and I need to talk about how to get out of here. Things have changed. This guy was trying to capture us, who knows what else the Devil has planned to keep us here. We need to figure out a way to get out of here and the country before the Devil wakes up.

Atria and Trus are in mid-conversation.

"We need to get help for Theo," Atria says urgently.

"You read the girl's note, Theo will be fine in a few hours," Trus replies.

"It said the potion would last for a certain amount of hours, but it didn't say what the after-effects might be. We need to get him to a doctor."

"We will when we get out of Brilla and back to Musalin. What we need to worry about right now is getting that girl out of the Devil's grasp and getting to Theo's jet."

I interrupt them. "Calm down, you two. We don't need to be wasting time arguing about what we need to do. We should instead be focusing on how we are going to get out of here **alive**."

Atria sighs and says, "You're right." Trus shuts his mouth and waits for me to share my plan.

"Did either of you guys notice ways out?" They don't say anything.

"Well, I did. Besides the front door — which we would obviously not have a good chance of getting out through — there's the garage, side door, and back door. But most of those ways have guards at every corner. We need to hurry and as silently as we can, take down the guards we pass before they alert any of the others. Now, Trus, grab your stuff; I'll go get Theo's bag." I turn to where Jez is watching our conversation from. "Now, Jez...Where's Jez?"

Atria and Trus stop what they had started to bicker about, and turn to see where Jez was; the spot is empty and the door's closed.

Atria starts to worry, "She wouldn't go on her own. She's scared. She would have waited for us. Where did she go? Did someone take her?"

"Don't worry, Atria; I bet you she's fine. Let's just continue with the plan and we'll find her on our way out."

Trus grabs his bag and Atria helps him with Theo. When I open the door to go out into the hallway, I do it carefully and quietly — just in case whoever took Jez is still out there. I look both ways down the hallway: no one. I start to Theo's room. When I near the door, there's a body on the ground. I kneel to check it out. Not Jez, it's a guard with a bleeding head. On the ground, there's shattered glass. And it smells like the guard is wearing perfume? Jez must have done this. She cracked the man on the head with her perfume bottle. A smirk comes to my face. Smart girl...but, where is she?

I crack open Theo's door, "Jez?" I say loud enough so she can hear me, but quietly so that I don't alert any other guards who could be near. Theo's room is completely silent. I open the door all the way. The light switches are right next to the door; I flick them on. No Jez, but Theo's bag is on his bed — still packed and closed. In less than a minute: I have Theo's bag on my back, my suitcase on my shoulder, and am heading back down the hall to get Trus and Atria. I meet them halfway to Trus 'room; they have Theo between them.

"I didn't find Jez, but I'm sure we'll find her on our way out. Come on." I lead them down many halls, to the side door that I had spotted. We don't encounter any guards. All the inside guards from this end of the house must have been in the dining hall. But, outside will be another matter; I must be ready to protect Theo. I grab my gun out of my pocket and make sure that it's loaded and that the safety is off.

"Let me go first and take down any guards. When I turn around, the coast will be clear, then you bring Theo out," I instruct Atria and Trus.

I point my gun, open the door, and step outside.

CHAPTER NINE

Jezebel

As I back out of the room, a hand grabs my elbow. I let out a silent gasp. The hand has a tight grip on my arm; it pulls me fully into the hallway. I no longer hear the guests 'voices as the door seals shut. The hand harshly turns me, allowing me to get a good look at my captor's face. It's a guard. Crap! There's no way I can escape from him.

"What's this? The Little Birdie trying to escape? Let's take you back to your cage." He laughs meanly and drags me down the hallway. We're nearing the room that the young man looked in for his friends; soon we'll be where I can't escape. I need to find a way to escape the guard before it's too late. I can't hit him — he's much stronger than me. I can't kill him — I don't have the knife anymore. This is hopeless.

I'm thinking and motioning my anguish with my hand; when it bumps into my pocket, hitting the bulge that is mother's perfume bottle. I don't want to do this. It belonged to my mother. But if I want to escape the Devil, I have to do anything. Besides, I've already killed the Devil's sidekick, it's not like I'm still innocent nor can I go back. I pull mother's perfume bottle out of my pocket without the guard noticing. When we come right in front of the door to the guest's room, I fall into it. The guard loses his grip on my arm and fumbles; he wasn't expecting me to fall — he must've been thinking of all the riches he'd get by turning me in. Before he or I know it, my hand's over his head and I wham the perfume bottle as hard as I can into his skull. He falls to the ground, knocked out cold.

There's so much blood. But I don't think about that. I start to run as fast as I can. I need to get out of here. The longer I stay, the more I turn into the person I never wanted to be: a killer, like the Devil.

I run faster than I ever knew I could. I don't care that it's hard to breathe, or that everything hurts. I just keep on running. I run all the way to the kitchen. Once I get in the kitchen, I put a chair under the doorknob and make sure no one can enter. I stop to catch my breath and think.

I need to get out of here by myself. I can't rely on the guests to save me. I wouldn't want them to anyway. I didn't survive torture from the Devil this long just to be a damsel in distress like the ones in my fairytale book. No, I want to be a knight who even though has nothing, turns out to be the hero in the end. I want to be the hero of my story. I'll not let any other person be the hero who does the heroic act.

Right before I decided to give them some space, I heard the guests mention something about Musalin. I've no idea what Musalin is. Maybe a place? Perhaps it's where they live? That might be the key to my escape. I can't stay in Brilla and have a normal life if I have to fear the Devil finding me. I'll have a better chance in another country, so I'll leave this place and look for a way to Musalin.

Now that I have a plan, I'll venture somewhere I've never been before: the outside. I don't let any fear get into my mind. If I think about it, my nerves will never let me leave. I clear my mind and only focus on my mission.

There's a door at the back of the kitchen that leads to a part of the outside that's not heavily guarded. But it's kept locked at all times. It's only used for the rubbish to be taken out.

When the Devil went away, my tutor taught me more than just how to use weapons. He also taught me how to pick a lock and go undetected. He said all I'd need are my wits and the lock picks that are used as pins for my hair. When the woman brushed my hair, I had to take them out. They hid easily in my mess of hair — the only good thing that came from my hair never seeing a brush.

Also one time, my tutor accidentally let slip that when he wants a break or to leave the house for a mission without the Devil's people finding out, he leaves via the kitchen — there are no guards there. But it's also the most complicated lock to pick, it has to be in order for no guards to guard it. My tutor had a key to it; sigh, if only I had it now. I could unlock it instead of having to pick it. But picking it is the only option that I have.

It's going to be tricky, but not difficult because as with knives, I excel at picking locks. I know how to pick this one quickly. One time, when I was cooking a very nasty-smelling but delicious pie that takes a while, I tried picking the lock on the door to the outside. I had a chance because the guards were outside the doors that go from the kitchen to the hallways so they could avoid the worst of the smell. Anyways, while I waited for the pie to cook, I tried to understand how the lock worked and how to pick it.

It had taken me all of 20 minutes to figure it out and unlock it. I'd have escaped then, but until now, I never had the motivation to leave — or people who were going to help me escape. Until now, I thought I was a hopeless case who deserved all the punishment that the Devil gave me. But recently, I remembered my mother **had** loved me; with her being dead, I have to make sure she didn't die in vain. Now, I'm going to do what she always dreamed of: my escape from the Devil. It's just too bad that I can't take her with me.

I start to pick the lock. I put one pick into place, make sure the right amount of pressure's on it, then I put the other one in. I jiggle them into just the right niches. And not a moment later, I hear the click that indicates the door's unlocked.

I look down at my dress; it has lemonade stains all over the front. That'll make me not blend in at all. I look around the kitchen to see if there's something I can use to cover up. On a stool at the counter where people eat breakfast, I see a coat. I grab it, put it on, and step outside.

As soon as I open the door, something blinds me. It's so bright outside. I shut my eyes the second I step out. I take a whiff with my nose, and right away, it's bombarded with smells. Mostly the rubbish. But beyond that nasty smell, there are many others. They must be the smells of outside. They smell so good. I wouldn't know what they all are; I've never been outside before. I wish I could focus on the smells and follow them to find out what they are, but I have to focus on leaving. Escaping is my number one objective. If I don't leave, by now I've done enough for the Devil to decide the punishment's death or worse. I don't want to die yet. I just stepped outside; I want to discover everything the world has to offer.

I open my eyes and can see — the light isn't so blinding anymore. I step all the way out of the door; it closes behind me and relocks. I look around. The rubbish is in a huge bin that's taller than me, and way wider. The rubbish space isn't very big, it's just a little, almost-closed-off nook. Really, it only fits the bin with a little bit of walking space. The exit's just big enough to fit a person slightly bigger than me. It's off a corner opposite the door. I walk over to it and before I go through it, I look everywhere for guards. I don't see any, so I step through the exit.

I have no idea where I'm going now. I've been in the giant building behind me my whole life. There are woods behind it, I don't want to go that way because, thanks to my fairytale book, I know what waits in the woods. In front, there's a large thing made of stones as the ground, and there are weird-looking machines on it. I don't like the look of them. The machines look like they could swallow you up. But on the side of the house, right near me, there's a thing. It has similar features to the scooter I had when I was little — my tutor would let me ride it around the halls when the Devil was out. Except this one's bigger and looks to be a machine too. But unlike the giant things, the scooter doesn't look like it'll swallow you.

I go to it; it's mint colored — like the ice cream I've seen in the freezer. There's a weird-looking thing hanging on the place where you put your hands with a note inside of it.

The note says: *Jezebel, this is your 19th Birthday present. I wish I could give it to you, but it will only be found if you escape. It's an electric scooter. It will take you wherever you want to go. The thing on the handles is a helmet — it goes on your head — and the buckle goes under your chin. Once you put the helmet on, you sit on the flat part that has padding. You will see a fuzzy thing sticking out of the top — the key to the engine. You turn it and the engine starts. To go, you must turn the throttle — the handlebars. You will need to steer it. To go one way, you turn the front with your hands on the handlebars in the direction you want to go. On the screen, it shows a number; while on roads, you will see signs with certain numbers — the speed limit. The screen number and sign number must match. There will mostly be cars — the weird machines on the stones. Your passport, license to drive this and money for a plane ticket are in the envelope. Good luck. I hope you get to live a normal life — that's all your mother and I have ever wanted for you. Love — ~~~~ ~~~~~~.*

The note is in my tutor's writing. Whatever he wanted to sign it with, is scribbled out. I pick up the helmet. As I do, a pouch that was hidden under the note falls out. I open the pouch; it has a folded thing in it. I open the folded thing, it has a picture of me with the name Iris Arch. My name isn't Iris, it's Jezebel. Why did he put Iris on it? Maybe so that the Devil can't track me? The folded thing must be what my tutor called a passport.

Then there's a card, it says license. The license has the same name but the picture on it is me at an older age than the passport. Then there's a bunch of bills. And a card that says credit. I'll use the credit card at my destination.

I put the helmet on my head — with the buckle hanging on either side of my chin. I then buckle the helmet, put the shield down — masking my features — and turn the scooter around to face a path leading forward, but not towards the stones with machines — cars? — on it.

I swing one leg over the padded flat part so that I'm sitting facing forward. Oops, I didn't have to swing my leg, I could've just sat down. I move my legs so that they're right in front of me on the flat part at the bottom of the scooter.

Wait, I need to make sure that I still have everything — my hat's still on my head and being crushed by the helmet, Spyglass necklace is secured, and my pockets are full of everything. Oh no! Where's my fairytale book? I thought I had it. I must've set it down or dropped it somewhere. Crap! That was my favorite object. I loved reading it. Hopefully, the others will find it, and one day when we meet again, they'll give it back. I've had it since I was 9 years old.

At least I have everything else; it's time to go. I turn the key to start the engine. The screen starts up, and it shows a map with 2 dots on it. There's a blinking one and a steady one that are quite a distance from each other. All of a sudden, a voice starts speaking — it's my tutor.

"Hello, Jezebel. Happy Birthday! The 2 dots are you and your destination. The steady one is an airport. You must look at your blinking dot once in a while, if it is moving towards the steady one, you are on track. If it is moving away, change course. When you get to the blacktop in front of the airport, park your scooter in an open spot next to a car. Remove your keys, put them in your pocket, and enter the building. Once inside, go to Gate 5, there should be a man at the desk with the name Checker on his shirt. Show him the inside of your passport and tell him, "I buy ticket to Musalin". You must say those exact words in that exact order. He'll take you to an airplane, and get you set up. The plane will not stop until it gets to Musalin. Once there, you must go to 42 Baker St, knock on the door, and ask for Soppy. She'll get you set up with a new life. Good luck, my sweet Jezzy."

I do exactly as he says — he has never given me a reason not to trust him, he has always been nice to me and never once steered me wrong. I put my hands on the handlebars and start the throttle. The scooter starts to move really fast. I look at the map, it shows the blinking dot moving in the direction of the steady dot — I'm on the right course. But it's going to take a while. I hope that whatever this thing's running on, doesn't run out.

...

After about half an hour, the path I'm riding on ends and a black road with a yellow line begins. There are machines riding here, cars my tutor called them. He said to go with them. So I turn right — the way the cars in front of me are going — but they're all going straight, not right. After I turn, I check the map on the screen; it shows me heading in the direction of the steady dot. The cars are going faster than me; I turn the throttle again, and the scooter starts to pick up speed.

Soon, a sign appears with numbers on it and, at the top, are the words "speed limit". I compare the numbers on the sign to the numbers on my screen. The ones on the screen are a bit higher than the ones on the sign, but I'm going at about the same speed that the cars are going. So I don't change my speed — still breaking laws!

After an hour and a half of riding altogether, the blinking dot's halfway to the steady dot. But further up the road's a sign that says detour; none of the cars are going straight by it, they're going in the direction that an arrow's pointing.

Oh no! What if this detour makes me go in the opposite direction than my destination? I hope it doesn't. But, even if it does, I can't do anything about it, I need to go with the cars.

When I get to where there's no more detour, I check the map; I'm still going in the direction of the airport. I thought for sure that the detour would take me in the opposite direction, it's a good thing that it hasn't.

The sky starts to darken; I hear a faint boom. What's happening? I hope it's nothing bad.

In a few minutes, water starts dropping from the sky. What the? Why's water falling from the sky? It starts falling faster and faster. A sudden strike of light crosses the sky. It's quickly followed by another boom, like before, but way louder.

What's happening!?

I look down at the map showing my destination. I'm so close. But then, the screen starts acting funny. It fizzles and makes a bad noise. Then the screen goes dark. How am I going to find my destination now? I've never been outside the Devil's house before. I've no idea where I'm going. I don't even know where I am. All I know's that I was following my tutor's orders and a map he left for me. Now I have nothing.

My clothes are soaked. It's completely dark except for the lights coming off the cars, and I don't know how much further it is to the airport. The universe is against me! It doesn't want me to escape from the Devil! Should I listen to it and turn back?

No! How could I even think that? There's no way that I'm ever going back; I'll just keep on riding and maybe, I'll eventually see the airport.

After another hour of riding straight, the rain has stopped and the sky is brighter. There's a sign that says food and is pointing to a path leading off the road I'm on. I really shouldn't deviate from my mission, but I'm so hungry. I need to make up my mind quickly, I won't be able to turn off in a few seconds. My stomach grumbles and gurgles. My decision's made. I turn onto the path.

At the end of the path's a giant building, there's a sign on the front of it. The sign says McDonald's. What's McDonald's? Is it somewhere to get food? I hope so, I'm starving. By now, I would've eaten what little was left of the soup and bread.

The cars are all parked individually inside 2 lines. I copy them and park my scooter inside 2 available lines. I do as my tutor said to do and take my keys out of their spot. The scooter stops making the noise that it did when it started up earlier. I put the keys into my pocket and go to the door at the front of the building.

The doors are different than the ones I'm used to. All of the doors that I've seen until now, have had knobs. These doors don't; how you open them? They have flat things in the middle of them.

While I'm standing — trying to figure out how to open the door — a person comes up and opens the door next to me. All the person did was push the door inward — so, that's how you do it. I try pushing my door, it opens and I step inside.

CHAPTER TEN

Bryce

As I step outside, a gun discharges; the bullet hits the wall right next to my head. *Crap! That was awfully close.* I put my gun in my pocket, duck, and run for cover while shot after shot is fired. There's a giant crate under a window, behind which I position myself so that I can see where the shots are coming from. I get my gun back out of my pocket.

I quickly poke my head up to see where the guards are. There's a guard in the window of the garage, and another on the rooftop. I duck my head back down as a bullet whizzes past. I use the reflection of the window above me to find out where more guards are located. There are 2 guards opposite the door in bushes. I can't shoot the one on the rooftop from my location, but I can shoot the 2 in the bushes.

I double-check that my gun is loaded, making sure the safety is off — both are good. I aim my gun at the guard in the right bush, and shoot, ending with him unmoving in the bushes. The guard on the left starts shooting at me; I move to the furthest end of the crate from where the guard is shooting at. I aim my gun at the guard, shoot, and he's down too.

Now I just have to deal with the guard in the window, plus the one on the roof. The one in the window is a sniper — I'll have to act fast before he delivers a killing shot. I aim and shoot, but miss. I try again and my bullet hits the sniper; he's not dead, but he's down for a little while.

Now, for the one on the roof: I need a better vantage point to shoot him. I look around for a place that will cover me, there's a rubbish corner to my right, but nothing else — just open land

and woods. I look back to Atria, Trus, and Theo inside the door. I motion with my hands to inform Trus of what I'm about to do — I need him to cover me. He nods in understanding, has Atria take all of Theo's weight, and gets out his gun. He runs to the side of the house and starts shooting at the guard on the rooftop. While the guard is busy trying to shoot him down, I run for the rubbish corner.

Once there, I duck behind the rubbish bin and get into position; I need to take down the guard with just one shot. I whistle to Trus. Once he runs back inside the door and takes half the support of Theo from Atria, I point my gun and shoot the guard on the rooftop. He falls forward and off the roof, landing with a sickening crunch in front of the opened door. Atria emits a shrill scream.

I begin to rush back to the three in the door. On the way there, my foot goes over something on the ground. It's probably rubbish, but something compels me to pick it up. *Oh my god: it's Jez's Fairytale book.* She must have come out this way and dropped it. I place it in my pocket and continue back to where Atria and Trus are struggling to position Theo correctly. We meet back up and head in the direction of the woods.

After clearing the house and no more encounters with guards, the four of us continue in a rushed walk, but a little less worried than before. I look behind me to see Atria and Trus walking while pretending that Theo and the bags are not a strain. I am supposed to be going ahead and making sure that the way is clear of guards, but I walk back to them.

"Trus, stop pestering me. I'm fine. Theo is my son, my baby. I can handle his weight. **You're** the one who doesn't look so good." Atria looks very annoyed — Trus must have been pestering her for some time.

"I know he's your son, that you can handle a lot. But I think you should take a break. I'll carry him the rest of the way. It's not that long of a journey to where the uber can pick us up." Trus snaps back.

Today's events are weighing on them. Trus really is just

trying to protect Atria. Both of them need a break, we have been walking for 15 long minutes through the woods.

"I'll take his weight. You two walk ahead. You both need a break, your strength is gone. We can't walk slowly — we don't have long before more guards will come. And you taking Theo's weight is slowing us down; you need to focus on yourselves. Theo is my charge, I must carry him." The only way to get back to Musalin is if I take complete control. This would have gone South without my interruption; Trus would have done something regrettable. Do I need to remind him of what happened to his last charge?

They both grumble in protest and look like they want to shoot my eyes out...but they know that I'm right. They hand Theo over to me and start walking ahead of us. They are still going slow, but not as slow as before. At least they no longer look like they are going to collapse from the pressure of holding everything up.

As we continue walking, the trees become more spread out. When we left the house and saw no more guards, the trees were everywhere. After we walked for 5 minutes, we were in the thick of the woods; but now the trees are sparse — we must be nearing the road. When I called for an uber, I told the person to pick us up on the other side of the woods behind the Devil's house. The person said it would be almost an hour until the uber could pick us up; when we get to the road, an hour should have passed.

Hopefully, the uber will be there waiting. We don't have much time to waste; we need to get out of the country before the Devil wakes up. It will be much harder for him to take us out in our own country.

It's just too bad that we still haven't found Jez. I promised her father I would get her out. But knowing Arch, he probably had an escape all planned for her. I hope she found it and is getting out of Brilla. Once I can ensure Theo is home safe, I will start looking for her. There can't be that many people in the world who fit her description.

After 10 more minutes of walking — we still aren't that close to the road — a shot rings out. Atria falls to the ground. Shit! Atria's been hit.

Trus drops his bag and gets his gun out. I put Theo on the ground and get out my 2 pistols. More shots. Very close, but luckily no one else is hit.

"Where are they coming from?" I hear Trus mumble.

I don't know from which direction either. I look around, and for a second I see a flash of something in a tree. I motion with my hands to Trus to tell him "in the trees". I don't say anything, I don't alert the guards to the fact that we know. I duck behind a fallen tree and look for a guard in the tree that I saw something flash from.

There's a guard in the middle of the tree. He's got a musket, but there's only one guard and one gun. Should be easy enough. I aim my gun at the guard's heart. I shoot, and a second later, the guard falls to the ground. But before he fell, a sound rang out. It sounded like a wire snapping. Whooshing sounds come from every direction and the trees are lit up by flaming arrows. The man falling must have set off a booby trap. Shit!

"We need to get out of here now! Trus, grab Atria! I'll grab Theo!"

Trus grabs his bag and sweeps up a bleeding Atria into his arms. I pick Theo up the same way, and we both start running like mad toward the road all the while more booby traps are going off.

When we finally reach the road — 6 minutes later — both of us are finding it difficult to breathe. There's a car waiting for us. I open the back door, Trus gets in with Atria, and I throw Theo in. I slam the door and get into the front.

The driver looks into the backseat at Atria, then he looks at me. His eyes are full of fear and questions.

"Drive! I'll tell you the directions in a few minutes." The driver starts the engine. I turn around in my seat. "Trus stop the bleeding. Where was she hit?"

"In the shoulder. But the bullet went right through. I

don't know if anything was hit, I'll have to look when we get on the jet." Trus has a waver in his voice and he looks very worried. Atria is his charge. If she dies, it's on him.

When we are 10 minutes away from the Devil's house, I give the driver directions. "St. Andrew's flight field. How far?"

"Ffffive miles, sir. No traffic should be out at this hour. Maybe 10 minutes?"

Ok. 10 minutes. It's been about 2 hours since the Devil ate the potion. That means we still have 4 hours give or take. That should be enough time to get on Theo's jet and land in Musalin. I just hope Jez made it out. I don't break my promises. Promises are a weak thing, a vulnerability. But I did give Arch my word and I never go back on my word. Jez will get out of the Devil's place and live a normal life in Musalin or wherever she wants. I need to find her though. She's probably huddled somewhere scared, shaking, and waiting for us to come and get her.

The minutes fly by really fast. In no time at all, we arrive outside St. Andrews flight field. A place reserved for private jets. The Royal Family comes to Brilla all the time; Theo's uncle actually owns the flight field. Lord Andrew of Roseed — a small region near Musalin. Theo's allowed to land his jet whenever he wants, as long as his uncle gets to have a law passed at once in that same year. Theo rarely uses the field so that none of his uncle's laws are passed.

Trus and I get out, grab all the bags, and pick up our 2 indisposed royals. Both of our charges are down. How the bloody hell did that happen? We are some of the best The Circle has today. We never have a charge down, and now both of us have our charges down?! Today is not our day.

We go to the closed gate on the side of the building in front of where the jets are held. There's a booth in front of the gate with a guard inside. The guard is sleeping...but it's only a fake sleep. Let the intruder think the only guard is asleep when in reality, he's not and there are at least 3 armed guards alert and ready for when the switch near the sleeping guard's hand is flicked.

When we are right in front of the guard in the booth, I say the password. "TRFER." Every person who has a jet here has a specific password used only for them. TRFER means Theo Royal Family Edward Robin. Edward is Theo's middle name and Robin is his branch of the royal family's symbol.

"Enter. His uncle arrived an hour ago, said when his nephew is up for it, he's got a law ready."

"Well, you can tell his uncle to—"

"Thanks. Will do. Let's go, Bryce." Trus interrupts me from letting out my frustration about the day and showing just how much I hate Theo's uncle. I unclench my fists and make my anger seem to disappear.

The guard opens the huge gate for us to pass through.

Right after we clear it, the guard closes it with a loud *clang*. There are tons of jets here, all ranging from big to small. For an airfield that only allows certain people, you wouldn't expect so many. But Theo's uncle runs the best private airfields and everybody knows it. Theo's uncle uses that to his advantage. The airfield was just supposed to be for the royal family, but if a rich person offers Theo's uncle a good price, he'll allow anyone in. And the price is not always money, like with Theo, the price could be something to do with government and politics. It doesn't matter just as long as Theo's uncle comes out on top.

We pass at least 10 jets before we come across a small, modest one. It doesn't show how much money Theo has in his private bank account; he could buy at least 30 giant private jets, but he doesn't like to spend a lot. "As little as possible" is his motto for spending money on anything other than Musalin. He would rather have money for his people and their future than spend it all on the now. That's one of the many reasons why I am grateful that the future king is Theo and not someone like his uncle.

Theo's jet on the outside doesn't look like much compared to many others in the field. It only fits 9 people. The outside is plain white and has 2 windows on both sides. The front — where Musalin's own best pilot flies the jet — isn't very big. But

Theo takes pride in it. He takes pride in everything he has that is much smaller than anything owned by everyone else in the royal family. It's all he needs — why would he spend the money on unnecessary additions?

He loves the fact that his family sneers at the small things that he loves. "Because what makes a person is not spending left and right on the most extravagant, expensive things. What makes a person is one's actions, one's personality, what's on the inside" — at least that's what he always says to me after he sits alone at a café in town on Friday nights, watching life go by.

As we near Theo's jet, the door swings open. The pilot comes out, sees Atria and Theo, and hurries to help get them into the jet. In less than 5 minutes, the pilot is starting up the jet to take off; Theo is lying fully on the sofa; and Trus is healing Atria on the wall. The interior of Theo's jet is a little less modest than the exterior. But that's so that it can function for many different things. There is a row of 4 seats on one side. The other side is a medical center, it's got what we call "the wall". The wall is really a bench for a patient to be laid down upon, with tons of wall storage holding medical supplies. And last but not least, there's a sofa, which takes up the whole back of the jet — it doubles as seating for many people and a bed. Right now, it's being used as a bed while Theo is still under the effects of the potion. I go from the sofa to the part of the wall that is used for baggage.

After I make sure that all of our baggage is secured, I go to the front of the jet, sit in the seat next to the pilot, and put on the other headset.

"How long until we land in Musalin?" How much of a head-start will we have when the Devil wakes up?

"About an hour, sir."

"Can you get us there any faster? Atria and Theo need to see a doctor."

"If there's not much going on and no problems, I can make it 40 minutes."

"Ok. Do that…please."

"Will do, sir."

I don't need to stay in the front, then. I can leave everything to the pilot. I take off the headset and go to the back of the jet. Once more, I check on Theo — he's still got a pulse and is breathing faintly. I go over to Trus.

"How's she doing?" I hope Atria wasn't hit too bad. It's not the first bullet she has taken, so she will get through it. I just hope that it didn't hit anything.

"It went right through everything. I don't believe anything was hit, but I can't know for sure without the right equipment."

"We'll get her to a hospital as soon as we land in Musalin."

"What about Jezebel? We didn't find her on our way out. I hate the idea that we left her to get captured by the Devil's people."

"We had no choice but to leave her. She's not our priority, Atria and Theo are. I found this outside in the rubbish corner." I pull Jez's book of fairy tales out of my pocket and hold it up so that Trus can see.

"So, she dropped it. But did she drop it while escaping, or when she was struggling against a captor?"

"I don't know. Once we get Atria and Theo awake and know that they are fine, then I'll search for Jez. Why hasn't Atria woken up yet?"

"She doesn't seem to be in critical condition. She was awake way before we left Musalin. The bullet made her pass out. And now, she's getting the rest that she so badly needed. She should wake up before we land, but I hope that she doesn't. The pain will be excruciating."

"I'm going to get some rest. Wake me up when Theo wakes; if he doesn't, then do it when we are about to land."

"Will do."

I go to the chair closest to the sofa, get into a comfy position, and try to fall asleep.

CHAPTER ELEVEN

Jezebel

There's color everywhere. There are colored booths with tables; different colored chairs at tables; and colored stools at counters. I've never seen so much color in one room — it's awesome!

I want food, but I don't know where to go to get it. At the front, there's a giant counter with weird-looking machines on it and a person behind each machine. The person that came in before me is at the giant counter talking to a person behind a machine — that must be where you get the food from. The other machines are busy. I go up behind the person and wait for my turn.

I overhear what she says: "I'll have the Big Mac — no pickles; Red Leicester Melts; Cadbury Dairy Milk McFlurry; a Blueberry Muffin; and a Mango and Pineapple Iced Fruit Smoothie."

The person behind the machine replies, "For here or to go?"

"For here." She hands him a card, just like the one my tutor left for me. That must be how you pay for it; I should pay for mine that way too. The young woman stands aside once she gets her card back and I move up. There's a giant kitchen behind the machines. I wish I could work in a kitchen like that, but it looks nothing like the one at the Devil's house — I wouldn't know how to use it.

"What would you like?" The man behind the machine asks me.

While the young woman was ordering, I looked at the

ceiling and saw tons of delicious-sounding food. I say a bunch that I saw, "Filet-o-Fish, Quarter Pounder with Cheese, Crispy Chicken and Bacon Salad, Apple Pie, and a Strawberry Milkshake. Please." As I say every item, words appear on the screen facing me. When I finish talking, a number shows up at the bottom of the screen. It's $35. Wow, that's a lot, I guess. The young woman next to me waiting for her food looks at me curiously or strangely — I'm not sure which.

"For here or to go?"

"For here."

I pull the card that was in the envelope out of my pocket and pass it to the man. He takes it, swipes it on the machine, hands it back, and pulls a tray out from under the counter. He places the tray next to the one for the young woman's food.

I'm very surprised that my voice worked. Besides the fluke this morning, my voice hasn't worked when I wanted it to in a long time. I guess the further from the Devil's house I get, the better my voice becomes. I'm still very scared because I'm not yet out of the country. But I'm a teeny tiny bit more relaxed than I have been my whole life.

The young woman's tray starts filling up. First comes a small bag that says Red Leicester Melts. Then a muffin in paper and a drink that looks kind of like the smoothies I'd make for the Devil in the summer — but this one looks way more delicious. Second to last comes a box like none I've ever seen before, it says Big Mac on the top. Lastly comes a small blue thing that says Cadbury Dairy Milk Mcflurry and has stuff inside that looks sort of like the homemade Ice Cream I'd make the Devil. But this looks so much better — now I wish I had ordered one. What's a Mcflurry?

Once the young woman's tray's filled, she picks it up and goes to a booth near the windows on the right side of the building. Now my tray starts to fill up. Everything put on my tray smells so good. Once it's full, I grab it and go to a stool at the counter in the middle of the room, near where the young woman put her tray. But the young woman isn't at the table where she put hers. Where did she go? She better eat her food before it gets cold.

Oh! There she is. She's over at another counter with more weird-looking machines. I wonder if I need anything from over there. I go to where the young woman is, and see that she grabbed a weird-looking stick thingy — I think it's a straw. I've only ever seen one in a magazine about food and drinks that my tutor let me read once. I think I need a straw too — I need it to drink my milkshake. I grab one and go back to the stool facing my tray full of food.

I stick the straw through a hole in the lid on top of my milkshake, sit down on the stool, and get started on my food by opening the box that says Filet-o-Fish. It's got a white sauce on it that I've never seen before. I wonder what it tastes like. I take a bite...Wow! That's a good taste. Best fish I've ever had. Until now, the only fish I've eaten was after it had gone bad. The Devil wouldn't let me eat any good food. This is like my first proper meal.

I finish the Filet-o-Fish and get started on the next box. This one says Quarter Pounder with Cheese. A quarter pound of what? I open the box. Oh! A quarter pound of hamburger. I've never had a hamburger before. If the Devil eats hamburger, then he doesn't get it from me; I've never cooked hamburger. I've only ever seen a hamburger in that food magazine. I take a bite. Oh... My...God! This is way better than the Filet-o-Fish! I can't believe I've never eaten a hamburger before. Boy, have I missed out. It's so delicious. I finish the whole thing in less than 3 minutes.

I take a sip of the strawberry milkshake while I open the salad. I've cooked bacon before for the Devil and his people for breakfast, but I've never been allowed to eat it. Bacon's so good! I love salad because it's healthy and the lettuce is earth grown — you can't go wrong with something you can grow yourself. I was able to grow small things in the kitchen, like mint and parsley.

When I get to where I'm going to live, I hope to grow a big garden. I finish the tastiest chicken I've ever had and the bacon salad. There's less than half of my milkshake left. I want to get another one, but I don't think I should. I really want to try a Mcflurry. I open the box that holds the apple pie. My first-ever dessert! It smells so good. It's nice and hot. Apple's delicious, and even better when put into a pie. I finish it in less than a minute. All I have now is rubbish, what do I do with it? I look over at the young woman. She's almost all done with her food. I think I'll go and order a Mcflurry and see what she does with her rubbish.

I go to the counter at the front of the room and get in line. There's only one person in line in front of one of the machines; I stand behind him. When he's finished ordering, it's my turn. I order the same thing the young woman did: A Cadbury Dairy Milk Mcflurry. I stand next to the guy waiting for his order. Mine comes first. Someone working in the back hands me the blue cup that says Cadbury Dairy Milk Mcflurry, along with a spoon. I take it back to my stool. When I sit down and start to eat my Mcflurry, the young woman stands up and grabs her rubbish. I don't take my eyes off of her.

She walks over to a bin by the door, and empties the tray into it, but doesn't put the tray in it. Instead, she places the tray on top of the bin. Ok, now I know what to do and can go back to focusing on eating my Mcflurry and leaving the country. The Mcflurry's so good. Way better than any of the other stuff I had. Who knew a Mcflurry could be so good? It doesn't even sound like a flattering name. And yet, it's so frickin delicious! I can't wait till I have another one. But not today, I don't know how much more time I have before the Devil wakes up. The sooner I leave, the better.

I finish the Mcflurry, throw away my rubbish, place the tray on the bin, and go back out to my scooter. It's in the exact same spot I left it. I take the keys out of my pocket and put them in the keyhole. I get on the scooter, turn the key, and start the throttle. The engine starts up. I back out of the spot and drive to the path that indicates the way back to the main road.

...

After driving for about 10 minutes, the screen on my scooter comes back to life. The map with both the blinking and steady dot's there. Yay! Now I have an idea of where the airport is; I forgot to ask someone at McDonald's for its location.

To be fair, I wasn't sure if my voice was going to work. I was lucky that I was able to get out as many words as I did.

I'm very close to the airport. The blinking dot's like 5 centimeters away from the steady one. But, that's on the screen, I've no idea how far away from the airport I am in real life. But, at least, I'm almost there; I've definitely made a lot of progress since I escaped from the Devil's house.

As the blinking dot continues to near the steady one, a car pulls up next to me. The windows are tinted so that I can't see who's in it. I don't like the looks of this. I pull my scooter away from the car and into the next lane. The windows on the car open a little and something like those weapons that the guests had poke out. I hear sounds and see things flying through the air. I think they're trying to hit me! What the heck!? Why?

I don't want to be hit by whatever those things are — I think it'd hurt a lot. I make the scooter go faster. The cars aren't going that fast and all the lanes are filled up. I go between the cars — my scooter can fit, but whoever's in the car can't. I need to get to the airport and get out of this country as soon as possible. I'm not safe when I'm in the same country as many of the Devil's people.

I look at the map; it shows that the airport's very near. I look around and don't see it. Where's the airport?!

I keep riding my scooter in between cars while looking for the airport. The blinking dot's literally on top of the steady one. I see a sign for an exit and go toward it. I want to get off this road; it's not taking me to the airport. I get off at the exit and start going in the same direction as all the other cars. I think I left behind those people who were trying to hurt me — at least I hope I did.

The map shows the blinking dot moving in the opposite

direction as the steady one. I can't go this way — this isn't the way to the airport. I need to ask someone where it is.

The further I go, there are more buildings and fewer cars — looks like people don't like to be out at night. The few cars that are out, are going slower than on the road I was taking. I make my scooter go slower. There's a little building with weird-looking things outside. The cars go up next to the weird things and something goes into a little thing on the side of the cars — connecting the car to the weird thing. Is that what makes them run? Maybe I need to fill my scooter up. Perhaps someone in that building can help me find the airport and get my scooter to its fullest. I make sure that no cars are coming and that there's an opening for my scooter. I then turn in the direction of the little building with cars at weird things.

The entrance is difficult to spot, but I find it before I would've had to go back. It's a little break in the grass on the side of the road. I turn into it and spot those little lines where some cars are parked — just like at that place called McDonald's. I park my scooter in between two open lines, take the keys out of their place, and go to the door. This door's just like the one at McDonald's, a weird one, without a doorknob — how do they lock it? Inside there are rows and rows of merchandise. But I didn't come here for anything in the rows; I came for directions to the airport.

There's a counter to my right with a woman behind it. But she's busy; another person's facing her, with the counter separating them. I guess I'll have to wait my turn. I go over and stand behind the person. After a few minutes, the person finally says "thank you" and "goodbye" to the woman. Now, I can ask where the airport is. Also, maybe where their toilets are, I have to go — must be that milkshake and Mcflurry.

"Yes." The woman says. She doesn't seem too friendly.

"Where's the airport?"

"You don't know where the airport is?"

"Um. No?"

"Do I need to spell things for you too?" She says in a voice

I've never heard anyone use before. It seems like she's making fun of me. I wait for her to stop enjoying what she said.

"Can you please just point me to the airport?" I think I'll wait to deal with the toilet situation until I get to the airport.

"Fine. When you leave here, go in the opposite direction than the one you did to get here. Drive straight — don't get on any highways or go to any other exits — and you should be at the airport in 15 minutes."

"Ok, thanks." I pull out a piece of paper that was in the envelope that my tutor left for me. The number on the paper's 5. It must be worth 5 of whatever people here use to pay for things. I hand the paper to the woman and go back out to my scooter. What's a highway? The woman said, "don't get on any highways". How will I know that I'm not on one if I don't even know what one is? But she also said to just go straight, so I think that if I just go straight, I'll reach the airport with no problems whatsoever.

I get back on my scooter, put the keys in, turn them and the engine starts up. I pull out on the opposite side from where I entered. How do I get to the other side of the road to get to the airport? I follow the cars and continue to go in the wrong direction. But after a few minutes of riding, all the cars stop at a little light in the sky. The light's red. I see a spot to my left where the cars look like they'll be turning to go the way I need to; I get in line with them.

When my lane gets a green light in the sky, they go. The cars turn and go in the reverse direction than before. I follow them. It's a bit tricky trying to turn my scooter like that, but I'm able to do so.

I look at the map. The blinking dot's now going in the direction of the steady dot. Yay! I'm back on track; I might actually have a chance to get out of this country before the Devil wakes up. I hope that I'm able to. Because if he catches me, the torture will be way worse than before. This time it'll be worse than death. It'll be so bad, it'll make me wish that he had killed me. I don't want that. I want to experience the world. I finally got out; I'm not going back. Not now, not ever. And nobody can make me.

Although the Devil can — he way more than scares me. There's not a word strong enough for the level of fear he makes me feel. He's just so bad, nasty, mean, and a bunch of other words that I don't know. I mean, he tortured my mother all the way to her death. People aren't supposed to die as young as my mother did. At McDonald's, I saw a lady who could've been like 35 years older than my mother. And my tutor's older than my mother was when she died. I hate the Devil. If I weren't so scared of him, I'd kill him.

CHAPTER TWELVE

Bryce

When the jet finally lands, we are bombarded with chaos; it doesn't help that everyone is in a panic. We have to get Theo awake, Atria patched up, and the rest of us really need some sleep. Today's events have been more than I have seen in a long time. I think the last time that something this bad happened was when Linris was taken and the king was killed.

That was obviously way worse than this. But this is pretty bad; we've got a shot royal and the ruler of a kingdom down, possibly on his way to being dead. There's no way of telling what was in that potion and what the side effects will be. We just have to wait and hope that he wakes up.

We get into the car that was sent from the palace. On the way to the palace, we stop in the Town Centre to drop Trus and Atria off at the healer — she should be able to patch up the bullet wound so that it doesn't become infected and make sure that nothing was hit.

About 20 minutes after landing, we arrive at the back door of the palace — the front door isn't an option, people will talk and The Red List may find out. I carry Theo from the car to his room in the palace. The palace is not very big. It's bigger than a normal person's house, but it's not the biggest palace in the royal family. It only has 10 bedrooms, 15 bathrooms, a few closets in every hall, and a good-sized kitchen. There's also a grand hall which is used as a lounge. But the thing that the palace is for sure lacking, is a dining room. There's a huge screened-in patio with beautiful beech wood flooring and ceiling — lined with a very long dining table that seats at least 20 people; that always has so much light streaming in, it's as if you were in a spotlight — that is used for dining in the warm months. During the chillier months, barely any guests come, so everyone just eats in their rooms or the kitchen.

Theo's room isn't the ruler's room; his mother still sleeps in the king/queen's room. She has been sleeping in it since she and the king were dating. I believe that she would change rooms, but Theo doesn't want his father's room and so Atria kept it. It reminds her of the king; it looks like he still lives in it. It's both painful and a pleasure to her. She sees it more as a pleasure though, having all of her husband's possessions.

I go to Theo's room, open the door, and put Theo on his back on the bed — this way the doctor can see if Theo will heal or wake up or whatever. I need him to wake up; I don't want to be a failure. I can't be a failure or I will get kicked out of The Circle. Once you get kicked out, there's an even bigger target on your back. You won't have The Circle's resources to help you, you will be compromised and dead in a week — if you're lucky.

Once Theo is safely on his bed — he looks like all he's doing is sleeping — I go to get the doctor. The doctor has an office and a flat somewhere in town, but because he mostly serves the royal family, he has a room in the palace and lives here. He works at his office during the week and stays in his flat when the royal family is on holiday. But today is Friday, so he's bound to be somewhere in the palace.

I will look for him in his room first; his room is all the way on the first floor. There are 4 floors — not including the ground floor — Theo's is on the 4th. All the bedrooms are like suites, they include a bathroom, bedroom, living space, and another room that can be used for whatever you wish. Theo's extra room is a dining room, so that he, Atria, and Trus can all eat together. Sometimes I join them. But most of the time, I just eat in the kitchen when I finish working — like all the other guards.

When I get to the doctor's floor, I go to his door and knock on it. No answer. I knock again. Nothing. This time I open the door and say, "Doctor, you in here?" Absolutely nothing.

Next, I try the patio out back and the gardens. The doctor's not here either. I check many more places before I finally find the doctor in the kitchen. He's on a stool at the counter eating dinner. Looks to be goose with mash. I'm glad we weren't here for that, we just had goose and mash 3 days ago.

When I walk through the doorway to the kitchen, the doctor stops talking to the person who works in the kitchen at this time of day. They both look at me, waiting to see what I need.

"Doctor, we are in need of your assistance. Theo isn't feeling too well."

"Ok. Just let me finish my mash. Will only take but a moment. Judy, I'll have to have dessert later. Be a dear and save a slice of that delicious-smelling apple pie, please." He follows that with a wink.

The doctor shovels the rest of his mash down, burps, and wipes his mouth with a cloth napkin. He stands up, picks up his medical bag, and walks over to me. I turn around and walk out the door. The doctor follows me out.

We go from the kitchen to the grand hall, to the staircase right in the center of the entrance. We go up the staircase and pass the first floor, second floor, and third floor, and arrive on the fourth floor.

I arrive on Theo's floor quickly, the doctor is still on the stairs — I can hear his labored breathing. I go to the only door on this floor that is closed — all the others are open because nobody lives in them, only when visitors come are they used.

I go into Theo's room and leave the door open for the doctor. A minute later, the doctor walks through the door slouched over, breathing heavily, and barely holding onto his medical bag.

"Still...not...used to...all those stairs," he says between breaths.

I ignore what he says and get right to the problem at hand. Now that there are not as many ears up here, I can tell the doctor what happened to Theo. I can't tell him everything of course, but

I will tell him what he needs to know to help Theo.

"He ate something that knocked him out. He's been out for a while. He hasn't woken up since. Do you think you could check him out?"

"I'll check his pulse and breathing."

The doctor pulls a stethoscope out of his bag and checks Theo's breathing, he then puts his fingers first on Theo's neck, followed by his wrist.

While putting his stethoscope away, he speaks, "Everything seems to be fine. There's not much else I can do until he's awake." He closes his medical bag and picks it up. "When he wakes, come and get me. I should either be in the kitchen or my rooms."

I nod my head in thanks and the doctor leaves, with the door closing behind him. I sit down on a stool near the fireplace in Theo's room.

Now all I can do is watch the door and wait for Atria and Trus to get back or for Theo to wake up — whichever comes first. I hope that it is the former, then Trus can fetch the doctor while I talk to Theo.

It's been a long day. Fatigue is starting to take its toll on me; my eyes are taking a lot of strength just to stay open.

As the fatigue is starting to win and my eyes are about closed, the door opens; the noise that it makes startles me awake. Apparently, 4 hours of waiting with nothing to do is tiring. Round 1 goes to awakeness, goodbye fatigue.

Trus comes in first, with Atria close behind. Trus looks like he got into trouble with Atria — he must have been fussing too much and she snapped at him again. He must blame himself for her getting hurt — as I do with Theo — he can't help but feel the need to make sure she's healed up good and perfectly fine.

Huge bandages are now covering the bullet wound. I hope she'll heal up in no time, who knows what we are going to have to do with Theo. She might need to help heal and watch over him.

Atria goes to Theo, sits down next to him, puts his head

on her lap, and starts to stroke his hair. Trus comes my way and stands next to the fireplace.

I ask him silently how Atria's going to be. He replies that she'll be fine in a few days, she just needs to have the bandages refreshed twice a day.

When training in The Circle you have to learn how to read each other's thoughts by looking into their eyes. It's very effective when on a mission with the enemy within hearing distance. Trus and I did it just now so that Atria wouldn't get even more upset than she already is. She's very worried about Theo — I didn't have to read Trus 'eyes to know that.

After a while, Trus pulls out a stool from a nook in the wall and places it next to mine. He calls Atria over. She puts Theo back into his resting place, walks slowly over, and lowers herself onto the stool. Trus remains standing.

Atria is the first to break the silence. "How is he? Did you get the doctor to look at him?"

"I had the doctor check on him. He said that he can't really do anything until Theo wakes."

That ends the conversation for now. Atria shakily nods her head. She seems out of it — I'm not sure if it's because she's worried for Theo or if she was given something for the pain her wound brings.

We remain as we are, stuck in our own heads for the next hour. I may or may not have dozed off, but when I am paying attention again, I look over to Theo's bed and spot movement.

"Look," I say to Atria and Trus while pointing to Theo's bed. Atria exclaims and goes to the foot of Theo's bed. There's a smile on her face and she doesn't look so tired anymore. Instead, she looks overjoyed.

Atria starts talking to Theo at the same time that I do. All the while Trus is saying very loudly, "It's a miracle! He's awake. I told ya, Atria, that he'd be fine. You didn't have to stress yourself out over it."

From the bed comes a voice that doesn't sound like Theo. But it's one of his favorite few words he says when he can't hear himself think. He tells everyone to shut up. I silence Atria and Trus.

Trus pours Theo a glass of water, Atria grabs it out of his hand and makes Theo drink it. Now, he should be able to talk more clearly.

I begin to ask him how he's doing when he says the light is hurting his eyes. It must be because he hasn't had his eyes open for a long time and who knows how the potion is making him feel or act. I go to the light switch and turn it off. Not exactly dark, but not as bright as it was.

I continue trying to explain all that happened at the Devil's house, but before I can get anywhere, Theo shouts that he can't hear what I'm saying. The potion must be affecting his ears. I send Trus to go and fetch the doctor. I don't need to tell him where he is — everyone knows that the doctor spends all his free time in the kitchen. That fact slipped my mind in my haste to have Theo checked out. There are rumors that it's because he drank a potion that turned him into an actual pig; he stayed that way long enough for the eating habits to rub off on him.

My theory is that it's because the doctor likes the serving lady — the very one who was in the kitchen when I brought him to Theo's room the first time.

As we all wait for Trus to get back with the doctor, the room is very silent. Theo looks like he's deep in thought; Atria just keeps staring at Theo with a tired, but happy smile on her face. I am busy debating how long it will be until I can go to my nice, comfy bed.

I need to get as much sleep as I can tonight because tomorrow I need to go back to the Devil's country — Brilla — and start looking for Jez. I can't break my word to her father. Where am I even going to start? She might not even be in the country anymore. Nah, she most definitely still is. How could she get out? She has no money, and no idea of the outside world; she has nothing but the hope of us coming back for her. She's probably somewhere hiding, just wishing for us to find her — if the Devil's men haven't captured her yet.

I don't want to even think about what the Devil will do to her once he finds out she attempted to escape from him. I really need to find her fast. Usually, I wouldn't care, I only care about my charge. But there's something about Jez. Maybe it's the quality that I saw in her, the one to be a great spy. Nah, it's mainly because I gave my word to her father.

When I finally start to relax, the door opens, and in comes Trus — with the doctor a little ways behind. Trus comes over to where I am currently standing near the window. As the doctor steps into the room, he's panting as bad as he was earlier, "we...seriously...need to...consider getting a lift installed". After his complaint, the doctor starts doing tests on Theo...poking, prodding, and using instruments. As he works, I hear him mumble, "too many stairs" at least twice.

Theo looks annoyed by the time the doctor finishes with him. The doctor then turns to me and says that "Theo will be fine, the effect will wear off in a matter of time". I thank him with a stiff nod. Now, time for Theo to get the truth — oh boy.

I am saved from having to tell Theo the truth, for as soon as the door closes behind the doctor, he blacks out. The doctor said that might happen. Now, I have time to decide what exactly to tell Theo — it's not like I can tell him all about The Circle and everything. The first step to proving yourself to The Circle is being able to withhold all information and never say a word about it to anybody on the outside. Atria only knows because she had to be informed after her husband was found dead at the hands of a Red List Agent. She needed to be prepared, both she and her son would be in even more danger than anyone had realized.

I shoo Atria and Trus out — they look even worse than I feel, they need rest.

...

When Theo wakes again, I tell him almost everything. I tell him about Jez — without saying her name or really anything about her — what she did to the soup, and my promise to her father. I make sure not to show any emotions, but Theo — like always — can see that not saving Jez is getting to me. I don't like leaving innocents defenseless, that's one of the reasons why I signed up to work at the palace — more of a chance to go into the city and save other people from everyday bullshit.

Now that Theo is awake, informed, and going to be all right, it's time for me to finally get some rest to be fresh for my next mission. I say "Night" to Theo, go out his door and descend the stairs to the first floor. My room is only one room with a small ensuite. I lock the 3 locks behind me and turn on the screen of my computer on my small desk. All the surveillance cameras are up and running. I check all the halls inside and the paths outside the palace — no strange activity or unknown person. Lastly, I check the footage from the one outside Theo's door and the one in his private hallway: all clear.

I think I'll take a hot shower before bed — for my tenseness, it's been a very long, difficult day. I go into my ensuite and turn on the water in my shower. While the water heats up, I take off my shirt and check the wound on my back. I got shot last week by someone near the palace; afterward, I checked everywhere and couldn't find anyone. It was probably a hunter with a bad shot, but you can't ever just think that and believe your charge to be safe; your charge is never safe, they always have a target on their back.

The wound looks like it's healing well — no infection or anything; it's almost completely scabbed over, and there's barely any sign of blood or shattered bone. I go back, check the shower's water — scalding — and turn it down a little. I take off the rest of my clothes and get into the shower. I just stand under the water for a while, letting it warm me and soak my hair. It feels good; after a long day, nothing is better than getting clean in a nice, hot shower.

I soap myself, put shampoo/conditioner in my hair, and finish by rinsing out my ears. I dry myself off, put on my dressing gown, and wash my face with a washcloth. I end my nightly routine by combing my hair and brushing my teeth.

I leave the bathroom feeling clean and tired. I turn on the telly — low volume — and pull the sheets back on my bed. I get in and try to fall asleep. I try for so long that after a while I get sick of it and pick up my phone off of my bedside table to see what time it is. I have been trying to fall asleep for an hour. My mind never shuts up — good for the job, not good for sleep. I pick up the book that is on my bedside table — "The History of Musalin", there are many different versions and copies; I have almost all of them, but this one I found in an antique store on a day out checking the city with Theo. I will read until I fall asleep.

CHAPTER THIRTEEN

Jezebel

I keep on going straight, with the blinking dot slowly approaching the steady one. There are cars to my left and right, in front and behind. The one in front of me stays in the same lane as me — they don't get off at any exits or anything. Their car looks fuller than it should be. Where are they off to?

Will I know the airport when I see it? I've never seen an airport before, not even in the magazines, articles, and such that my tutor utilized to teach me to read. I keep on driving, the dot keeps moving, and the car stays in front of me. As the blinking dot completely overlaps the steady one, I see a building that looks different than the others. It looks almost the same, but it's bigger and has more land. There are tons of cars in front of it and it looks to have a lot more to it than the buildings I've seen.

This building must be the airport. Yay! I've found my destination. But how do I get into it and how do I know if it's even the airport?

One of my questions is answered when I get closer. There are giant words on the building facing me, it says a word I don't know how to pronounce and a word that looks like "airport". The car in front of me turns on a light that blinks on the same side as the airport. They must be going there. I'll just follow them then — solving another one of my problems.

Now, I just have to find the person my tutor told me about, and get on a plane to Musalin.

The car in front of me turns into a giant blacktop through a break in the grass on the side of the road. I, in turn, do the same. I need to pull into a thing — like the one at McDonald's and the place with the weird machines— with a line on one side, a gap, and a line on the other side. I try to look for an open 2 lines near the door to the building. I've no idea where the door is; I can't spot any knobs, and there are windows that look like doors everywhere. I just ride my scooter into an open spot near the building.

I turn off my scooter, take the keys out, put the keys in my pocket, and wonder if I'll ever see it again. I'm never coming back to this country — I never want to see the Devil again — so I probably won't be seeing my scooter after this. My vision begins to blur, it was a gift from my tutor and I finally got the hang of how to drive it.

I leave my scooter and go to find the door to the airport. When I get closer to the building, people start coming out of a door. I run over to that door before it can close — it blends right into the building!

Once inside, the door closes behind me. A pit forms in my stomach, I feel so out of place; there are so many people. Too many people. I don't know what to do. Everyone's busy and has somewhere to be, I don't know where I'm going. I forgot everything that my tutor told me to do. Did he say where to go?

My mind's blank; it's difficult to concentrate. So many people, they're all staring at me. I wish I knew what they are thinking. They know I don't belong. What am I doing? I can't handle this many people. Never mind, I don't want to know what they're thinking, they're probably thinking mean things about me. Is it better to know the bad things that they're saying about you, or to worry about it? I don't know. My heart is racing so fast and my throat is beginning to close up. What am I going to do?

Jez, get a hold of yourself. You can do this. I believe in you. Your journey's not over yet.

Those words sound like the wind, but the wind can't talk. It must be my head trying to get a grip. Ok, head, I'll try very hard not to focus on how everyone else looks normal and what they're thinking about me.

I can't do it! It's too hard, they're all staring...Or maybe, it's just in my head. I actually look at the people; barely anyone's looking in my direction — they're all too busy going about their business. Just a very few are looking over here, maybe it's because I still haven't moved from right in front of the door. They could be waiting for someone or just interested in seeing who comes through. I wish I could sit and just watch life go by.

I go over to a bunch of seats and sit down where nobody else is. I sit in a chair facing the door. A family comes through the door loaded with storage things that are similar to what the young man had. There's a mother, a father, and 2 children. The girl looks older than me. And the boy, oh wait, that's another girl — she just has very short hair. The other girl looks to be younger than the first but still older than me. The family looks like they've somewhere to be, yet are still pleasant to each other and are smiling while they talk. I wish I had that: a family, happiness and not having to be worried.

Wait, what am I worried about? Aren't I supposed to be doing something?

I'm escaping from the Devil! How could I forget that!? I have to get out of this country as fast as possible!

I jump out of my seat and start walking in the opposite direction from where I came in. I still don't remember what my tutor said to me. I look at everyone else going the same way as me. They all have some sort of paper; they keep looking up at the ceiling and then back down at their paper.

I look up at the ceiling, there are words every so often with numbers. A word that begins with a "g" and ends with an "e". What's that word?

A voice comes out of the sky. The voice says, "Last call for Vertyrc. The plane leaves in 10 minutes. If you are for Vertyrc, go to gate 8."

Gate! That's what that word is. I already passed gates 1, 2, and 3. What gate am I supposed to go to? Let me think. Airport...Airport...Plane...Musalin...Gate...... 5! I'm supposed to get something called a ticket at gate 5. Tickets must be the papers that everyone keeps looking at — they keep looking up because they're all trying to find their gates.

I walk further into the airport while looking up at the ceiling. I pass gate 4 and keep on walking. I walk about 30 steps and still no gate 5. Where's gate 5?

I walk more and more, going deeper into the airport, and still no gate 5. For some reason, I look to my right where there happens to be a little dark nook. Above the nook's a sign that says Gate 5. I stop going forward and walk back to the desk under the sign.

As I approach the desk, the man behind it stops what he's doing and looks up.

"Can I help you?"

"Yes, can I get a ticket please?"

"You either have to book ahead of time or get a ticket at the front of the building."

An idea pops into his head that causes pride mixed with cruelty to replace the boredom in his eyes.

"Passport, miss."

Something doesn't seem right.

"What's your name?"

"Maryice. I need to see your passport in order to be able to sell you a ticket. Hand it over."

Something really isn't right. The man's supposed to know me; I don't need to give him my passport. And this man seems evil. There's something off here. I don't want to say the catchphrase and give away my destination. I look at his shirt, there's a name on it. It starts with an "M". I don't remember what my tutor said, but I'm pretty sure that he didn't say a name that began with an "M". I need to go...but I don't want it to look suspicious.

"Sorry for wasting your time. My friend said she bought me a ticket and to pick it up somewhere. I don't remember what she said; she probably already got it for me and is waiting at the right gate. Thanks for your help."

I walk as quickly away as I can without it looking like I'm running. I see a sign up ahead that says help. I'll ask whoever's there where I can buy a ticket to Musalin. It looks to be far enough ahead that the guy can't overhear.

Goose pimples form on my arms and I get a prickly feeling on the back of my neck; it feels like someone's following me. It must be that man. I turn my head around. He's still at his desk, but he's watching me. There's a group with a girl at the back coming up on my left.

"Mary!" I call and go over to join the group. Now, it looks like I found my friend. Nothing suspicious here. I pass the girl and go to the other side of the group, making sure I'm blocked from his eyesight.

Once I'm out of his vision, I pick a scarf out of a lady's overflowing bag and place my hat on a man's head who's asleep against the wall. I fix my hair and put the scarf around my neck. Hopefully, I look different from the back. I leave the group behind and walk fast to the desk that said help. I try to keep hidden on the other side of people so that the man can't see me.

There's a woman at this desk; she has a bright smile on her face and nothing but mirth in her eyes.

"Hello, miss. How can I help you?"

"Do you know where I can buy a ticket?"

"You can do that right here. Where to?"

"Musalin."

She looks at the screen of a machine in front of her.

"Ok. A direct flight will cost you $1,000. But, seeing as you are buying it last minute, and all we have are a few business seats, that will be $2,500."

I don't know if that's a lot, but it sure does seem like it. I hope the card I was given by my tutor has that much on it. I hand the lady my card. She swipes it on a different, smaller machine next to the other one she previously used.

"Will that be all?"

"Yes." She hands me back my card. I put it back into my envelope and keep the envelope in my hand — who knows if someone could take it from my pocket; it's all I have to get to my new life.

"Gate 10 is your destination. Just keep walking for 12 more minutes. Don't worry; your flight leaves in 25, so you shouldn't be late. Have a nice day."

"Thank you."

I leave the desk and get in the middle of a large group passing by. I walk with them until I see the sign that says gate 10.

The gate's just a desk and then a passage behind the desk. There's a line of people at gate 10. I'm going to have to leave this group — they're going past my gate. But that means no more camouflage. I see a door that has a girl wearing a dress painted on it, it has a sign above it that says "Toilet Room".

I enter the toilet room and check my wrist — I found a thing that tells time in the envelope my tutor gave me. The thing says it's 23:38, and I think my plane leaves at 23:51. I have time to finally use the toilet. I find an empty stall and go. Good thing I only had to wee, and not poo — that would've for sure made me late for my plane. I look in the mirror when I leave the stall. My hair looks so nice; I brush my hands through it. My hair feels so smooth. I've only ever seen what I look like once — in an art lesson with my tutor, I was to do a self-portrait. He gave me a small mirror to use so I could get the portrait accurate. That girl looked completely different from the one in this mirror.

This girl has nice hair, but also dark circles under her eyes and they're filled with fear and uncertainty.

I wash my hands and check the time, 23:43. I better hurry or I'm going to be late. I wrap the scarf around my head — masking my hair and features — then rush out into the hallway. I go to the desk at gate 10. The lady looks nice but impatient. I hand her my ticket.

"You better hurry, you have 7 minutes. You're lucky, any later and you would have missed it."

She looks at my ticket and lets me enter the pathway behind the desk. There's a group of people up ahead, I go and join them. We walk the rest of the hallway and go through a door into a narrow passage that has seats filled with people on either side. The group all sits together and I sit down in a chair by itself in the middle of a row.

I put my envelope away and start to relax; the door has already closed. But, my attention is drawn to the window by huge, bright, red flashing lights. The door to the airplane opens back up and the man from gate 5 looks in. Through the door, comes the sound of something very loud — it must go with the flashing lights. I duck down and get onto the floor so that the man doesn't see me. There are gaps under the seats, into which I can just about fit. I scurry under and move farther back on the plane. I look up as far as I can and see a door at the back of the plane, before a curtain. It must be a toilet.

I don't have to go anymore, but it could offer a good hiding spot. I look back down the aisle: the man's coming closer. I don't have time to get into the toilet room. It's too great of a risk. I ball up and make sure none of my limbs are sticking out from under the seat — I'll have to stay here until he leaves.

I check the time, it's almost the time that the Devil should wake. He might even already be awake; somebody must've found him, the body of the Devil's sidekick, and the body of that guard I knocked out. I knew it! This man works for the Devil — good thing I caught on that something was off and didn't tell him where I was going.

The door to the toilet room's closed — there must be someone in there. The Devil's man goes to it and the look on his face says he caught his prey. Good thing I didn't hide in the toilet room, I never would've gotten in and it's an obvious place to hide.

The Devil's man waits for the person in the toilet room to come out. He pounces on the person, expecting it to be me. From my vantage point, I can only see his legs and feet, but it sounds like an old man. The old man screams and then falls back into the toilet room — I hope he's not hurt. The Devil's man doesn't look ashamed or anything, he just looks disappointed and mad.

The Devil's man storms off the airplane and the door closes behind him. I crawl back to where my seat and get out from under the seats. Two women are helping the old man, they get him out of the toilet room and lead him to an empty seat.

The same 2 women then go on either side of the aisle and start checking people's papers and tickets. The lady from the gate gave me back my ticket, I get that and my passport ready. The woman who's doing my side of the aisle has found a family of 3 who don't have seats, and they want to sit together. The row I'm in has 3 seats and 2 of them are empty. I feel sorry for them, but I don't want to move. I just want to get to Musalin safe and sound.

When the woman gets to me and looks at my ticket, her face evolves. I don't know what I did wrong, but apparently, I did something.

"Honey, could you please get up and come with me?"

Oh no, I did something. I nod my head shakily and get up. She then motions to the family of 3 and tells them to sit down where I was. After she makes sure that they're settled, she then leads me in the direction of the toilet room. She goes through the curtain and to the other side. I stop before the curtain. What's going to happen? What's on the other side of the curtain? I can't stop my legs from shaking.

I don't want to get kicked off this plane! I can't! I can't stay in this country and get caught by the Devil! I'd rather kill myself because staying here will make me wish for death to take me.

The lady comes back through the curtain and impatiently motions me through. I step through the curtain.

The sight's breathtaking; I'd look around in wonder and enjoy all of it if I wasn't so scared of being taken off this plane. She leads me to an empty seat and tells me to sit down.

"You were in the wrong part of the airplane; this is business, which is what your ticket's for. Whatever were you doing in economy?"

I don't answer, I just sit down in the seat and wait for her to go away. My face must be as red as a tomato; my new life's not starting off as good as it would've for anyone but me. Only I could get my seating on an airplane wrong and have to be outed for it; everyone in business is looking at me. I don't even know what economy or business are, all I did was follow the group of people who were in front of me. My face feels enflamed...their staring makes me ashamed of my mistake.

The lady's done talking and goes back in the direction of the curtain. A voice comes on something that can be heard throughout the airplane. "Good evening ladies and gentlemen. Tonight you will be flying with Goifa Lines, we will safely get you to your destination. Just sit back, relax, and we will be arriving in no time."

A person in a suit comes up to me, puts a tray in front of my seat down, and places a plate full of food on it. They ask me what I want to drink. "A smoothie," That young woman's at McDonald's looked so delicious.

The same person brings me a glass full of smooth liquid that's pink. I uncover the plate of food: meat, vegetables, fish, fruit, cheese, and potatoes. I want to ask the person "who am I supposed to share this with," but I don't want to embarrass myself again; everyone else seems to have their own plate and has started to eat.

My stomach's still full from McDonald's and I don't think it can take any more food or I'll puke...but I eat some anyway. There's no need to be rude.

I eat as much food as my stomach will hold and drink the smoothie to wash it down. The smoothie tastes like bananas and strawberries — must be a strawberry banana smoothie. I've made them before for the Devil, but they never looked as good as this.

I'm so full and the day's events are starting to catch up with me. I feel so tired and this chair's so much comfier than my bed at the Devil's house. My eyes start to close, and within seconds, I'm fast asleep.

...

As I'm sleeping, strange things happen and I remember information. I dream about my tutor being the one to save me, not just his voice, but actually him; he escapes with me. He tells me that we'd get to the airport in a few hours and that his man named Checker'd be waiting for us with 2 untraceable tickets to Musalin. Once there, we'd start a life of our own, with him being my father, my family. And I have more family. Not a mother — she's dead. But I've aunts and uncles and cousins, we even have a horse named Spirit and adopt a puppy named Pooka. We have a giant house; we don't have to work. We just do hobbies and stuff that we love while living a luxurious life.

But then the fantasy turns into a nightmare and the Devil arrives. He kills my father and turns up with my mother's broken body — which he flaunts over me and taunts that that's what'll become of me. Then he gets his whip out and starts hacking at every part of me — my punishment for escaping, not one centimeter of me is unscarred.

As I scream a blood-curdling scream in my dream and lose consciousness, I wake up terrified and shaking, not knowing where I am. There are so many people! Where am I?!

And then it all comes back to me: I'm on a plane to Musalin. I lean back into the chair and try to calm myself. It was just a dream. Only a dream. I know it was, but it just felt so real. I can still feel the pain from the whip all over.

I won't close my eyes again, every time I do, I'll just see the Devil. He's going to catch me. I can't even imagine the horrible stuff he'll do to me. The whip's just the beginning.

I don't know how long I was sleeping. How much longer until we get to Musalin? I look at the time on my wrist, it's 02:00. We've been on this plane for more than an hour. Wow, it doesn't feel like that long. I must've slept for most of it. That's the only good thing about my dream turned nightmare. What does it mean? Is the Devil going to capture me and make my torture even worse?

No, it was just a nightmare. None of that's real, it's all fiction. My tutor would never be my father or have taken me away from the Devil, or else he would've done it instead of just giving me a bottle with a potion in it. Plus, I've no family; I'm all alone.

I look out the window and watch the stars go by. I can't go back to sleep, but I don't want to worry. I just clear my mind and look outside, unaware of my surroundings, focusing on nothing but the stars.

I stay like this for a while, in a state between awake and asleep, just peaceful. I stay like it until the voice comes back on, announcing that we'll be landing in Musalin soon and that we have to put something called a seatbelt on. I don't know what a seatbelt is.

I bring myself back to reality and see what everyone else is doing. They pull something from either side of them and buckle it near their middles. I look on either side of me and find weird-looking fabric straight things with buckles on the end of each. I pull them out and make them longer. I then pull them up and around my middle and try to put them together. How do you do this? Do I just push them together and they'll connect? I don't know. As I'm trying to figure out how the buckle works, the plane starts rumbling and going down. I about slip out of my seat. I quickly push the two ends together and tighten it on my stomach as far as it'll go.

Before long, the plane's on the ground and everyone's starting to get up and grab their stuff. I unbuckle myself and make sure that the scarf's still in place. I wait for somebody to get done grabbing their stuff and follow them off the plane.

As I get off the plane, I look around and find that there's no building in sight. There's just a big space that has many people and a gate leading to many cars and the world beyond. Other people who just got off, go to where workers are piling people's stuff. I don't have any stuff...so I don't follow them. I go to the gate and up to the person at it. It's a man. As I get closer, he looks up and stares at me for a little while before he starts to talk.

"Do you need anything?"

"I was wondering if this is the way out to Musalin."

"It might, it might not be. You need to pick up your luggage over there." He points to where I saw all of the other people go.

"Everything I need's waiting for me at my house — I got it sent over here first."

"Ok. Can I see your passport?" I hand him my passport. He looks it over. "Where to?"

"I just need someone to drop me off near Baker St. I'd rather walk the rest of the distance to my house."

"What's on Baker St?"

"Nothing. That's not my destination. I just know that it's a good walking distance from my house. I haven't been here in a while and just want to enjoy the sights and refresh myself of my beautiful home."

"All right. Whatever." He hands me back my passport.

He opens the gate for me and I step through. I pause for a moment and look around. This is the beginning of my new life.

Beyond the gate are lots of things. I see grass; flowers; and woods in front of me; along with many cars on blacktop. How am I going to get to 42nd Baker St? It's too bad that I don't have my scooter. What other mode of transportation is there? I can't drive a car, so that's not an option. I don't know where anything is in this town. My tutor might've had another map telling me on my scooter, but I'll never know if he did or didn't, will I?

The man who controlled the gate comes out of his booth and over to me.

"I'll get you a cab, there should be one available."

He goes over to the blacktop and sticks his thumb up while whistling. A yellow car comes over. The driver gets out of the car and goes to the back of it; he opens a part of it and lifts it up, exposing storage space. He comes over to me. Once he's able to look around, he gets a confused look on his face.

"Where's your baggage?"

Oh. The storage thing must be for my stuff.

"I don't have any. Can you drive me to my destination?"

He looks dazed for a second and then clears his head.

"Sure can." He goes over and closes the storage thing. "Hop in."

Does he literally mean hop in? And do I really have to get in a car? I don't want to, it's going to swallow me and I'll never survive it. But, I got this far; I won't turn back now. I open a door on the side of the car and get in.

As I sit down, my shaking is intensifies. What if this thing kills me? Riding my scooter was one thing — this is completely different. The man gets into the front of the car, starts the engine, pulls out of the blacktop, and out into the world.

"Where to?" He asks me. I don't know what to say. I want him to take me to Baker St. But I don't want to be traceable, then the Devil would for sure find me. Baker St shouldn't be far from the center of town, right?

"Center of town, please."

"How will you be paying, cash or credit?"

I don't know what either of those things are. The only thing that I do know is I'm paying with my card, but which option's my card?

"Card."

"So credit then."

"Yep."

The conversation stops there. We drive on in silence. I look at my wrist, the time's 04:30. How did it get so late? That plane ride took a while. There's no way that the Devil isn't already awake. I bet you he woke up not even 2 hours into it; his evilness made the potion wear off early.

I look out the window, enough worrying for now. We pass everything by in a blur. But I've never seen blurs so bright; the grass and trees are so green, they shine in the dim lighting. Everything here seems very healthy, natural, and alive. Unlike the Devil's place, where everything's dead.

After a little while in the car — I'm still alive, it didn't eat me, phew — we start to get closer to tons of buildings, the lighting becomes brighter, and more crowds of people appear. There's one building that towers above it all, it looks like a castle from my fairytale book.

"What's with the castle?" I ask my driver.

"It's where the royal family lives. They have been ruling over Musalin for as long as anyone can remember."

Interesting, it's like something out of a fairytale. I hope I can visit the castle, it'd be a dream come true. I've always wanted to be transported into my fairytale book and live there.

When we get to the town, the car slows down. We keep on going, but at a slower rate. When we pass a lot of buildings and seem to be in the thick of the town, the car comes to a stop. The man turns around in his seat and has a machine similar to the one that the lady at the airport used to buy my ticket.

He sits there for a moment looking at me. It's becoming very tight in here — who knows what's going through his head? I just want to get out, but I can't until I pay him. Do I pay him by giving him my card? Will he give it back? Does it even have enough to pay for this?

"Card please." I hand him my card. He swipes it through the machine and a little click fills the silence. What does that mean? Is there anything left on my card?

The man doesn't look upset or anything, so hopefully, nothing's wrong. He hands me back my card.

"Have a good day." He turns back around and seems ready to drive off. I get out as quickly as I can; I step onto something that I believe's called a sidewalk. I look around for signs, just need to find the one that says Baker St. I know how to spell baker — there's one in my fairytale book. As I'm looking around, I spot 2 familiar people across the way.

I gasp. It's the lady and older man from the Devil's house; this must be their home. They got here before me — so much for them rescuing me. I bet you that they've already forgotten about me. The lady's holding up her arm, it's covered in something weird-looking. I hope she's not hurt — that's the only explanation I can think of as to why she'd be acting that way with her arm.

I duck behind a person who's just standing on the sidewalk looking at a tiny machine, like the one the young man used back at the Devil's place. I hope that the guests don't see me,

I don't want them to take me back to the Devil. And I don't want them to stop me from figuring out what a "normal" life is.

They keep on walking, they seem to be going in the direction of the castle. What are they doing? Do they live at the castle? I gasp. Are...are they Royals?

Is that why it was so important that I serve them? The Devil wanted to show how evil he is through his power over his servants? Is that why my tutor waited until these guests came for my escape? Because they have power in another country and could've protected me here? Well, never you mind, I'm going to protect myself. Once I find this Soppy, I can get my new life in order and find a way to stay away from the Devil forever!

After the 2 guests are completely out of sight, I continue looking at the signs that name the streets. I see "Whomper" "Windle" "Rhine" "Scarlet" and "Bansher". I don't see one that says "Baker". I should ask somebody if they know where it is. I don't want the Devil to be able to trace me, but if it's a random person, he shouldn't be able to guess who I asked. There are many people around — it is after all the Town Centre. There's a man walking slowly my way, he looks like he's determined to be somewhere; I try to stop him and ask for directions, but he doesn't even look in my direction. There's a young woman at a sign that has some sort of big car on it. I go up to her.

"Excuse me, miss? Do you by any chance happen to—"

It's as if my words are falling on deaf ears — oh, no is she deaf? I hope I didn't insult her. How does one determine blind and deaf people from everybody else? I've never had to even think about these questions before. If it hadn't been for my tutor, I never would've known that there's a giant world out here filled with people.

A giant half-black-half-white car that has some sort of banner with people on it pulls up, I jump back — it's huge! As the young woman passes me to board the car, I see little things in her ears. Oh, that must be why she didn't acknowledge me; what are those things?

There are many more people, but they all look busy too, or

have things on or sticking out of their ears. I guess I'll just have to figure out my own way to Baker St.

There's something in the middle of the sidewalk. I walk closer to it. Oh! It's a map! It looks like the one on my scooter, but bigger. I can find where Baker St is on it. Yay!

There's a giant red thing near where it says "Town Centre", that must indicate where you are. I look at all the words and try to find Baker St. I see a bunch of streets, but no Baker. I scan the whole map twice and still don't see it.

A young man comes over to the map. He doesn't seem to have any things around his ear. He puts his finger on the map and seems to trace a route made up of many streets.

"Excuse me, sir." He looks at me.

"Oui."

"Do you know where Baker St is?"

"Laquelle?"

"Baker St."

"Voulez-vous dire—"

"I'm sorry, but I don't understand what you're saying."

"Je suis désolé. Sorry, I just got back from Etloré. I was saying that you must mean Holmes Ave. It was changed a while back."

"Ok. Thanks."

"Do you need help finding it?"

"Yes, that'd be very helpful. Thank you."

He puts his finger on the red circle on the map. "We are here." The same finger on his other hand points to a street further up on the map. "This is Holmes Ave." Now I see the words that are the name of the street. "You need to take all these roads." He moves his finger from the red circle until it connects with his other finger.

"That's a lot of streets. I don't know how I'm going to remember it all."

"I can walk you there."

"Can you? That'd just be lovely. I'd totally get lost if I were to go on my own."

"Sure thing. Just let me call my family and let them know I'm gonna be late."

"I'm very sorry. But can you please not? Time is of the essence. If I don't get there as soon as possible, bad things'll happen."

"All right. You're probably not going to tell me what those bad things are, are you?"

I shake my head. I can't tell a stranger all about me. I hate that he even knows my destination. What if he works for the Devil? At least I didn't tell him what number house. I'll just leave him at the end of the block, wait until he's gone, and then go to the house that says 42.

He picks up his bag from the dirty ground and starts off. I follow him. We walk for a few minutes; he walks so fast, I have to do something in between running and walking to keep up. We pass many streets, and yet, we stay on the same side of the road. When I was looking at the map, Holmes Ave was on the other side of the road.

When the young man looks back at me once in a while, his face is scrunched up in worry. We pass many more turn-offs from the street we're on. Why are we not crossing the street?

The young man looks at his arm — he's got something like I have on his wrist that tells the time. He starts to get jittery, bouncing from foot to foot as he walks. The young man keeps looking around, he looks up and down streets. "We're almost there." He says over his shoulder to me.

He stops looking back at me and keeps walking forward, almost at a run now. This is really starting not to feel right. What if he does work for the Devil? Why else would he offer to help me? And why haven't we crossed the street yet?!

Think, Jez. Remember the map.

I look back at the map in my mind. When the guy did one finger to the other, there were about 15 streets in between where we were and Holmes Ave. We've passed more than that — I think. I look around for something, a sign, to tell me where I am. The closest street sign says 'Napoleon Ave'. I don't remember seeing Napoleon Ave on the map. There was a whole section that didn't have any streets labeled. It seemed like there was nothing in that section. It was labeled Hellion Alley.

I look behind me at the previous street sign, it's hard to make out. But I see a T in the first word and it ends in a V. The second word seems to be Fri. I remember the last street labeled on the map before Hellion Alley was a street called Leitmotiv Fri. I can only make out one 't 'on the sign, but there could be 2.

There are no roads from here that lead to Holmes Ave. This guy works for the Devil! What?! But he seemed so nice. I can't have him taking me back to the Devil. I'll not go back. I won't!

When I know for sure he's not looking back anymore, I find a vacant side street. I silently slip into it and go deeper into the darkness until it swallows me whole. I see a giant rubbish bin and hide behind it. I look under the bin — there's a space in between the ground and the bin, I can see out but no one can see in or through.

A shadow passes the opening, it comes from the man's direction. The shadow pauses at the opening and stays there for a minute. My heart's starting to beat really fast. I keep my breathing as silent as I can. I hope he can't hear my heart. I really don't want to be dragged back to the Devil. Not yet!

The shadow passes. I wait a few more minutes and don't hear anything. I leave my hiding spot and try to find another way out.

My heart stops. There's a figure a little ways down the road. I freak out. There's something to my right. I grab onto it and start climbing up to the roof. I go so fast that halfway up, my foot slips. I hang on — with all the little bit of strength that I have — to the bars. My head swings downward, the ground's so far away. My stomach drops and all the food I've eaten today comes back up my throat.

I take a deep breath, swallow the food back down, get my foot back on the step, and continue up at a little bit slower pace than before.

When I get on top of the roof, I turn around and look back down. The height makes me dizzy and sick. But I look past that and find the figure down below; it's in the same spot and doesn't seem to have moved nor to be looking up. Phew, it's not the young man.

I stand up and look around. There are many roofs here, one for each of the buildings that I passed. The buildings are close together, I believe that I can get back to the Town Centre without using the roads. There's less of a chance of the young man finding me and dragging me back to the Devil if I use the roofs as streets.

I start back the way I came, jumping from one roof to another. What if he doesn't work for the Devil?

If he didn't, then why'd he take me to Hellion Alley, which is nowhere near Holmes Ave? No, he was working for the Devil. You can't trust anybody. Everyone works for the Devil. The men who were in cars trying to kill me, the man at the airport, and now this young man who seemed as friendly as a giant fluffy bear. And bears are the friendliest thing out there; their hugs are better than anybody else's, with all their fur. I hope I get to meet a bear. I want it to be my friend and protect me from danger.

Get your head back on the task, Jezebel.

Right. I'll have time to greet a bear later and become its friend. Right now, I need to focus on finding Baker St — Holmes Ave — and starting my new life with the help of Soppy.

I look back, I must've been on top of at least 10 buildings. That doesn't help, we passed way more. I wish I had my scooter, this would go so much faster.

I start to run. I'll just go forward with no thoughts in my head. I force my mind to go blank and stay like that for a while until noise filters through my ears in the form of many voices. I stop running and crouch down on the roof — I wouldn't want someone to look up and spot me. I go over to the edge of the roof and look down.

I gasp. It's the Town Centre! Finally! But it's different now. All the people are lined up. There's a group on one sidewalk, one on the other, and 3 lines in the street. What's going on?

There are men in red, keeping everyone in their lines. There's only one red man keeping an eye on the group on the sidewalk under me. All the other groups seem to be getting searched by many red men.

I crawl over to the side of the roof — there's a structure like the one I climbed to get up here. I look down and make sure nobody's in the street. It looks different than the one in Hellion Alley, this one's wider, brighter, and more colorful. I don't see anyone and start to climb down, at way slower a pace than when I went up.

I get to the ground without slipping or falling. I look up and down the street, there's not even a rubbish bin to hide behind. This street smells fresher and cleaner than the closed-off one in Hellion Alley.

The smart thing would be to go to the left, away from the people being searched. But I need to know what's going on. Has the Devil found me?!

I take a right and go out of the side street and onto the main road. There are no red men near where I come out. There's a young man to my right and a lady to my left. I've had enough of young men today — they're the worst! I turn to the lady.

"What's going on?"

"They're searching for someone. This hasn't happened since the king was killed. And then it was the royals, not these red men."

"Thank you. Is there such a thing as Baker St?" I whisper in her ear so that no one else knows my destination.

"Yeah, it's in the Royals 'private neighborhood. But nobody's supposed to know it exists."

"Which would be where, if such a thing did exist?"

She turns to look at me and smirks.

"I like you. You have to go to the palace and then turn left at the 45th street sign and a right at the 3rd street leading off of it."

"Thank you very much." I open my envelope and take a

piece of paper out of it. This one has the number 10 on it.

The red men don't notice me as I slip away. This time there's no loud noise alerting me that they know I was there. I go back through the side street and out the other end.

CHAPTER FOURTEEN

Bryce

The crow of a rooster startles me awake. For a second, I forget where I am; I open my eyes and the sunlight coming in through the windows reveals my surroundings: Atria's jet. She let me take it so that I could look for Jez. I have been searching for about a month now. Every day I wake up, go outside to new surroundings, and search for Jez. So far, I've checked Toorun, Mapl, and Attorie — some of the countries from Musalin to Brilla, the Devil's territory.

At this rate, the Devil's going to find her first. Why did I have to give my word to her father? I have set my own doom. My word is one of my few weaknesses.

I get up and go to the front of the plane. The pilot is still asleep. I look at my watch; the fact that it's only 5 in the morning makes me groan.

Being careful not to wake the pilot, I lean over him and push a button on the dashboard. With an almost silent whoosh, the door is open. I throw on a jacket, lace my boots, and leave the jet.

As I step out into the silence of the landing field, I imagine finding Jez and saving her from a horrible fate. And then finally being promoted to guarding the palace and no longer being just Theo's bodyguard. All I've ever wanted since I was first training to be a spy, was to work protecting the palace and to stop an event like what happened to the king from going forth.

Once I am fully out of the jet and the door has shut behind me, I close my eyes and take a deep breath. It's a fresh, new day. I breathe back out. *I will find Jez today; today I will go home.* Every day since the end of week one, I have thought this motto when I step out of the jet. I open my eyes.

I go to the small building through which you enter and exit the landing field. As I pass the guard at the desk, there's a clearing of a throat. I keep on walking; the guard speaks up.

"Sir...Excuse me, sir?"

I look over my shoulder; it's very irritating when someone bothers you early when you're focused on a mission. "Yes, what do you want!?" I throw the guard a disgusted, irritated look — I'm not really a morning person.

The guard quakes a little, and his hand goes under the desk. "Th...th...," he clears his throat again.

"Well, out with it boy!"

The boy coughs and continues on. "There's a package here for you, sir. It arrived late last night. Do you want it or should I —"

"I'll take it." I walk briskly over to the young guard and take the package that is offered.

I leave the landing field and go to find a spot to grab breakfast. Not many places are going to be open this early. But we're not talking about just any city. This is Ostki, the capital of Normindi — a city and country that supposedly never sleeps. What's in the package? I'll open it while I eat.

Several shops are open. The most famous cafe, Nuovo Inizio, opened at 03:00. But that's not the best way to go, Normindi is full of Red List agents and they frequent the good places. So instead, I turn down an alleyway and find a small cafe. Roos is run by the Nowak family — peasants from past generations who scraped enough money together to be at the very bottom of the middle class.

The door isn't even really a door, I step through the tallest window on the ground floor. I find a table with a menu and an upside-down decanter. The only table with such stuff is in the corner closest to the actual window on the other side of the entrance and opposite the counter. Once I sit down, a lady who was at the counter goes into what must be the kitchen.

There are hushed conversations in the kitchen and out comes a teenage boy.

"Wat will sie иметь Monsieur?"

Ah, the Normindian language. I haven't spoken it in years. Early on in my training, I learned 5 different languages, Normindian being one of them.

I look over the menu. "Ochtend-Spezialität avec фасоль." Breakfast specialty with beans. I wonder what is in the specialty, the menu does not elaborate.

"En zu boisson?"

"чай" I'm pretty sure this means tea; I'll just have to wait and see.

The boy goes back to the kitchen, with more voices and shouting. Sometime later, the boy comes back with a platter full of food. I would have opened the package while waiting, but I didn't know how long it would take for the food to be prepared and I don't want anyone to know what's in it.

The boy is stronger than he seems, all of the food on the platter must weigh a ton. He sets the platter down on the other end of my table and goes back to the kitchen without a word.

I hear more shouting and this time it is not as hushed. I am a little rusty with the language so I can only pick up a few words here and there. "Red...killers...wanted...Him!...why? ...who?...call."

A female voice shouts at the others. "Nein! тишина! We zullen not! Il est ein клиент! We unterlassen Sie beurt im люди. Rappelles toi what wij benutzt être!" Something about me being a customer and not turning me in? If I am correct in my translation, I only have one question: turning me in to whom?

During all the shouting, a young girl scurries out of the kitchen with a giant pouring jar in one hand and a clean-looking glass in the other. She comes over to my table with her head down, turns the decanter right side up, and pours half of the liquid from the jar into it. She sets down the glass in front of me and scurries back towards the kitchen; but instead of going into the shouting match, she leaves through a different door.

I took in enough of my surroundings to know I am safe. I hear my stomach growl and look at the food on the platter. Toast with a spread that looks like Vegemite; ham and cheese on bread, but cooked a peculiar looking way; dim sum; some kind of soup; and the beans I asked for. Wow, not even Theo and I working together could finish all this.

I start to eat. While I do so, a head pokes out of the kitchen: it is an older woman. She is younger than the one that was at the counter but older than the one who brought me the liquid. I notice her out of the corner of my eye and try to memorize her face.

Once I finish as much as I can, I pour the liquid from the decanter into my glass to wash down my food. Some kind of flavor to the drink. It's not poison — I already smelled it for that. But it tastes weird, it tastes like tea but there's a kick to it.

I don't drink all of the liquid, just to be safe. I make sure that the package is still in my pocket; place the amount of Normindian currency that the menu said, plus a little bit extra as a tip for the beans onto the table; and leave the building through the same door that I saw the young girl go through.

I find myself in a dark alley with only one window very high up on one of the buildings, no ladders in sight, and no other escape routes except for the door that I just came through. This was a bad idea. I'm supposed to be finding Jez, not getting myself into trouble. Bryce, really? No matter what or how I think, I continue ahead. There's a noise to my right, like someone tripping over a tin can and it smacking against the wall. Through the darkness, I can just make out a dumpster, and is that…a shadow? Is there someone behind the dumpster?

"Hullo? Anybody there? Come out, I'm armed." I pull my pistol out from inside my coat.

There's a crash behind me, I turn to see what it was and something comes down hard upon my head. Before I black out, I see someone. It's the girl who was in the cafe. But it looks like…

"Jez?"

CHAPTER FIFTEEN

Jezebel

I try my best to follow the lady's directions, but without being able to use the main roads, I've no idea which way I'm going. The buildings on the side streets are so tall that I can't see the palace. If I can't find the palace, I can't find Baker St. Whatever, all I can do now is to keep walking and hope that I spot it.

I walk until I no longer feel my legs. I stop once I'm walking as slow as a snail and look around at where I ended up. The buildings look nicer than the ones in Hellion Alley, but they aren't as nice looking as the ones near the Town Centre. These ones are very dirty and worn-down looking. Most of the buildings look empty and seem to have no life to them.

I lean against the brick wall on the left and look through the stuff in the envelope that my tutor left for me. There are just a few things of paper money left, my card, passport, and keys to my scooter. But there's something I never noticed before, there's a flat thing that's lit up and a circular-looking thing, I pull them both out. The circular object has very skinny triangles on it pointing in different directions to the letters "N" "S" "W" "E" in bold and "NE" "NW" "SE" and "SW" in small. On top of that's an arrow that's constantly moving, but it stops in one direction when my feet move. I look at the flat thingy.

Oh! It's a map! There's not as much on it as the one that was in the Town Centre, but it does have 3 words: "Palace" and "Baker Street". Looks like I didn't need to ask that lady after all, my tutor left me a map to my destination. How very kind of him, I wish he were here with me. My heart aches thinking about what the Devil's doing to him — he's bound to have found out what my tutor did for me.

I can't think of my tutor now, tears are already forming in my eyes; thinking of him will just make me distracted. I'll see what happened to him later; for now, I must make my way to Baker St. I close my eyes, try to calm myself, and get back to normal — I need to focus.

While I straighten up from leaning against the wall, I hear the faint echo of broken footsteps. They seem to be heading toward me. I open my eyes and look to my left, there's a man stumbling this way. There's something wrong with him. What's his problem, what's happening to him? Does he need help?

When the man comes close enough to have my shoes in his vision, he looks up and his gaze slides slowly along my body. I shouldn't be afraid of him, I know how to kill a man — heck I've already killed one. But there's something about this one that strikes chills down to my core. Maybe it's the way his gaze seems hungry as it drinks in my figure.

He makes me almost as afraid as the Devil — he has the same air about him. The man comes closer. I tell my feet to move, but they stay glued to the ground. Go! Feet Move! I'm frozen. The man's almost in touching distance, I don't like this. I don't like the look of this or his hungry gaze.

"What have we here? A pretty little thing. Where's your mamma and papa?" He slurs.

He comes even closer, he's now in touching distance. His hand comes toward my head. No! Feet move! My heart keeps picking up speed, and I still can't move. What's wrong with me!? Go! Everything seems to come to a stop, and all of a sudden I realize how alone I am. How there's not a single soul near and I don't hear any sounds, not even birds. The man's hand touches my head, his other arm leans against the wall, entrapping me in the process.

"How lucky I am to find a pretty little thing like you," he drawls in a slur. He brings his face closer to mine. My legs are still frozen and I can't even move my arm to hit him. Everything's frozen. What's happening?! His mouth touches mine and he's doing something to my lips. As he does this, he growls. His tongue touches my lips and forces them open. I'm immobile, he must be doing this. He has powers!

"Such sweetness, open up." He mumbles from my mouth. His tongue strokes mine. As he's doing this, his hand has moved from my head and has moved down. He fumbles with his trousers and then moves to push the skirt of my dress up. I'm screaming inside. This isn't right! No! Stop!

I don't look down, I can't. I try screaming for real, but I can't. His mouth's still covering mine.

What the Hell?! Right before he can go any further, something happens to him. All of a sudden everything he's doing stops and he falls a little, dropping my skirt in the process. He slides down and lands on the ground; he doesn't move. There's blood coming out of his clothes where his heart is.

I'm still standing frozen. Even his death doesn't release the hold of something on me. It's got to be a spell for sure. I must focus on figuring out what's holding me so that I don't break into hysteria for what just almost and what did happen. I hear the impact of something on the ground to my left, like something or someone came off of the roof.

Out of the corner of my eye, I see the shadow of a person. The person comes over to the man who's dead on the ground. The person crouches down and makes sure that the man's really dead. When the person stands up and turns to me, I get a good look at him. It's definitely a him, I've never seen him before. He pulls a knife slightly out of his sleeve, so that it's easily available in case he needs it, but not enough so, that a normal person who wasn't trained to spot every little movement, would notice.

"Are you all right?" I try to answer, but I can't.

"You can move now, you're safe; he's dead. You don't have to be scared anymore." Well, duh. Of course, he's dead — even an idiot would know that. I try to say something, but I'm still frozen. I try to struggle against the hold on me. The young man — he seems just a little older than me — crouches down and picks up the stuff that I dropped. The documents that let me drive my scooter and passport have fallen out of the pouch, along with my card. The circular thing and map aren't far from my feet, both of them are cracked and broken.

"Iris. Is that your name?" I don't respond, I can't.

He picks up the circular thing and the map, stands up, and tries handing them to me. When I don't reach out to take them, he gets a little bit of an impatient look about him.

"Look, I know that he almost raped you, but I need you to come back to reality; nothing bad happened. I killed him before he went too far. Sorry that it took me so long; I lost his trail a few streets back. It's actually harder than you think to keep up with a drunk bastard." He tries to look humorous.

I try to speak with my eyes, to tell him that I can't move. I'm not sure if he understands or not. I look at the man lying dead on the ground in a heap.

"Oh, if he was your client, I can pay you. If that's what you want. Don't worry, this won't get back to your mistress." My mistress? Why would I have a mistress?

"Gevan, she is obviously not a prostitute. Look at how scared she is. And you more than anybody should know what a Lacstris victim looks like." A lady comes down from the right and starts searching the dead man for something.

"Victa, I was handling it. Of course, I know that she's being affected by a Lacstris. I was just about to search for it."

The lady called Victa snorts. The young man — Gevan? — crouches back down to search the man too. Before he can start, Victa pulls something out of the dead man's pocket. It's small, I can't really make out the details of it. She breaks it into pieces while she stands back up.

Suddenly, it's like my free will was given back to me. I fall back against the wall, clench my eyes closed, wishing this is a nightmare: it's just a nightmare. Yeah, I fell back asleep on the plane and my horrid dreams of the Devil prompted me to start thinking of all the bad things that could happen. When I open my eyes, I'll see the plane's interior and all of this will be gone.

I open my eyes. I scream a scream that's not silent, but also not the way normal people scream. Everything's still here. I pinch my arm, but it doesn't work. I pinch it again and again. I keep pinching it until the lady grabs my arm.

"Stop. All you are doing is hurting yourself." I can't shake her off, I don't have the strength to. I start to bite my arm, I'm willing to do anything to wake up from this nightmare.

"Victa, get out of the way; let me handle this." Victa doesn't look at him, she just tries to look into my eyes and make me stop.

Gevan pushes Victa out of the way and all I see is a flash of something coming down over my head and an angry look comes over Victa's face before the blackness takes over.

...

When I come to, I'm not in the street anymore. Instead, I'm on the floor of a building with just a pillow under my head. I open my eyes to find the lady and young man a ways away. The lady has her eyes closed and tear streaks on her face. The young man looks like he wants to comfort her but doesn't. Instead, he's looking out a window and keeping an eye on the lady.

I don't know what's going on. I don't think that I should alert them to my awakeness — I might learn a thing or two if they think I'm still out of it. I close my eyes back up and fake being unconscious.

The lady starts crying more, and I hear the young man's footsteps go closer to her. I think he might be comforting her now.

Once she stops crying so hard, he talks to her in a gentle voice.

"Victa, why are you crying. Who is she?"

"I do not know who she is!"

"Then why are you crying? You've been doing it since you got a good look at her."

"She looks like someone who disappeared a long time

ago."

"Who? The only person who ever disappeared was Arch."

"No. Remember his wife: Linris."

"She wasn't his wife, they were just together."

"Well, whatever they were, she looks just like Linris."

"She's not her; she's only 18 and her name is Iris."

"You know as well as I do that documents and passports can be forged."

"But she's not as old as Linris would be. Why is this so important? Why would someone who looks like Linris make you cry?"

"Because Linris was my aunt. My mother's closest friend. She came over all the time before she disappeared. She was my favorite person; I loved her even more than I loved my mother. Because Linris always acted as if she loved me."

"Your mother does love you, she's just very hard on you. She has to be in order to lead us and keep everything in balance."

"I know, but...I think she might be waking up." Victa sniffs and stops herself from crying.

I guess I need to wake up now, but I don't want them to think I was eavesdropping. I give a gasping indrawn breath and fake open my eyes as if they hurt. I sit up as if I'm lightheaded. I hold onto my head and once I'm in a sitting position, I do the thing that'll end my fake wake-up. "What happened?" I say in a faked groggy voice — to prove that I'm out of it.

Victa has dried her eyes and cleaned her face; she doesn't look like she was crying. She comes closer and looks me over to make sure that I'm ok.

"You hit your head. Do you remember anything of what happened?"

I shake my head.

"You do not remember anything?"

"No," I say in a weak voice.

She seems to fall for my act; she comes in close, hugs me, and seems to want to comfort me. "It is all right. That is all right. You are going to be ok."

104

"Who am I? Where am I?" I might be overplaying it a little. I hope they don't realize that I'm lying.

"You really do not know?"

"No. Do you know who I am? Do I know you? Are we friends?"

"No, sadly we are not. And I am so sorry that you do not remember anything." She looks with anger in her eyes at the young man — she must think he hit me on the head so hard as to make me not remember anything.

"Hey, don't look at me like that, she's lying. I didn't even hit her that hard on the head." He says while holding up his hands in defense. I need to get out of here quickly before they do anything bad to me.

"I'm sorry that I don't know who you are." I stand up. "I'd really just like to leave." I need an excuse. I gasp.

"What? What is wrong?!" Victa seems to be a very caring person. I feel bad for deceiving her. You've no choice, just continue on and don't think about it.

"I just remembered something. My mother, she's waiting for me. I was supposed to come right home after school; she and I are going to the spa and then the bookstore. She promised she'd take me to the bookstore if I agreed on a mother-daughter spa day."

"Your mother, what is her name?"

"Uh…I forgot. Just mum?" She looks at me very worriedly.

"I really do need to go. Thank you for taking care of me, but she's waiting and I don't want her to think something bad has happened to me." A look passes between them. "Nothing bad has happened, right?" Sadly, I remember everything that happened. My first kiss was with a drunk bastard and I was almost forced to do something disgusting with one too.

"Right." She's quick to make me feel better.

"Ok. Well, bye." I go out the door and start heading in a direction. I check my pockets, crap! The pouch that has all my stuff in it isn't here. It's a good thing that I took some of the paper money out and put it in my pocket. I took the big bills out because the pockets of my dress are harder to get to than the pouch.

I look back to make sure that they aren't following me. I don't see anybody, I don't detect any movement or see any shadows/play on light. I see a ladder to my right that goes up to the roof — it should be easier to find my way to the Town Centre up there than down here.

I climb the ladder quickly and am on the rooftop in less than a minute. I look in all directions and see similar things as when I was up on the roofs the first time around. But I don't need the Town Centre this time, I need the palace.

I look in all directions, the palace is in the direction that I just came from. Hopefully, I don't run back into Victa or Gevan. I walk to the next building in the direction of the palace, this one's a little taller; instead of just jumping over a tiny gap, I reach up to the next building and pull myself up and over the roof while the muscles in my arms shake. The rest of the buildings are all about level, with a few here and there that are a little bit taller or a little bit shorter. When I get to the shorter ones, I jump down onto the roofs and when I reach the taller ones, I pull myself up and do the exact same thing that I did the first time. Hopefully, there aren't many more tall buildings — my arms could barely hold my weight the first time.

With every building that I run across, I get closer to the palace. So far, so good. The palace seems to be only a few streets away and I haven't heard anybody spot me. Nor do I hear anybody following me or up on the rooftops with me. The only sounds that I hear are birds calling out to one another and the sounds of life going on down below on the streets.

When I seem to be getting to the end of buildings, I realize that I've no idea how to get down. I don't see any ladders like the ones I've been using. I can't have people seeing me come off of the roof, but I don't want to go into any more side streets — SIDE STREETS ARE EVIL!

Thinking about side streets sends a disgusting, revolting shiver through me. I don't think about what happened, I don't let myself think about what happened; if I do, I've no idea what the effects on my sanity will be.

At the very end of the buildings, there's a place with something sticking off of it — I think it's called an awning. The awning's in between the roofs and the ground, it'll make the landing easier. I go to the edge of the building, sit down, and dangle my legs over the edge. I look down and make sure that there's nobody down there. My first look is very blurry and not focused, but as I stare at the ground, my vision becomes clearer: not a soul.

I swing myself off of the roof and hope with all my heart that I land on the awning. I hear the wind very loudly and feel my hair coming out of the scarf and getting messed up. As I get closer to the awning, it feels like I'm falling faster. I put my arms out in front of me and try to position myself so that I land on my knees instead of my feet.

I land on the awning with a great impact sound. It's a good thing that the awning's very strong. From the rooftop, it looked very flimsy and not strong at all.

I look up and across from the awning — I was so STUPID! The building across the street has a ladder. In fact, it has several. WHY?! It looks way harder to cross the street up there, but there's a rope coming from a window on the building across the street, and is hooked to something on the building I just came from. I could've crossed it and came down the ladder.

Oh, well. The fall was fun. I laugh a little out loud. It feels so good to be able to use my voice. Going mute before was my choice. But on that side street, my voice was taken from me. I HATE it when things are taken from me, as was my first kiss! My mind starts to go fuzzy and I get the sudden urge to scream. I force myself to stop thinking about what happened and think about what I'm going to do now.

I look over the edge of the awning; nobody came out to see what the sound of my impact was. I slide off of the awning to the side — if there are windows on the place below me, I don't want people to see me. This time, I land on my feet; they quake and I almost fall, but I support myself by putting pressure on the wall next to me.

I shake myself off, remove my scarf from my hair, shove it in my pocket to burn later and try fixing my hair as best as I can. I don't care what people think; I don't care if it's messy. But I need to look normal in order to find Baker St. without anyone causing me trouble. And normal people apparently like having nice, not messy hair. Every lady I've seen or met so far has well-kept hair: the guest, Victa, and the lady who gave me directions.

What were the directions she gave me? I'd close my eyes and try to remember, but the last time I closed my eyes and left myself vulnerable...my mind goes fuzzy again. This time it's also shaking and I see colors, not nice ones. I force myself to forget what happened. Focus on your mission! Find Baker St, find Soppy!

I shake my head to clear it and head out of the side street onto the one that leads to the palace. There are many people out, but not as many as were in the Town Centre. It's lighter now than when I left Victa and Gevan, I look at the time on my wrist — luckily Victa and Gevan didn't take it, it's bad enough that they stole my pouch — it's 07:50. Wow, this early in the morning and people are up and about? What day is it? Is it like this every day or only on days like today? I don't know what to do; I can't remember the directions that the lady gave me in order to reach Baker St.

The only thing I can think to do is go to the palace and ask directions, but I don't want to run into the guests, and that lady said that nobody was supposed to know about Baker St. Maybe she was just messing with me, maybe everybody knows about it and she saw that I was easy prey to pull one on. I've no other choice, I have to go to the palace and ask for directions. But it's really early, maybe I should wait until later. People tend to be most cranky late at night and early in the morning, at least that was when the Devil was at his worst — and that's saying something, he's always at his worst.

If that's my final plan, then I'll need to find somewhere

to sleep. My stomach starts going in knots. Why's that? What about the idea of finding a place to sleep worries me so? Oh! Right! My face becomes all scared feeling, I wonder if people can see what's going on in my head.

I don't want the same thing to happen to me again. And this time, Gevan and Victa won't be there to kill the person. I breathe air shakily out and put my hands to my temples. I widen my eyes, take a deep breath, and try to walk confidently to the palace gate.

While walking to the gate, I take stock of everything: 4 guards near the front of the palace — obviously many more elsewhere — only one guard behind the gate, but there must be more to open it. The gate's closed and not much life activity seems to be going on behind it. I don't see anybody suspicious on the road or sidewalks. And though a few people might be stumbling home, I don't see any that seem to be like — ugh — the side street man.

I have to keep pushing those thoughts aside, it's just so hard not to compare everything to it. The Devil never did anything like that to me. It was worse than torture. With torture, all I get is pain, none of my will not being mine. Whereas I was literally frozen and who knows what would've happened if Gevan hadn't killed him. GO AWAY THOUGHTS!

I put my mask back on and approach the gate.

"Hullo, good morning, sir."

The guard just turns his head to look at me.

"I need directions. Can you help me?"

The guard looks away from me.

"Please, I can pay you. I just need to find a certain street that I didn't see on any maps. But I know it's near here." I'd like to say my destination, but you can't be too sure about anybody. The guards could be working for the Devil.

The guard sneers at me. "Get the hell out of here. We don't deal with your kind." He spits through the gate, his spittle lands near my feet.

"I was just asking for directions. Sorry to bother you. Have a nice night."

I keep my head down and scurry as best as I can away without it seeming like he won and that I'm frightened. I...am... not...frightened! I ungracefully sit down on a bench not far from the gate, but also far enough that if tears come out, the guard won't be able to see.

The day has just been way too much, way too difficult. Real life's worse than torture. I think it's time to admit defeat. I left the Devil for the cruel world and its people. I'll never get out of this; I'll never end up finding Soppy or having a normal life. Why don't I just kill myself now? Why not? I tried and I failed. All that's left now is for the Devil to find me and take me back to a fate worse than death. I'm going to kill myself.

"How do you kill yourself?" I mumble miserably. Tears are coming out of my eyes now. My mask has left me. I created it for the predictability of the Devil, not for actual life. It's a good thing my hair's so long, it's covering my face...not having my mask doesn't matter. Nothing matters anymore. What little bit of life I had is over.

"Hey, don't think like that." A voice that I've never heard before comes from above. I keep my head down. I'll accept whatever this man's going to do to me. "It's just one bad day."

He sits down on the bench next to me. "Look up, come on. No reason to give up, tomorrow will be better. You can make tomorrow better. All that matters is not giving up."

I snort, what cheesy lines and why would I ever believe him? He doesn't know what I've been through. He doesn't know who I am. But then again, nobody has ever tried to lift my spirits or cared about me not killing myself. Who is he? I sneak a peek out of my hair to look at him. I gasp inwardly, but don't show any reaction on the outside. It's the young man! The one from the Devil's house who ate the poison. I look away.

Now, I feel even worse. I poisoned him, if he knew what I did to him he wouldn't have said any of that — or if he still did, he wouldn't actually mean it.

I get up and try to walk away from him; I hear him get up too. He doesn't come after me, but I think he wants to. I let more tears fall and start making sounds. While trying to get away from the young man who was given ill by me, my legs become all shaky and collapse under me. One second I was walking away from him, and the next I find myself on the ground. My legs are killing me, they couldn't even hold me up anymore. I cry even more. Today's the worst!

The young man came closer when he saw that I was falling, but he didn't catch me, he didn't have to. I'm sitting on the ground, at least I didn't fall into an embarrassing position. He comes and sits down across from me. I keep on crying. Through my hair, I see his hands move — he's trying to fight the urge to do something with them.

He wants to strangle me. I knew it! He found out I poisoned him and now he wants to kill me. Well, at least now I don't have to figure out how to kill myself. I can just let him introduce me to complete darkness.

He loses the battle and moves his hands toward me. I close my eyes and breathe out, "just kill me".

But instead of his hands going towards my throat, he pushes my hair out of the way and lifts my chin up. "Please stop crying. I'm not going to kill you. I just want you not to be so miserable. I hate it when people are miserable when there's no need to be. People should be happy. Why are you crying?"

I don't respond. But he's being so nice to me, nobody's ever been nice to me. Not even my tutor looked at me like this young man is — like he seriously cares about my well-being. I don't want to tell him anything about myself or what happened to me. But I don't want to give him the silent treatment — he doesn't deserve it. I've already wronged him by poisoning him.

I stop crying and start to sniffle.

"That's better. There's no reason for you to have been crying, is there?" I shake my head. "My name's Theo. What's yours?"

I wish he hadn't just told me his name. Knowing his name

and then knowing who he is, makes the fact that I poisoned him worse. He might fall dead right here in front of me. Knowing that I poisoned him and made his life shorter makes me hate myself. I wish he'd hate me, but a part of me doesn't want him to. He's very handsome. He reminds me of the Princes from my fairytale book. He's probably not a Prince, but still, he looks like he came out of my book. Maybe he did.

"Iris. My name is Iris."

"Well, Iris, it's nice to make your acquaintance. Although, I am sorry that we had to meet like this."

"Like what?" I forget everything when he looks at me with his eyes like that. How can someone show so much care and possible love to a stranger?

"With you looking like the nicest, most innocent," — innocent, I killed a man! — "person I've ever seen but with so much sorrow. More than someone our age should have. Are you ok now?"

"I believe I am. Now that you're here." What am I saying? Am I flirting with the one person who should hate me because I poisoned him? I can't think when he's near. So much for us possibly being friends. I'm probably revolting to him now.

He laughs. Why is he laughing? I don't know, but he has a very good laugh. As is his voice, they're both so warm and caring; I just want to get to know him, maybe kiss him. What?! Why am I thinking this? With what just happened to me. I need to get away from Theo, he's muddling with my head. I need to find Soppy and Baker St.

"I overheard your encounter with the guard. He shouldn't have acted that way. What street do you need to find?"

Should I tell him? He doesn't know who I am, which means he has no reason to hate and wish ill on me. And I don't think he works for the Devil. How could he, with those dimples and smile and handsomely caring eyes? I shake my head to clear it, right I need to focus.

"Baker St."

A shadow comes over his face. "Why would you ever want

to go there?"

"I live there now. My new family's there. My father just died." Best first impression: lying.

"Oh, I'm so sorry. My dad's dead too. I know how you feel, I always notice his absence." I doubt he knows how I feel, I don't even know who my father is. And at least he has a mother, I never even had that. "I could walk you to Baker St. if you'd like?"

What if it's like the last time I took that offer from a man? I should say no. But I've no reason not to trust him. I mean, I was the one who poisoned him, not the other way around.

"Ok." He stands up and offers a hand to help me up.

I take his hand.

CHAPTER SIXTEEN

Jezebel

I don't notice Theo leaving nor do I notice the people on the other side of the gate until it's too late. When I stop at the marker, something takes over my mind. It's like a scanner...but it seems to take my whole life; my memories; and everything that makes me, me and keeps them for itself. While it holds me hostage, it opens the gate and forces my legs to walk through. The people on the other side aren't the welcoming party I was hoping for. When the captive leaves my mind, I'm lost, swimming in old memories. The Devil whips me, my mother comforts me, my tutor trains me and wipes the blood off. That's why I don't notice all the people with scars both on the inside and out. They give me hostile or uncertain looks. And two of the people in the crowd are familiar: Victa and Gevan. But what exactly happens to me is a mystery. All I know is that I black out and will never be the same again.

...

The first thing that I hear when I come to is people talking, but they're not in the same room, house, or even country. It sounds kind of like static, but real people's voices. I open my eyes and in front of me is a lit-up device that I somehow know is a television. That thing that held me hostage may have taken a look at my essence and taken all of me...but, it left me knowing more than I did, more about the world.

It let me keep my memories, but also gave me the history of the world — and The Unknown, which is what I've always been a part of. My mother — Linris — was, as was my father —

Drew Arch. Linris 'mission was to collect Drew from The Circle and bring him to The Unknown, but she got pulled into The Circle and fell in love with Drew. They had me and she was never able to complete her mission.

I saw her struggle all those years in the Devil's house; I even saw him break her and her spirit leave her dead body. I saw her spirit join mine; she'll leave me once I've completed my mission. But even when my mission's over, I'll still live. Because my fate's more than just my mission; not all spies are the same. Most just have their missions and nothing else. I have everything else in store for me.

Uh, my head hurts so much, I can't make all these images and facts go away — that cursed captor! Why the hell did it have to give me everything!? I need to try to distract myself, thinking about what it gave me will just make the pounding worse.

I turn my attention to the television — that's where the voices are coming from. There's a lady on the screen along with a man, they're both sitting at a giant desk and have more screens behind them. The lady says, "There was a giant fire that started yesterday at the Bouglia Woods in the Devonish Territory in Brilla. It was said to have come from the house in the woods of which there's no record of an owner. But apparently, people hiking in the woods have noticed people coming out of it all the time".

The lady stops talking and the man instantly picks up where she left off, "One such person's description is different than all the others; people have said that he was the Devil incarnate. He had scars all over and blood-stained skin." I gasp. That's the Devil! His house was on fire. The place where I was born and have lived my whole life?!

The man on the television is still talking. "The fire is still raging, so far the substance that started it is still undetermined. We have reporters on the scene right now. Let's switch to Jane."

The image on the screen changes and now there's a different lady — Jane, I assume — in front of the Devil's house. "Thank you, Billy. Yes, the fire did start here. Firefighters have tamed the fire; now, the only thing still burning is a small section of the forest. But scientists are still uncertain as to where the fire originated. If you will follow me, I can show you one of their theories." Jane walks into the house, and the cameraperson follows. They go through the entrance and all the way to the kitchen.

The interior's so much different from what I remember it being; it's all black, scorched, and looks to be ready to fall down with a very strong wind. Jane goes over to the oven. Oh, no, I know where this is going.

Jane motions for the cameraperson to aim the camera at something in the oven. "What scientists have found is a vial that contained a foreign substance. They have no idea what the substance is — there wasn't any left in the shattered vial — but it did have a peculiar scent to it. They believe that when somebody turned on the oven, it overheated the vial to shattering, which spread the substance and fire everywhere."

Yep, that was my vial. I DID THAT!!! NO! I'm the reason for the Devil's house and the woods to be on fire. I hid the vial in the oven. It's all my fault, everything's my fault.

I start dry crying and rocking back and forth. I close my eyes, wishing to scream. I can't think. I hear something snap — I'm not sure if it's my sanity. All I can do is rock back and forth, shaking, and making noises out of the back of my throat.

I don't know how long this episode lasts — it just seems to go on forever and ever. I'm officially broken; time passes by, but I don't notice it. I don't notice anything anymore. I should've known that escaping from the Devil would be too much for me. I was never cut out for a life full of adventure and freedom; I was never made for a life at all really.

After what seems like days, my mind starts to calm and my voice starts to break and leave me. I stop rocking; sit up; and for the first time, I notice a hand rubbing my back. I'd jump away and scream for help, but I don't care anymore. Let this person kill me; I fooled myself into thinking that I could ever live a normal life. I...give...up.

"Shhh. It's okay. You're ok now." The person notices that I've stopped freaking out. "That's better. Now, why don't you have a glass of water and we can sort everything out."

A glass comes in front of my eyes, I tell my hand to take it...but, my hands stay limp at my sides. Now that I realize it, everything's limp. It doesn't feel like that time in the alley, it just feels like exhaustion has taken over my body, and the will to live is too much to bear.

"You don't trust me, I understand. I wouldn't trust me either if I were you." The glass goes away. The voice comes from my left, the woman's sitting right next to me.

The energy it takes just to turn my head to look at the speaker is all I can do. It's probably the last of my energy. At least I'll be able to see the person who'll watch me breathe my last breath.

She seems to be old, but not too old. She looks younger than my mother would be now. Her eyes show a life full of struggles and that she's wise beyond her years. Her eyes are also full of sorrow, so much sorrow, it drowns everything else out. She has short blond hair drawn into a loose ponytail behind her head. Her eyes are the greenest that I've ever seen — I didn't know that one could have such green eyes.

Well, if I'm going to die, I might as well know this lady's name.

"Who're you? Where am I?" I try to speak, but all I can do is mouth the words. I try to clear my throat, but nothing happens. The lady's still holding the glass of water in my direction. I command my left arm to reach out; it feels like pins or sand — I believe it's waking up now. My arm actually moves, it reaches out to the side but doesn't go much further than that. The lady moves the glass so that it hovers just above my outstretched hand.

I flex my fingers, grab the glass, bring it close, lower my head down, and take a sip. A sip that turns into me chugging the whole thing down. My throat feels moist and like it might actually work. I clear my throat and a little noise comes out. I try to talk again.

"Ww….." I clear it again, the lady refills my glass, I gulp it all down.

"Wwwhho arre you?" My voice goes silent before I get the last word out.

She takes the glass from me before speaking. "Well, I would tell you my real name, but protocol prevents me from doing so. You can call me Soppy. Now, what is your name?"

"Iris…um," I look around and spot a landscape hanging from the wall. "Iris Rome."

A weird look goes through her eyes, it's only a flash, but I notice it. "Nice to meet you Iris Rome. Do you happen to know where you are?"

I take a moment to decide what to tell her; nobody's supposed to know about Baker St. Is she friend or foe? Her name's Soppy, my tutor told me that I'd be safe with Soppy. But is she the same Soppy or an imposter?

"I don't know. There was a man following me, it might've been a woman, but I had a feeling that it was a man. I went as fast as I could to get away from him without looking suspicious. I wasn't looking where I was going, I just had to get away from him. I turned down a street and must've fainted. That's all I remember before waking up here with the tv going."

"Ok, well you are at house 23 on Louis Lane. Some people passing by saw you collapse and called me out. I had them bring you here so that you didn't wake up in the middle of the street with everybody staring at you."

If she made this up then she must be foe.

"That's very kind, thank you. I'm fine now, can I please go?"

"Go where?"

Why does she need to know? Did the Devil hire her to find me and take me back?! I WON'T GO BACK!

What am I saying? He wouldn't hire her, he'd scare her into submission.

"Home, my shift ended and I was heading home." Throw

in something about home, always put normal words in so that you don't seem suspicious. "My mother's making a feast for me, I got all As on my tests. She even invited the cute boy who lives across the street, Dreamy Theo." Do people really reveal all of this about themselves on a normal basis? I shrug mentally. No wonder nothing's private these days and people get hurt a whole lot more — they're not at all secretive with important stuff.

"Would you like my driver to take you home?"

"No, thank you. I can make it just fine on my own. I've lived here my whole life; I could walk the streets blindfolded." I couldn't walk them before, but now I have the map seared into my brain.

I stand up; my legs shake a little, but they hold. "Thank you, again. Could you point me to the exit?" You take a left out of the door to the west and go down a hallway that goes south. The front door is straight in front of you. It's an old-fashioned-looking door, but really cool and has modern touches, you couldn't guess how old it really is. It's 100 years old! The layout of the house is also seared into my brain; apparently, there's a dungeon at the very bottom of the house — on the same level as the subway.

Let's see if she passes my test: she's friend if she says left, foe if she leads me to the dungeon. If that happens, it's too bad that I don't have a knife. But the hallway to a back door is only 2 doors down if we head towards the stairs to the dungeon — which is hidden behind a portrait of some pig lady.

"I'll walk you out. I have errands to attend to."

She stands up and opens the door for me to head through first. I stop and wait for her to lead the way. We take a left and walk to the end of the hall. The door looks different than the one in my head; this one's greyish-brown, it used to be white. She switches at least 5 locks and puts her finger to something on the wall before I hear a click and the door swings open. She lets me walk out first.

The door closes with a loud bang behind me; I don't turn around. The street's absolutely deserted. It must be that nobody wants some stranger to know all of their secrets. Well, too late for that, the gate gave me everything about all of their missions. Thankfully, it didn't give me very personal images, just missions.

Before long, I'm at the gate; I can see the real world on the other side via a screen. "Get me away from this crazy — not real — world," I mumble. A second screen lights up at my voice. It starts to talk. I jump back and then peer closer at it.

"Would you like to leave Baker St?" There's no keyboard to type in my answer. I think "yes" and before I can say it aloud, another question comes out. "A mission or a visit?" Visit? "Eyeball S'il vous plaît." Oui. I put my face in front of the screen and open my right eye wide.

I hear whirring coming from the bars on the gate and the almost-silent machinery working within the gate. The gate opens slowly and just barely enough for me to fit through. I step through and am back to reality.

CHAPTER SEVENTEEN

Bryce

All of a sudden, I am soaked and very, very pissed. I open my eyes and am about to go full steam engine when the worried look in the pilot's eyes stops me.

"What happened?"

"Yesterday, you went out like normal and then I went out. I came back to you being unconscious. I thought you were sleeping and must have just been really tired. Then I went out again today; hours later, you were in the exact...same...spot. It's been more than 20 hours."

"The last thing I remember is seeing a girl."

"That's good for you, but I don't see how that is relevant."

"No, it wasn't like that." I run my hand over my eyes and face. I close my eyes for a second and reimagine what the girl looked like. "I think it was Jez."

The pilot goes over to the side table and picks up a large envelope. "That explains this then." He hands me the envelope. It just says "Theo's bodyguard".

"I'm going back out, we're leaving now that you're up; we need more fuel and supplies."

I wave him off and open the envelope up. I'm not sure whether I should be fearful or what. There are a bunch of objects in it, but most importantly, there are two pieces of paper, 2 letters.

Bryce, I'm fine. These people captured me, but they didn't harm me. All they did was tie me up. Then a very beautiful and sweet girl saved me. She's the best, her name is Roma Arch.

She's got the most luscious blonde hair and beautiful baby blue eyes. She's very tanned and very wise for someone our age. She's got old soul eyes. Sometimes I catch her looking into the distance with such sadness and terror. Then she looks at me and smiles — it's as if she's more than one person. She started working in the palace right after you left, then she saved me. We've gone out a few times. I think she's the one, Bryce. She doesn't see me as the Prince, she just sees me. But what makes me sad is that I met the one before Roma. This one's name was Iris; I don't think she told me her last name but, it could have been Arch. She and Roma have some shared characteristics and looks. Don't hurry back, I've got Roma to protect me.

With Princely Authority —Theo.

Oh no, whoever this Roma is has got Theo tied around her finger. Roma and Iris must be the same person, she's just disguised as Roma. She must work for The Red List and the Devil! I must get back and destroy her before she has a chance to destroy the last good monarch.

I look at the other letter; it has neater handwriting on it — seems feminine.

Bryce, it's me Zej. Please stop looking for me, you won't have any luck. I hide where no one expects me to. I found this letter in a country I visited recently, the owner didn't seem to mind losing it. Theo is really nice and he doesn't deserve what anybody has planned for him. I tried my best to warn him, but he didn't listen. I can't stay in one place for too long, or they will catch me. Theo is in danger! I can't say from whom, you just have to trust me. I'm sorry for leaving how I did; things just happened so fast, and before I knew it, I found my own escape. I wish I hadn't; life in hiding and on the run is much harder than being tortured by the Devil. At least then it was just physical pain. Seeing enemies everywhere and jumping at every little misdeed or suspicious question is starting to make me go crazy. Please just get back to him as soon as possible. I have given you a few items that you can use to decipher who is after him. I didn't want to say it outright just in case you don't get this. What I have written is enough for a death sentence if I am caught.

There's no signature. Zej is Jez backward, sooo clever.

I look out the plane's window while I am pondering Jez. We are still in Normindi and the airfield doesn't let any jets leave until 13 hundred hours. My watch says it's only zero-nine hundred, we still have 4 hours to go. What to do in the meantime? I won't be able to concentrate on anything except worrying about Theo and taking down Roma. I look over at the envelope from Jez; the pilot said we needed supplies, maybe Jez left us some. The envelope is really thick and made of a kind of recycled material that I have never encountered before. I don't want to shake everything out — something might break, so I put my hand in and pull out the first thing it hits.

My hand comes out of the envelope; I glimpse something small and cylindrical through the gaps in my fist. I open up my fist; in my palm lies a more advanced-looking carrier of messages than The Circle uses. The machine is supposed to only work with the DNA of the person it was meant for. Its messages are coded, but with a cipher, it isn't impossible to crack — unless you are not the person it is meant for.

I grab a butter knife off of the table and cut my finger — the DNA of my blood is the kind it wants. I press the wound to the cylinder, it makes a creaking sound — one of clogs whirling. The top section of the cylinder pops up, but instead of a message, there is a scanner, it whizzes around the room until it reaches one of my eyes.

After it is satisfied that it is actually me, nothing happens. There's no message, no paper, I don't think there's actually anything in the cylinder. This girl is sending me on a wild goose chase!

A few minutes later — right before I chuck the cylinder into the wall of the plane and grab another item from the envelope — the cylinder makes a beep and the audio starts.

"Hullo, Bryce, it's been a while." I hear someone drawing a breath in. It takes me a few moments to realize that it's Jez and that she is talking to me right now; it's not just a recording. "You look good, well, not good exactly, you seem more haggard than the last time I saw you. The months have been rough on you I presume." Months, what is she talking about? It's only been 6 weeks.

"You look confused. Don't be so fearful, I know how to read masks. I, myself, have had one for so long, it's easy to read what other people are feeling. I take it you didn't realize that it's been 6 months. I was told that after the last experiment, your memory wouldn't be too sharp for a while — the 'side-effects'." She says the last part with sarcasm. "I can't believe I trusted them," she says in an angry, mumbled breath — if my memory isn't sharp, at least my hearing still is.

"What I'm about to tell you, I will only say once. I have secured the plane so that nobody can hear us, but it won't last long, as advanced as this technology is, it's still developing. Or, at least it was when I took it and ran, right after I found out what they really wanted." Who are they? Who is she talking about? The Circle?

"Do not trust anybody, not even The Circle. They are all corrupt, every single spy organization. Nobody is pure anymore. The people I worked for had it in their heads that they were saving the world by keeping peace and balance. Peace? Yeah, right! How is the king's death peace? It is not."

"You know about Theo's father's death?"

"I've done my research. We don't have long, remember. So just listen and memorize. I see everything that you do, DON'T write anything down. Now, as I was saying, the king's death was just one of many signs that they were corrupt. I'm still figuring things out, but what I do know is that they have a plan for the Prince. Why else would they have kidnapped him and forced me to save him?"

"Are you Roma?" She continues as if I hadn't said

anything.

"I need you to go to a location for me, it will have all the information we need to take them down."

"Who? To take whom down?"

"Everybody." She says the last part as if I'm an imbecile.

"Will you do what I ask, please? Theo's life depends on it. 50 degrees, 75 degrees, that is all I can give you. The pieces in the envelope will help you with the rest of the coordinates. Watch your back; don't worry about Theo, he's safe for now. They need him alive for whatever their plan is. It was good to see you again, Bryce."

"But I just saw you, when you knocked me out a day or two ago."

"Shit! It's started."

"What? What's started, what's going on Jez?"

"That wasn't me; you're lucky they let you go. They are probably monitoring you, tracking you. They mustn't follow you to these coordinates, they can't know that you know. Bryce, don't trust ANYBODY!"

I hear a loud bang, it comes from the other end of the cylinder device.

"They're here, I have to go. Promise me, Bryce, that you will do this."

"I pro..." I hear gunshots; the cylinder beeps and goes dark before I can finish. I hear a ticking; the cylinder bursts into flames, burning my hand. I drop it to the table and rush to get the fire extinguisher. When I get back to the table, the fire is out, and there's nothing left of the device except for ashes.

I put the fire extinguisher down and hold up my hand...it doesn't look burned at all. How can that be? The cylinder exploded right in my face, it was truly on fire — how can my hand be unscathed?

I really am losing it. I still have a solid 3 hours until we can leave. If I take a nap, my mind will be back to normal in no time. The envelope will be gone; it will be Maye; and I will be able to stop my search for Jez and go home.

A few hours later:

Right as I am about to be knighted, my dream ends abruptly by shaking. I open my eyes and find that I can not move. The pilot is the one shaking me, but besides moving my eyes, I can't do anything.

"Good, now that you are awake, we need to go. People are following me. I went out for supplies and there was this black car following me everywhere, I fear they mean harm. We must go, I got everything in a rush, so we might not have enough of anything, but we can always stop somewhere. Buckle up."

The door to the plane is closed but knocking comes from the outside.

"Hullo, open up. You are in danger, I am here to help." It's a woman's voice. Is it Jez? No, it doesn't sound like Jez. And why would she go through all that trouble just to come and talk to me in person? I move my eyes in the direction of the screen showing cameras to the outside; she has dark hair and I can't see much of her face, but she seems familiar. "Something is wrong with one of you and I know how to fix it. Just let me in and then I will leave."

The pilot looks at me, he sees how I haven't moved — he knows it's not like me to just sit still. He looks to be weighing the pros and cons of letting her in. In the end, he relents and the door to the plane opens; the woman walks in. The pilot scans the airfield before closing the door.

She comes right over to me without even bothering to introduce herself. She does something in her pocket and then pulls an object from my hood before breaking it in half; I can now move more than just my eyes.

The woman holds up the object, "It's a Lacstris, it takes away free will and movement, it makes a person vulnerable."

I clear my throat. "And you are?"

"Victorious, but everyone calls me Victa. I heard on the

deep web while I was undercover, that you were the next target of one of the most wanted criminals: a one Iris Arch."

"What is she wanted for?"

"Murder, Stealing, among other things."

Her hand went into her pocket before pulling the Lacstris from my hood...what if she put it there to begin with? Jez said she wasn't the one who knocked me out, what if it was Victa; she turned the Lacstris on after she discovered that I was in contact with Jez. The thing that she had in her pocket might have been the control for the Lacstris; she turned it off right before she broke it. She faked saving me to get into my good graces — to fool me and to get to Theo.

"Well, thank you. But we really must be going, we're expected by my family."

I stick to my morals; I must not be impolite, but I want her to leave.

"Can I come with you? I can protect you, I have resources that would be of use to you."

"I live in another country and it's a family-only event. I can protect myself, thank you very much."

She looks crestfallen, "Ok. Well, it was nice to meet you. Sorry for bothering you."

She could not have left any sooner. The pilot had been sitting in his seat the whole time, getting the plane ready while also listening to the conversation.

"Let's get out of here. We won't find Jez here."

"Where to sir?"

"The place."

He starts flicking switches and the plane starts. As the plane finishes getting ready to take off, I sit down in the chair at the table with the envelope and buckle up. I can figure out the coordinates on the way to the secret hiding place used when my family is in trouble. Theo's family has a different place, but the pilot knows what I meant and where mine is because he is a distant cousin of my mother's.

As the plane enters the air, I hear an almost silent ringing coming from the envelope. I pick it up and look inside: there's a burner phone. I pull it out and look at the number. I don't know it, but it is set into the phone as Zej; I press the accept button and put the phone next to my ear.

"Hullo?" I hear heaving breathing on the other line.

"Bryce?" Her voice is very faint.

"Jez, what's wrong?"

"Nothing, don't worry about me. You have your mission, find the destination for me." Her voice disappears as she talks and by the end, it's just air.

I hear a scream that sounds like Jez and then a person trying to get their voice back.

"Don't trust Victa. She's one of them. She's evil....Don't... let...her—" Another scream, this one more painful than the last. "Know...that you...know about their plan...They...they would kill you...ii...ff...if they find out."

Another scream and a curse. "GODDAMMIT!"

"Jez, why won't you tell me what's wrong? Why do you keep screaming?"

"Oh, it's not me, there's an interrogation in the next room." I might have believed that if I were an idiot and if she didn't sound like she was in excruciating pain.

I pull my state-of-the-art laptop out of its protective case and open up the program I created that traces supposedly untraceable phone calls. I put in the info from the burner and it pinpoints Jez's location. She's not in Normindi, but she is very close — she's 2 countries over in MosGravich. The program also shows everywhere she's been — looks like she wasn't lying about never being in one place too long and being on the run. But her path shows that she's never been in the same city for as long as she's been in Sitterai, a hamlet in the middle of nowhere in MosGravich.

I unbuckle and go up to the front of the plane to talk to the pilot. "Change of destination, aim for the airport in Sitterai, MosGravich."

"But that's in the complete opposite direction than the

place. Are you sure?"

"Yes, I'm sure. We don't have long, people could die. Step on it."

"Whatever you say, Bryce. You're the one who went into the family business, not me. The fastest I can get us there is an hour, is that alright?"

"Let's hope so."

CHAPTER EIGHTEEN

Victa

6 Months earlier:

"Gevan, why did she do that?" My vision is blurring again after Iris fled.

"I don't know, Vic. Maybe, she's not who we are looking for. The Devil losing someone doesn't mean we instantly run into them. This girl seemed normal, while the Devil's girl is a stranger to any kind of world."

I am still holding onto the girl's stuff. "She left this, why would she leave this?" I sniffle and get a hold of my tears. "The only person the Devil has taken in nineteen years is Linris, that has to have been her."

"She looked about 18 — which is what all of her documents say. There's no way Linris could have stopped aging."

"But it had to have been her, who else would escape from the Devil?"

"There is another option, that girl is..." I gasp as my mind comes to Gevan's conclusion on its own. "Linris 'child," he finishes.

"Do you really think so?... Could it be that I have a cousin?" I mean, she did look exactly like Linris; now that I think about it, the parts of her that were different looked like Drew. Her tinted skin, her eyes, all scream Drew; but her hair and facial shape are the legacies of Atributous — our ancient family who created The Unknown.

"I don't know, Vic, it's the only option that makes sense. Can we please just leave now, she obviously didn't want our help;

we need to report back to your mother."

"Do not talk with that voice, she is your mother-in-law; you knew what your responsibilities would be when you decided to marry me."

"In my defense, you proposed to me. I never wanted the responsibility of telling your mother all the failed mission assignments — everybody tells you because she won't punish you. I still have a horn sticking out of my back from the last time and a scar from the time before, from telling her that we didn't find the Devil's sidekick. I only said "yes" to you because the punishments would be worse had I said "no"."

I get up and stand next to him, "And because you love me."

"And because I love you." He agrees with me, puts his arm around my waist, and pulls me closer to him; he leans his head on my shoulder and sighs. "Can we just get this over with quickly? All I want to do is go to sleep — it's been a very busy and long day."

"I can tell my mother by myself if you would like. But you would then have to check in at a rundown hotel so that she does not know that me lying, is really me lying."

"Thanks, I'm not rested enough for a punishment this morning. You're the best."

Gevan and I walk out of the building together and break apart at the corner of the street. He goes in the direction of Potter's Town — where all the artists used to live, now it is just a rundown dump — and I go in the direction of the palace, in the direction of Baker St.

As I arrive at the gate, I run into Warren — Gevan's identical twin. He beats me to the gate, it scans him and takes his memories from the previous day first, then it does me.

On the other side, he is waiting for me. "Hullo, Victa."

"What do you want, Warren?" He always wants something. With how he is, it is as if he was not raised by the same good parents who raised Gevan. There is no doubt as to who the evil twin is.

"A little bit nicer, please."

"Hullo, Warren, peachy day ain't it?" I say with sarcasm. "Now, what do you want?"

"There's just no hope is there?" Sigh. "Anyway," He falls into step with me as I walk past him. "I heard from a little birdie that my goodie-two-shoes brother is skipping out on his duty to Soppy. I could step in for him so that the punishment isn't so bad."

"Why on Earth would you ever do that? What is in it for you?"

"You wound me, madam." He clutches his hand to his heart. "I just want to help out is all."

"That is a lie and we all know it. Now, out with it."

"Well, since you beat it out of me, there's a girl that I'm looking for. Everyone knows that you and Gevan are the best trackers; I was wondering if you could find her for me."

"I might, what is her description?"

"Scrawny, weak, laughable, poor."

"I meant appearance, not insults."

"Fine." He pulls a pad of paper out of his pocket and reads off of it. "She has brown eyes, black hair, a small nose, and medium-colored skin."

That sounds exactly like Iris. Everyone in The Unknown is looking for a girl who escaped the Devil, is it actually Iris? But Warren does not work for The Unknown, he just lives on Baker St due to family connections. So, how does he know about Iris?

"Why are you looking for her?"

"Uh…" He seems put together, but any spy can detect a lie coming out to hide the truth. "A friend told me that she went missing and I said that I would look into it. My friend really needs to find her — it's his daughter."

"Who is your friend?"

"Drew Arch." Yeah, right, like he knows Drew.

I gasp. "You have heard from Drew? But nobody has heard from him in years."

"Yeah, well he got in touch. Guess I rubbed off on him." He

shrugs. "Can you please just find her for me?"

"Sure thing, but do not come into my house. Gevan will be fine."

"Whatever." He leaves on the path that will take him to his flat.

I continue walking until I come to a stop in front of 42 Baker St. I take a deep breath in, exhale, walk up the steps, and knock on the door. A space to the right of the door opens, and an object comes out and scans my eye; I place my finger on a screen and it scans that too; the machine clinks and the door opens.

There is nobody in the entrance hall. I take off my coat, hang it on the coat hanger, and place my purse on the side table. I walk down the hall to my mother's office. I knock on the door and wait. I stand for 10 minutes before a voice comes from inside the room, "Enter."

The door clicks open, and I walk through it to find my mother behind her desk with a pistol pointed at me.

"Oh! Victorious, it's you." She puts the gun away. I do not say anything; you do not speak unless asked a question or ordered to when on business hours — which in this family, is all the time.

She motions for me to come closer and puts her hands on the desk in front of her.

"Report."

"We have been looking all day for the girl. We had a minor setback."

"What kind of setback?"

"A different girl."

"Who?"

I put the envelope that belongs to Iris on the desk and wait.

My mother does not touch it. "What is this?"

"I encountered a girl who was lost, she was under the influence of a Lacstris and I saved her from a drunk. She had this, she left without it."

"What is the importance of this?"

"I believe her to be Iris Arch, Drew and possibly Linris' daughter."

My mother has a flash of something go through her eyes — unless you grew up with her, you would not have spotted it.

"Well, that's odd, Linris and Drew never had any children."

"I know, but you have to see her, she looks exactly—" My mother holds up a hand to silence me.

"Thank you for the report, go back out, find the girl who escaped the Devil, and bring her to me. You are dismissed." My mother is distracted; she did not even ask about Gevan or shout at me for failing our objective. I just back out of the room before she changes her mind.

I walk out of my house and back out onto the street where many people are wandering around; a crowd has gathered close to the gate, and weird sounds are coming from it. I walk closer to investigate; I spot Gevan as I near it — he is back from Potter's Town, why?

I come up behind him, "Hey, Gevan."

He turns around with a smile on his face.

"Vic, it's happening."

"What is?"

"The gate is making a new spy, I wonder which group the person is going to."

"Have you seen who it is yet?"

"No, you don't spot them until they come on this side of the gate."

"What are you doing here? I thought you were going to Potter's Town."

"Turns out they are renovating it…it was all closed off. Warren called me and said that you needed help. I got here as fast as I could; traffic was horrible." Poor Gevan believes that Warren is not evil; he believes him to be the same innocent, good little boy who played with him growing up. "As soon as I got on this side, the gate started the initiation process. I would have continued, but I knew you had your mother handled, and I just had to see who the new spy is."

I put my hand in his. "How will we know which group they are for?"

"When they leave the gate, the initials of the group glow on their forehead."

"What happens if they are for The Unknown; how do people not know about our group if it says it on their forehead?"

"For our group, a symbol appears on their head, but because it is mostly handed down through the bloodline, many of us are already programmed into the gate. The symbol is 3 hexagons with a dot in the center of one. I believe that the last person to be given the symbol was your great, great aunt."

"Oh, right, she grew up in MosGravich because her parents were killed here and she was sent to live with her uncle on her father's side. He lived on a farm in the middle of nowhere, right?"

"I'll have you know, she grew up in Sitterai, the location of the best fields on the continent."

It is not easy to forget that if Gevan never chose to be a spy, then he would be a farmer. He would be the cutest, best farmer out there. He is always talking about the harvests and weather. Our flat is never filled with cheap food, all of our food is the richest — with all-natural ingredients. Just once, I wish he would let me get a burger from McDonald's, but his home cooking is the best — if not a little old-fashioned.

My thoughts are interrupted as the gate opens fully with a loud creak and in steps — or should I say in falls? — the next spy for The Unknown. The light goes away and Iris falls to the ground with the three Hexagons burning on her forehead.

"I don't see a dot, there should be a dot. Where is the dot? What does it mean that it's not the full symbol?" Gevan is starting to freak out.

"Forget about the dot; we must get her inside before everyone starts asking questions."

I pull Gevan with me as I run to scoop up Iris. I take her shoulders while Gevan takes her legs. We rush to my house as fast as we can with an unconscious Iris between us. The door opens and my mother's lackey meets us at the entrance.

"Put her in the green parlor." We take her to the indicated room — there is a thick yoga mat all set up, we lay Iris gently down upon it. My mother's lackey follows us into the room.

"Get back to your mission." He dismisses us while glancing at Iris.

"Was this expected?" He looks at the other door to the room, waves us off, and ignores my question.

"Vic, let's go." Gevan pulls me from the room.

CHAPTER NINETEEN

Jezebel

What am I going to do now? Soppy was my only hope of finding a normal life, but I can't go back there and get corrupted by them. A normal life's not worth corruption. The Unknown's terrifying; I don't know much about the organization, but I've seen what their people have done. They've done some good, but most importantly, they've done bad, evil things: one of their agents killed the king!

I check my pockets after I walk all the way to the Town Centre, I still have some cash. The gate gave me a bunch of good cafés and restaurants that the spies like to go to before stakeouts. There's one that's low-key, that they don't go to often — I don't know why though, the food looked very delicious. It's called Krystal Café. It's located next to the old cinema — which plays black and white films. But it's not as popular as the new one right in the center of the town that plays newly released films in color. I might go to the old cinema and catch a film after eating a snack — that's what a normal person would do, I think.

Krystal Caf'és on an old-fashioned cobble road — you can tell that it was a part of the original town. The door's one that I'm used to, it has a knob! The sign on the door says that they're open for business; I open the door and step inside.

As I look around in wonderment, I realize it's not at all as I expected it to look. It's very retro and old-fashioned; it's as if I've traveled back in time to the 1890s. The decor and dining room look new but are of an older style. The only thing that proves I didn't travel back in time is all the little devices that people have out — I now know that they're phones and have many different functions: talking, looking things up, playing games, etc. Phones weren't around in the 1890s, only black and white films were — Oh! The theme on this old street must be the 1890s — I wonder if all the other streets are the same, but with different years. Well, I'll just have to investigate. If this is to be my new home, then I need to know what's here, where everything is — where I might hide if the Devil ever comes to town.

Although this is a really nice place — the images from the gate don't do it justice — I don't think that I should eat here; there are a lot of people. This isn't low-key! What if Gevan or the guests from the Devil's house spot me here? Uh oh, too late, Victa's sitting at a table off to the side. She has spotted me; she's not shouting out my name, but I must go to her, it feels as if there's an invisible rope connecting us.

Only once I'm sat down in the booth seat facing her, does she begin to speak.

"Hullo, Iris. How are you holding up?"

"Hi. Fine. What do you mean, why wouldn't I be holding up well?"

"The gate does not create a new spy every day, but when it does, the information is a lot to process."

"I'm a spy? How can I be a spy? I don't know how to be one!" My voice is starting to rise; I'm going into hysterics. One big, bad thing after another just keeps on happening. Today's the worst! People are starting to glance over at us — that's why she didn't call me over, she must not've wanted to draw attention to our conversation. Now I'm curious, what's so important that nobody can overhear?

"Calm down. All the information is messing with your head. Drew must have prepared you to be a spy. Did he not?"

Drew, who's Drew? I sort through all of my newly acquired information for the answer. Drew Arch: member of The Circle, boyfriend of Linris, father to Iris Arch. Oh, he's my father. But the gate is missing a little bit of information. My name isn't Iris, it's Jezebel, and my father isn't a part of The Circle anymore; he was my tutor and still is a henchman of the Devil.

That's why he taught me how to fight. Now that I'm thinking about it, he actually did prepare me to be a spy. But I won't tell Victa that — I still don't fully trust her, it doesn't matter how many answers she has.

"No, he was too busy doing the Devil's bidding."

She doesn't seem surprised per se as to what I said, but her eyes look like she officially cleared something up.

"So, you **are** the girl who escaped the Devil; everyone is looking for you."

"Why're people looking for me?"

"Because you are the new spy; everyone wants to know all that there is to you."

She really isn't good at formatting things in an un-creepy and comforting way, is she? There's more to the reason than she's letting on.

She gets an uncertain look about her — one of warring faces — before she asks, "How do you feel about joining the organization that I work for?"

"I don't know." She seems nice; it was Gevan who acted like I was an imbecile and then smashed his gun down onto my head. I do like her: I like what I've seen of her character, and something does draw me to her. "What organization do you work for?" Maybe she doesn't work for The Unknown.

She has an answer on the tip of her tongue, but at the last minute, she seems to change it. "Right now, I work for The Circle. So, what do you say?"

The Circle: both my mother and father were a part of it, it let them — and me — get captured, it didn't save us, and who they once were are now dead. I would've had a family if The Circle didn't exist. But I don't have much information on the organization besides that. They could be good. Maybe they tried to find and rescue my parents, but they couldn't. I shouldn't have underestimated the Devil — not even for a second.

Before I come up with an answer, Victa wins me over. "If you do decide to join my organization, then you will be able to live a double life, one for spying and the other will be normal," —

NORMAL! — "you will have a flat, you can even adopt a pet, and we can get you a job."

I know what I said about never going back, but it's not The Unknown, and I can have a normal life! I could never make a normal life on my own, not even with all the information in my head from the gate. Having a life trapped and secluded means you can't put words with actual things, you need to have experienced them with guardians older and wiser than you.

"You promise?"

"Yeah, just one mission and we can set you up with everything you need. I'll even help you find a flat and buy furniture; I can also drive you to the animal shelter."

An image of animals interacting with each other in bliss goes through my head, causing me to sigh in pleasure. I think I'd like that; I want a pet. A bunch of memories from the gate involved dogs.

"When will I know what my mission is and where?"

"I can take you back right now."

"Um. I kind of have plans, can we meet later?"

"I am free later, what time?"

"Here, around noon?"

"Alright, see you then. Welcome to The Circle."

As Victa welcomes me, a weird rush goes through me, like an infinite decision was made. The rush distracts me from seeing Victa leave and sending the waiter over to me on her way out.

What did I get myself into? Why will I do anything to get a normal life? I put my head in my hands in despair. I never should've escaped from the Devil.

"What can I get for you?"

I lift up my head to respond to the waiter. "What do you recommend?"

"Today's special is a delicious—"

"I'm short on time, surprise me."

"Will do." He goes to the kitchen.

I've no idea how much money I have left — hopefully, I

have enough to cover the food and a film at the old cinema.

In no time at all, the waiter's back, and balancing a tray with 2 dishes on it. He picks up one of the dishes — "Our famous Caesar salad" — and places it on the table. He picks up the next dish — "And today's special: Duck Confit" — he places this one right in front of me. "Is there anything else that you need?"

"Yes, do you have lemonade?"

"We do, yellow or pink?"

"Surprise me." I would've said "I don't care," but that's rude and these dishes look/smell delicious — he obviously put a lot of effort into it and chose very well.

I pick up my fork and knife and get started on the duck. Oh...my...god! It's absolutely delicious, incroyable! You can tell it's made fresh and old-fashioned, unlike McDonald's. Old-fashioned is better than fast food.

I'm more than halfway through with the duck when the waiter brings my drink — it's yellow, not pink. "The pink is good, but I prefer the yellow — it tastes purer and was made fresh this morning with lemons grown right here, in Musalin."

"Thank you, everything looks and tastes so good."

"Anything else?"

"I'm good for now."

He leaves, and I finish the duck. Without meaning to, I burp. It just comes out, I've eaten more today than I usually do in a whole month. I look around, so embarrassed that my face is enflamed again. Luckily nobody noticed, they are all wrapped up in their conversations, and the lone man in the corner didn't put his newspaper down.

The only salad I've ever had that was kind of fresh was the one from McDonald's, this one looks different. It's all leaves, no icebergs — they must grow it here. I've never had anything like the sauce, it has a peculiar taste, but it's good.

When I'm on the last bites of my salad, the waiter comes back. "How is everything?"

"Excellent."

"Do you want dessert?"

"Oui, s'il vous plaît. What do you have?" I think that I said yes, please — at least that's what I meant to say. But as the words left my mouth, flashes of light went through my head and I said that mumbo jumbo instead.

"Are you from Sirap?"

"Oui." Nobody from Brilla here. Sirap is the territory north of Musalin, it's on the Siquer Sea. Man, I love all of this information from the gate. Apparently, I can speak other languages now. Awesome!

"We have Sirap's most famous desserts: Macarons et Crème Brûlée. Our chef is from there; she creates the desserts with the finest touch. The people who live there would be proud of how her dishes represent the country's fine tastes. Which would you like?"

In my head, an image of both appears — how can I choose, they both look very delicious.

"I'll have both." He looks at me weirdly and whistles. "You've got some appetite." I ignore his comment. Hopefully, I have enough cash for all of this food that I wasn't expecting to get — it was just supposed to be a snack, not a whole meal + dessert — and the film. He leaves with that weird look still on his face.

He comes back with a plate full of treats, all the flavors of macarons, and a small bowl of Crème Brûlée. He's very generous — not every waiter would've given me all of the flavors to try.

"Compliments of the chef — from one Sirapian to another. She would like to speak to you later about your opinion. I'll be back with the bill if that's all."

I nod my head and keep on staring at the macarons while my mouth waters. Which one to try first? Lavender's my favorite color, I'll try that one first. It hits my taste buds and everything around me goes mute, all that's on my mind is DELICIOUS!

I shovel all of them into my mouth. With every bite, I feel a new explosion of flavor and taste. I look at the Crème Brûlée — it's a bowl of steamy deliciousness — and down at my stomach, which is sending pain, although not the usual hunger pains. For once in my life, I think I'm actually stuffed. Should I eat the Crème Brûlée? I'm paying for it whether I eat it or not, and who knows when I'll have another chance to try it. I pick up my spoon and with a heavy stomach, I begin to eat.

I eat the Crème Brûlée very slowly; with every spoonful, my stomach protests. I would be enjoying the unique taste of it, but all that I can think about is the pain in my stomach.

"That's it, I'm done." I drop the spoon into the bowl when I'm 2/3rds of the way through. You win, stomach.

I see my waiter and hold up my hand to call him over. My other hand's holding my stomach together. The waiter's talking to the man who was reading the paper, I can't see his face. I would be freaking out about it possibly being the Devil, but I can't keep seeing enemies everywhere — I'd lose my mind even more than I already have. Plus, I'm too full to care; if the Devil drags me screaming or kills me, at least I can go with the satisfaction of having a day of experiences.

The waiter finishes and comes my way with the bill — I think — in hand. I hope it's not a gun or anything. My eyes are finding it very hard to focus.

"You are finished, madame?"

"Oui, can I have the bill?"

"That gentleman in the corner paid for your meal." He motions in the direction of the faceless man. It takes a little while for my full brain to make sense of what he said, and when it does, my eyes bulge out, and my jaw drops.

"Why would he do that?" I mumble.

"What?"

"Never mind. Am I free to go then?"

"Yes, madame."

"Merci, here." I hand him a $20 bill.

He holds up his hands, "Tis too much, I couldn't possibly accept."

"Nonsense, I insist." I honestly don't have any bill values lower than that, and I don't want to stay here waiting for change, these people are starting to look suspicious — especially that guy with the newspaper, why can't I see his face?! Also, his service was pretty good, all of the ones in memories from the gate weren't as good.

He sighs and takes the money, admitting defeat. But I can see a shy smile come to the surface of his face, he fights it, but it shows through. "Thank you, madam."

He slips back to the kitchen and I head to the door. "Oy!" A shout rings out behind me. I turn to look. A woman's looking at me; she just came from the kitchen, and there's a chef's hat on her head. What does she wannnt? Why can't people just leave me alone? I don't feel so good, all I want to do is watch a film and find someplace to sleep.

She comes toward me. Everyone's looking at me now. I just want to cower behind my hair. My face is starting to turn beet red. When she approaches me, she holds up her hand — is she going to slap me? "Tenez ." She puts a package into my hand. "Comment avez-vous aimé les desserts?"

Oh, right. Didn't the waiter say she wanted to have my opinion?

"C'était très délicieux." She smiles a gigantic smile; she has very white teeth. For a split second, she looks like Soppy. I shake my head to clear it, this…is…not…Soppy! Why would she care to go after me? She wouldn't. But, now I know a lot of things about The Unknown. That's reason enough to kill me. You're freaking out over nothing, Jez. Just breathe and calm down. I didn't realize that I had started to hyperventilate.

I pretend to look at my watch. "Sacrebleu! Je suis en retard! Merci et au revoir." Without an excuse, I would come off as rude. Just because I killed someone, doesn't mean I want to be bad and rude. I turn my back and rush out of the café without running.

The old cinema's right next door, but if that was Soppy, I don't want her to follow me. There's an alley on the other side of the café, I jog to it. It's pitch black; I turn on my watch's torch — apparently, it's a smartwatch and can do a whole bunch of amazing things.

I shine the torch into the blackness, "Hullo? Anybody there?" Nobody answers or shows up in the torch's beam. I don't detect any signs of movement. It's safe to enter the alley. Halfway through, I find what I was hoping would be there: a ladder leading up to the roof. If I move quick enough, Soppy won't be able to track me up there.

Once on the roof, I remove my jacket and twist my hair so that it'll stay up. The inside of the jacket's a different color than the outside; I turn it inside out and wrap it around my head, oh how I wish for my scarf right now. I look around the roof to see if there's anything that I can use with my disguise. To my left, in the gutters, I see something reflecting the light of the sun. I crouch down and walk over to it. As I get closer, I can see that it's made of glossy metal. What could it be?

I pick it up and immediately drop it as if it had scorched my hand. I quickly back away from it. It's a gun! Guns mean shooting, shooting means killing, which means evil and bad. I don't want to be bad.

Pick it up, Jez — you can use it to protect yourself. You don't want to be fully raped this time, do you? I've no idea where that voice came from; I don't want to listen to it, but I can't help but answer it. *No, I don't want another man to ever come that close again!*

I cautiously go back to the gun and pick it up. I check the barrel, it's fully loaded. Who'd leave a fully loaded and functional gun up here? Whoever it was: merci.

I put the gun in my dress pocket so that it's easy to pull out. I scan the rest of the roof — there's nothing else. Hopefully, the jacket over my head's enough of a disguise. I'll keep my head down and walk confidently as if I've walked these streets my whole life. I follow the rooftop until I reach a spot where I can jump onto the cafés. The cafés roof is smaller, but I'm able to cross it without being seen and am on the ground in the alley next to the cinema in no time.

The alley smells like butter, popcorn, and what I think might be freshly brewed beer — maybe there's more to this street than meets the eye. I go to where I'll be able to get onto the street that has the front of the cinema. I look around the corner in both directions and don't see anybody. I step out of the alley and the first thing that my eyes see is the flashy sign across the street, it's for a bar and casino. I thought that only Brilla had casinos, none of the images or maps from the gate showed casinos being in Musalin. I'm not of age though; sadly, that'll mean I can't explore the whole street once I'm feeling better.

I cross the street to see the whole outside of the old cinema. It's got a giant sign stating the name: Borgne! It's got a gazillion flashing lights, screaming big time; yet, it also looks dated. I cross the road again and enter the building.

There are 2 doors as soon as you enter, but only one's open. I go through it and on the other side is a desk with a person sitting behind it. He's reading a book and seems not to be very busy business-wise. He's very interested in his book and is deep into the world of words. I clear my throat.

He bookmarks his page with his hand, closes it, and looks up. "Ahoj, Potrebujete trasu?" Uhhhh. What language is he speaking? How do I know what to respond with?

"Je ne comprends pas. Parlez-vous Sirapian?" Only talk in Sirapian, no such thing as Brilla here. What even is Brilla? Is it a place? The Devil'll never be able to find me if I don't speak the common language.

"Très peu, je parle principalement Trinipien."

Oh! He's from Trinip. I might know how to speak it, now that I know what he's speaking. Let's see. I close my eyes and envision what he said to me. "Ahoj" is hello; I think "Potrebujete trasu" is asking if I need directions. Ok, so I need to respond with "No, I don't need directions. What's playing and how much," but in Trinipien.

"Prečo by som potreboval smery? Má toto kino najlepšie staré filmy alebo nie?"

"Robí to, ale nikto ich nikdy nevidí. Jediní ľudia, ktorí prichádzajú, sú turisti hľadajúci orientačné body."

"Čo hráte?"

"Veľa starých čiernych a bielych tichých filmov sa bude hrať až do polnoci zajtra a môžete ich sledovať, ak chcete."

"Koľko sa pozerať?"

"Za celý čas: $20."

"Môžete zlomiť 50?"

"Áno, chcete akékoľvek nápoje alebo jedlo?"

My stomach has to choose this exact moment to send full pains and gurgle while digestion's taking place. I hope that I said the right responses, he doesn't look suspicious, so I must have.

"Nie ďakujem."

I hand him a $50 bill and he gives me change; he keeps 20 of it. He also hands me a very small, weirdly shaped piece of paper that says "Ticket; Cinema; Admit One," and has random numbers on it.

"Vychutnaj si šou."

"Urobí. Vidíme sa neskôr."

I walk in the direction that he motioned me to, it leads to a small and very creepy old hallway. I hope that this place isn't haunted. He doesn't even speak the common language, which must mean that nobody else wanted to work here. There must be a reason why. Mais, Je suis très fatiguée et j'ai trop mangé et tout ce que je veux faire, c'est dormir. So I'm just going to relax, enjoy the show and hopefully get some shut-eye.

I go to the door at the end of the hall, open it, and find myself facing a room with a medium-sized projector in front of the closed curtains of a stage and many rows of old velvet seats. This is what a good cinema looks like. Here's the prize of the past, a place where things literally don't age. Time's frozen in moving pictures; watching old films in an old cinema feels like stepping back in time. I go to a seat in the middle of a row in the middle of the room. I sit down and get comfy.

Now that I think about it — No, don't think, just watch. Let me just quickly finish thinking, inner voice. Alright, fine!

I've no idea what the guy said to me or what I said to him. The gate's intel is amazing — I can speak a foreign language and spit out words — but it's not much of an improvement because I don't understand any of it. But still, with all of these new words, conversations, and experiences, maybe not all people are bad. But that doesn't mean I should underestimate them; in fact, any one of those people from the café could work for the Devil. That guy out there could even work for the Devil.

"Ahoj!" I can hear the man talking to someone — silent films and thin walls make eavesdropping easy. What if he's talking to the Devil right now?! I need to get out of here! I jump out of my seat and am about to bolt to the exit in the front of the room — I believe that it leads to the same alley that I was in before — then, I hear more of the conversation.

"Ste Trinipien, áno?"

"Áno, čo môžem získať pre vás?"

"Veľký ľadový nápoj a stredná popcorn, oh a krabica cukríkov."

"Chuť nápoja, maslo na popcorn a ktorý cukrík?"

"Áno, prepáč. Teraz sa pozrime tu: hrozno, áno, ale veľmi málo. A čo máte sladkosti?"

I'm still standing frozen. It could still be the Devil, maybe? Possibly? I'm not so sure now. But I can't help but be scared.

"Máme Goobers, Sno-Caps, Chuckles a Black Crows."

"Všetky dobré možnosti." There's a pause for a minute or two — the person must be deciding which sweet he wants more. It's like me with the macarons et Crème Brûlée, I couldn't choose, so I went with both. More pain from my stomach. Although, I now regret that choice.

"Daj mi Goobers a Chuckles, Moje dve obľúbené staromódne sladkosti."

"Tiež sa mi páči, ale moje obľúbené sú čierne vrany, oni pripomínajú mi varenie mojej babičky."

I've no idea what they're saying — the information in my head allows me to speak and understand only when a person's talking directly to me. The only language I seem to have picked up was Sirapian, which is good if I'm to be one from now on. But hey, anything to get my freedom.

I know for sure that it isn't the Devil. He'd never converse that long with someone, and none of the tone or words seemed harmful; I don't even think that they were talking about me. I become unfrozen and less scared, sit back down, and start watching the film.

About 10 minutes later, I hear the door to the hallway creak open. It must be the same person who was ordering stuff from the guy at the desk. I heard sweets mentioned. One of the things that I was never allowed were sweets, the Cadbury McFlurry was kind of a sweet, but not like images that come into my head of the options that the man said. I think I want to try a box of Sno-Caps and Chuckles.

I'd turn around to see who just came in through the door, but I'm too tired and stuffed; my eyes are fighting to stay open. Besides, I've already ruled out it being the Devil, so it doesn't really matter who it is. I get absorbed in the film and let myself relax. Within moments, I'm fast asleep.

My dreams were always my escape from reality. Just because I escaped from the Devil, doesn't mean that my dreams are no longer as impressive. But tonight, they've decided to taunt me and take a turn into the nightmare realm. They drag me back to the place, with the drunk man, the alley, and the no free will. But, instead of seeing from where I did before, my perspective's now from up in the air. I'm watching it all happen — it's like my soul has wandered out of my body.

I see myself leaning against the wall, then a fuzzy outline goes around my body, and the drunk enters the side street. She opens her eyes and the man does it all again: forces her to kiss him, and reaches down to unbuckle himself. Oh, and here comes Gevan, he uses the exact same rooftops that I did. But he wasn't following the drunk as he said, he was couched on the rooftop behind a chimney, watching and waiting. He stood up only when the drunk started to go too far; he pulled out a pistol — not a normal one — fired, and the drunk fell. He jumped off of the roof while the drunk slumped dead.

Victa comes, rescues me, Gevan slams his "gun" into my head, and we leave. Time speeds forward, and I see movement on the rooftop — it's me, after I left Victa and Gevan and went on my way to Baker St. I see Gevan and Victa come out of the abandoned building and go their separate ways.

Victa heads towards Baker St, but Gevan comes back to the alley. He bends down and lightly slaps the drunk until a groan comes out of him.

"Get up, you fool."

The drunk groans again, but he opens his eyes and goes to stand up. I gasp. He wasn't dead after all? What, no! The man who took away my free will and violated me isn't dead?! I'm going to kill him! My vision blurs as tears come streaming from my eyes — everything just keeps getting worse. I don't want to see any more. Wake up, please? I try to pinch my arm but I'm still watching the events happen.

"You didn't have to shoot me." The drunk has an accent like one that I've never heard before. The gate has no memory of who he is.

"And you didn't have to take it that far." Gevan has a disgusted look on his face.

"I haven't been with anybody in a while and the new, innocent phase is when whores are at their best."

Gevan's face becomes even more disgusted. "She's not a whore!"

"Whatever, did it work?"

"I don't know. You were just supposed to threaten and pretend to kidnap her."

"It had the same effect: she was scared, you saved her. We completed Soppy's mission."

I knew it! I knew that Soppy and The Unknown are evil! They had someone attempt to rape me just to get me to trust their agent who "saved" me. What kind of sick, corrupted idea is that?!

"If Soppy looks at my memories, she'll get angry, it's her bloody niece!"

"You can always get this time erased. That's all on you, she won't be having my head, I don't work for her."

"I can take you down with me. Soppy knows who you are, Balor. She knows that I use you when I need someone that Victa doesn't know."

"She's not in on this?"

"No. In order to convince Jezebel to join our side, Victa has to be sincere and unknowing. Jezebel is Drew Arch's daughter."

"He was the best." I hear sarcasm in his voice. How dare he make fun of my father!

"Yep, and that's why you would expect nothing less from his daughter. She's just as skeptical and secretive." He checks his watch. "I have to go, she'll be a spy soon."

"Tell me which group she gets assigned to."

"Never in a million years would I tell you important intel like that." He turns away from the drunk and heads in the direction of Baker St.

"You know where to find me, the next time that you need me!" The drunk shouts to Gevan.

Gevan turns his head to look over his shoulder at the drunk, "There won't be a next time!"

"There's always a next time!" The drunk falls against the wall, slides back down onto the ground, and laughs. By his laugh, he might've actually been drunk, maybe he wasn't wholly faking it — or maybe he's a lunatic. A lunatic who doesn't deserve to live. If I can't kill him, I at least want him to rot in jail so that he can't violate anybody else.

The nightmare ends and I'm able to wake myself by pinching my arm. At least I thought that I could wake myself, but instead of opening my eyes to the cinema, I open them to the rooftop where I found the gun.

There's a man in a long coat, his face is covered and he's wearing a fedora. He looks like a detective, but in less eye-catching colors. Something about him's familiar. I don't know why, but there's just something about him. Maybe, he's helping me. He bends down, pulls something out of his pocket, and places it right where I found the gun. Oh! It was him? But, how'd he know that I would end up on that rooftop or even if I would need the gun?

Who's that guy? Is he following me?!

The scene ends and I finally open my eyes to the cinema. I hear the person in back eating and there's a new film on the screen. I check my watch, I've been asleep for more than 7 hours. How's that possible? The scenes didn't seem long enough to last 7 hours. Anyway, I should probably start heading out. It's possible that I missed meeting Victa back at the café.

I make sure that my jacket's still around my head, and that my cash is in my pocket, and I head to the long haunted hallway. The room's now freezing. Maybe I should take my jacket off of my head and use it for warmth.

The same man from the daytime is working the desk.

"Good Evening." Crap! I'm supposed to be speaking Sirapian, aren't I? I mean, "Bonjour."

"Dobrý večer?" Never mind, I'm supposed to be speaking his language. What was it again? I don't remember, maybe it'll just come to me.

"Dobrý večer!"

"Páčili sa vám filmy?"

"Oui?" No, that's not right, that's Sirapian. Let's try this again. I clear my throat. "Áno."

"Ktorý bol váš obľúbený?" What? Is he asking who was my favorite or which one was my fav? Or is he asking me nothing like that at all? I'll just say two answers in case I'm wrong.

"Špionáž a môžem si kúpiť cukríky?" There's always one about spies isn't there?

"Máme to isté ako včera v noci. Čo by si rád?" Which ones did I want again?

"Chuckles et Sno-Caps, prosím."

He grabs two packages of sweets from the compartment in the counter.

"To bude $10."

Earlier, he gave me change in the form of 10s; I pull one out and hand it to him.

"Ďakujem."

"Radosť podnikať s vami."

"Kde je toaleta?"

"Cez dvere doľava, hore po schodoch a prvých dverách vpravo."

I follow his directions and go through the door on his left, this hallway looks a little bit newer and less creepy than the one leading to the film room. The stairs are a cool spiral staircase. The doors are lovely beech brown and modern looking — this part must be where the owners live.

The toilet room's kind of small, it just has a toilet and shower. The shower has soaps, I wonder if I can take a quick shower. While I use the toilet, I make my decision. Once I'm done on the toilet, I lock the closed door, take my jacket off, and get into the shower. The hot water feels so good; the Devil only let me take a shower once a year — a few more days and I would've taken one in the Devil's tiny, gross shower.

I hope that it's ok that my dress is soaking wet. There are bottles of shampoo, conditioner, and body wash; they all smell fruity. I clean up thoroughly and am not able to comb my hair because there's no brush — so much for all the effort the lady put into untangling it.

Wait, there are scissors. Maybe I can jamb them — NO! I'll use them to cut my hair and nothing else. If given the opportunity, I'll have a normal life. I won't kill myself just yet, the future might hold something good.

There's a towel next to the shower; it's not that big, but I can use it to dry my hair and dress. After wringing out my hair and dress, I start cutting my hair; it's so dense that halfway through, my arms are quaking with the effort. I end up cutting it to my shoulders — it's a huge change from my knees. Now, I'm ready to go.

As I go to exit the toilet room, I feel carpet seep between my toes. That's weird — the toilet room had tile flooring, not carpet. I look down...all I see is my hair. I feel my eyes widen with fear. This isn't good! What do I do with all of this hair? It can be traced back to me, I must leave no proof for the Devil to find.

I look around for somewhere to put it. I don't see anything but candles near a basin. I grab a fistful of my hair, and a candle, and put the candle to my hair over the basin. The hair ignites and I drop it into the basin. I do the same to more fistfuls of hair until the floor is tile again — I don't leave even a single strand of hair. No more proof, and now I'll look completely different from the back. If I spot somebody that could turn me in, all I have to do is turn my back and they won't look twice.

As I leave the toilet room, I don't hear the whirring of the machines playing the films anymore. The man is still behind the desk, reading the same book as earlier.

"Prečo nie sú filmy hrané?"

"Prišli len 2 ľudia a druhá odišla." That man must've left while I was taking a shower. On my way out of the film room, I noticed that he was still watching the films with 2 empty boxes of sweets; I couldn't see who he was. I wonder if he liked the sweets and which one was tastier — I hope that the Chuckles are tasty, I bought a box and so now I have to eat them, whether I like them or not.

As I'm about to reach the doors, the man calls out to me, "Nezabudnite na svoje sladkosti."

"Dobre, Ďakujem." I go back and pick up the boxes, but I don't put them in my pockets. Good thing I forgot them, or else they'd be soaked and ruined.

I go out the door that I came in through. "Shoot!" My hand was checking my pockets to see if they are dry enough for the boxes, but instead, they are soaking wet and out comes a mushy, water-stained pile of paper — it used to be my cash.

"You don't have to fret about that, my dear." A figure comes out of the shadows, I jump but don't run. I've accepted whatever life throws at me, if he kills me, so be it. I get a closer look at him as he comes out into the light. It's the man from the café — the one who paid for my food — he was also in the cinema. In both places, I couldn't see his face, but now I can. His hood's pulled back — it's the older man from the Devil's house!

He says, "Your mother and father have tons of money put away, all of which is now yours," at the same time I say, "What're you doing here?"

"Can we go somewhere more private to talk? I can tell you everything that I know, but there are too many listeners here." I look around and don't see anybody.

"There's nobody here."

"Jezebel, please. Trust me, I won't hurt you. Remember: your father said that you could trust me."

If there are people listening, I wasn't supposed to speak the common language. Jezebel might be a popular name, but with my Brilla accent and use of the common language, people can connect the dots.

"Tu m'as laissé seul, tu m'as abandonné à Brilla."

"Is this like the silent treatment? Talking to me in a language not as simple as the common one? I'm trying to help you, why are you making this so hard?"

"Tu ne comprends pas Sirapian?"

"I understand it, I just can't speak it too well."

"Pourquoi n'essaies-tu pas de le parler?"

"We're wasting time; if I don't get you off of the streets, then The Red List's Agents will spot you."

"Les gens qui rassemblaient les autres?"

"Yes, they heard that you left the liveD, he contacted them as soon as he woke up. He knows that we live here — where else would you go? As far as he knows, you left with us."

"Je croyais que personne ne pouvait nous entendre. Pourquoi parlez-vous en code secret?"

"J'utilise du code et tu ne me fais pas asses confiance pour aller quelque part avec moins d'oreilles."

"Tu as dit que tu n'étais pas bon en Sirapian."

"Les merveilles du portail. Ils doivent l'avoir mis à jour récemment."

"Je me sens malade." I trust him, he seems very nice; my father did tell me to trust his group. He also told me to trust Soppy, but this guy gives off way better vibes. I just feel so miserable, it's a challenge just to hold my head up. Recent events have been too much for me, even more than 7 hours of sleep isn't enough to make the load lighter — in fact, it feels like I didn't get any sleep at all.

"Je peux tu emmener dans un endroit sûr."

"J'ai mal à la tête." My head's starting to hammer really bad. My vision is going in and out of focus.

"Je peux tu emmener au palais."

"Ce serait—" I can no longer breathe and my vision clouds over, I'm on the ground now — no, I'm in the man's arms, he must've caught me. I would be freaking out, but it's like my soul has detached from my body.

The man has me fully in his arms now and he's jogging to the end of the street; there's a black car waiting there, he places me in the back and gets in.

The car starts off without him saying anything; he's too busy trying to get me to calm down. My body's hyperventilating and starting to froth at the mouth and all of the stuff that's documented for seizures.

"Jezebel, you have to ride the wave, it's all the information. It's too much for your brain, the gate should not have given you so much. You have to calm down, let it take you over. Your body is fighting against it, all that will happen is you making yourself ill and you might possibly kill yourself."

He turns to the driver in front. "Adelia, can you go any faster?"

"För mycket trafik."

"Can we get off this road then?"

"Det är likadant överallt. Kvällsrusning."

"Sacrebleu. Euh, ça ne fait rien."

"Vad?" He dismisses an idea and thinks about something else before directing her.

"Kan du få oss på landsvägarna?"

"Varför?"

"We need to get her somewhere safe, far from the Devil. I was thinking Huset i Sheria."

"Bra idé. Djävulen." She spits after saying that word, I wonder what it means. "Vet inte om det."

"Just get us there as fast as possible and make sure that no one follows us."

"Ja, herrn."

He pushes a button: the windows close and tint, a divider comes up between the back and front of the car, and a compartment comes out of its hidden place in the wall. He grabs something out of the secret compartment; while he's getting it ready, he talks to me.

"I'm sorry that all of this happened to you. We should have taken you with us, but you were gone before we left and we had to deal with a bunch of guards — well, Bryce did anyway, I was dealing with Theo. And then it got even more chaotic, Atria was shot—" What, NO! The nice lady was shot?! And her name's Atria? Why's everyone's name so weird: Linris, Atria, Bryce, Devil, Gevan, Victa, Balor — I bet even this guy's name is weird; is the world also weird?

He stops talking without elaborating on Atria getting shot. He seems focused on what he's doing with the syringe that he set up.

He injects whatever was in the syringe into me. "All done, you should be better now. No more seizures." He's really nice, talking to and comforting me even though he has no way of knowing if I can hear him. I think I really do trust him. I won't speak in the common language once I'm back in my body, but I won't fight — as if I had even started to, I have given up. I don't fight anymore; but if I did, I wouldn't fight a caring person.

My soul seems to float back into my body and my perspective's no longer like a bird's; my body's calming down. When I open my eyes and sit up, he hands me a tea towel. I wipe the froth from my mouth; my head still hurts and I'm dizzy, so I lay back against the seat.

"Sommes-nous en sécurité maintenant?"

"Not fully, but there are fewer ears here. Once the barriers are put up, any listening devices will only pick up static."

"Qui es-tu?"

"Désolé, je dois avoir oublié de me présenter. Je m'appelle Guvnor Trus, je travaille pour le cercle protégeant Atria, Sa majesté royale: la mère du Prince Theo."

"Comment es-tu arrivé au Café?"

"Do you mind if I don't speak any more of Sirapian? The gate has updated since I've last stepped foot through it, but I am used to only understanding certain languages, speaking in them trips me up."

"Bien sûr, j'ai oublié comment parler la langue commune, je ne l'ai pas parlée depuis longtemps et je trouve Sirapian plus facile."

"You did seem mute at the Devil's."

"Ne lui montre jamais la supériorité. Vous allez entrer encore plus d'enfer. Il aime être le meilleur et avoir le dernier mot."

"You have changed a lot since leaving the Devil's house — you make eye contact and speak a lot."

"Je suis enfin libre. Non plus torture du diable."

"Did he beat you?"

I stay silent; I don't like nor want pity.

He seems to get an answer from my silence. The car goes on in silence for a while before he talks again.

"Do you still want help?"

"Qu'est-ce que vous avez à offrir?"

"With Drew and Linris being your parents, you are automatically a part of The Circle. You would just have to be assigned to a royal. There's only one local royal without a spy." He stops and gets a nervous look on his face.

"I know you didn't mean to, but it still happened..."

"Qui?" I already know that it's Theo. Even without knowing that my mother was the last spy to be taken away from a royal — my father was the guard of the whole palace — and the reigning monarch doesn't have a permanent guard, I could still understand who he's talking about: I didn't mean to poison Theo, but it could come across as an attempt on his life.

"Would you be ok with protecting Theo?"

"Je le ferais."

"We would get you lodgings, a new life that the Devil couldn't track, even with you staying in Musalin—"

"J'ai déjà dit que je le ferais." We can't have him keep on going, trying to convince me why to do it. We don't have time to waste; I need to know all that comes next before we reach the house.

"You did?" I nod my head. "Sorry, still getting used to hearing Sirapian spoken every time, the gate's update works faster on newer spies than older ones. I'm used to doing things the old-fashioned way: learning the language yourself and becoming fluent in it, not having a machine instantly make you fluent. And Sirapian was never—"

"Pouvons-nous s'il vous plaît continuer?" I'm not being rude — I said please.

"Oh, right. I talk a lot and get sidetracked — that's why Bryce takes up as leader of the missions." I tell him with my eyes and slow shaking of my head that he's doing it again.

"Get back to it, Guvnor," he whispers to himself. "Once we get to Huset i Sheria — a safe house that hasn't been used in at least 4 years — I'll contact my boss and she can get everything to us that you'll need to start your assignment."

"Et qu'est ce que c'est que ça?"

"It will mostly be protecting the Prince and staying under the Devil's radar, but you'll be given missions once in a while."

Missions, why's my mind bugging me about a mission? I just got into the spy business, I don't have any missions yet. I know that I'm forgetting something — the gate didn't improve my memory any. What am I forgetting?!

"Qu'est-ce que les missions ont habituellement à faire avec?"

"Making sure that The Red List doesn't do anything too disastrous, like killing the king. We would have prevented it if the Devil hadn't been in charge of it. We are usually one step ahead, but sometimes, for no reason, the bad seems to win."

Oh My God! Victa, The Unknown. The Circle couldn't stop the king's death because The Unknown did it. The Red List seems ahead sometimes because The Unknown helps them. I was supposed to meet Victa. It's so late in the day, she's probably no longer available. I feel so bad, I let her down. And wow, time moves really fast. At the Devil's house, time moved slowly; days were always the same, boring things. But boring was actually good, it meant that I could enjoy the few days that the Devil wasn't home to whip and beat me. I shudder just thinking about it.

You never have to feel the whip again, Jez. Never again. You escaped; you don't have to go back. Just breathe and focus on Trus 'intel.

"Quand serai-je de retour à Musalin?"

"We're still in Musalin, it's one of the biggest regions in the known world."

"Donc, où en étions-nous?"

"It's not really called anything different, it's just known as the centre or hub of Musalin."

"J'ai mal à la tête, puis-je me reposer?"

"You may."

I close my eyes and let the motion of the car take my mind elsewhere.

CHAPTER TWENTY

Victa

I feel bad for fooling Iris, I was not completely lying though — I am working with The Circle... it is just that I am undercover for The Unknown. She must believe that she just joined The Circle. I had to lie, my mother told me to. She said that Iris would not want to join The Unknown willingly with all the information that the gate gave her. Until I saw Iris being turned into a spy, I had no idea what my mother meant.

My mother was forced to tell me that one of our agents — in league with The Red List — killed the king. I do not fully agree with that action, the king was one of the best that Musalin ever had, but what can I do? I have been a part of The Unknown before I was even born — it is mostly hereditary and is for sure hard to get out of.

The only way to get out of it is if the gate puts you in a different organization when you come to a certain age. Unfortunately, when my day came, three hexagons with a dot in the center of the left one appeared on my forehead. Ever since I was two years old, I have had the burden of officially being the balance of the spy organizations — that is a lot for a two-year-old, especially one with a photographic memory; I never forget a thing.

I do not want to stay out, but my mother told me to find the girl who escaped the Devil — Iris. I do not want my mother to sink her claws into Iris; she seems like a good girl, I want her to choose to come to The Unknown on her own. I want her to come to terms with all the weight that she now has to bear before I give her to my mother.

I will give her some extra time to decide fully. She is smart, she will figure out sooner or later that she has no choice; we are all pawns in a game that started at the dawn of time.

As I walk to Baker St, all that I can think about is what happened to her in the alley, and the way Gevan was acting. Gevan never acts that way, why would he be snooty and mean? The Gevan I married would never slam his gun over an innocent's head — unless they were shot or something, and it relieved them of their pain.

And that man who Gevan killed, what kind of sicko thinks that it is all right to take away someone's free will? Who does he think he is that he can just choose to force someone into a traumatic experience?!

And what am I going to tell my friends? I promised the girls that I could meet with them last night, I was at their freaking house before I had to leave to be given a new mission. They saw me park and then instantly leave. They know that my job is crazy, but I have kept spying away from my normal life as much as I could. They know that a normal busy job would not make me instantly leave; they are starting to get suspicious. And adding this whole thing with Iris on top, just makes it worse.

But, most importantly: what am I going to tell my mother? She is not one to fool, she will know I am lying before I even open my mouth. She can smell lies. The only reason I could ever hate spying is when my mother becomes too harsh. I always complete my missions, so she is barely ever harsh with me; but, when it does happen, I do not even want to be in the same country as her. She gets very mad and my emotions just cannot take it, all I ever want is for her to be proud of me.

When I get to the gate, luckily there are not many people out and about. I arrive at the stairs to our house. I am so nervous! Shhhhe is going to be so mad, I just know it. I do not want her to be mad at me. She will stop talking to me, will no longer love me, and will kill Gevan just to punish me. Then, she will banish me to a remote location. I will never see my friends again; I will never be able to go on another mission. I will go from having a double life to having no life at all!

Stop having an emotional breakdown, Victa. You are overreacting, just get it over with and accept your punishment.

Ok. I take a deep breath, run a hand over my face to make sure it is put together, and go through the whole process of opening the door. I am freaking out so bad; the machine is taking forever to log me in. But I cannot let it phase me, I just need to keep on breathing and remain calm. My punishment will be even worse if I do not sell my failure the right way.

The door clicks and I step inside. This time a maid meets me by the door. She curtseys.

"Your mother is expecting you, miss."

Why? How? Ugh, what now? "Where is she?"

"If you will just follow me, miss." She turns around and heads in the direction of the long main hallway. She does not usually have me meet her in any of these rooms, they are mostly parlors for visitors.

The maid stops in front of the meeting room for family. The only people who ever use it are my two aunts: Linris and Melina. But Linris is gone and Melina has not visited since Linris was captured. I feel my face brighten, maybe Melina is here! I would love to see her again, she is way easier to talk to than my mother. I remember her being kind, caring, and not at all cold or judgmental like my mother.

I open the door quickly, I do not even wait for the maid to knock or open it for me. If Melina is really here, I have so much to tell her.

"Victorious Dellavina Atributous! How dare you enter a room without knocking!"

My brightened mood disappears instantly. Melina is not here, only my mother is. The TV is turned onto a news channel and there is evidence of people being in here: the floor is ruffed up and there is an empty glass knocked over on it. My mother is standing next to the closed window, with a very menacing and disappointed look on her face. Oh, no, does she already know that I failed the mission? I worry my bottom lip between my teeth — I cannot help it, it is a nervous habit, just like having emotional breakdowns.

"Yes, mother, what is—" She aggressively holds her hand up for silence. I back up into the door; I have not seen her this mad, EVER! I cannot believe I forgot myself and spoke before she told me to.

"What is this?" She motions to the state that the room is in.

Do I answer? Does she want an answer or has she already assumed something? I am assuming that this has nothing to do with my failed mission.

She is still standing there waiting, I better give her an answer. "Somebody was in here and left before meeting with you?" How am I supposed to know what happened? I was not even here for long. The only places I have been in today were my bedroom; the kitchen; the private hallway; the green parlor; and my mother's study.

"Don't play dumb with me, young lady! The security cameras were shut off. I know that somebody was in here and that you helped to create this mess. You know that nobody is allowed inside this house without telling me!"

"I know, mother. I—"

"Enough! You will clean up this mess and then I'll give you your punishment."

"But what about me reporting in about my mission?" I get out very quickly before she can stop me again.

"As I said, we'll talk after you clean this up." She says through clenched teeth.

What the heck is going on here? It does not look like anything is missing. Why is she so upset about a little mess in a room that is barely used? Why is she blowing up on me, when I did not even do anything?

Whatever. Just pick it up and do not give her any reason to get angrier.

I crouch down, smooth out the floor, put the floor cushions back in their positions, and pick up the glass. I go to power off the TV, but, before I can, my mother steps in. "Don't. I want to listen to this. Go clean that glass and meet me in my office." She is still angry, but at least she is no longer talking with her teeth clenched.

"Yes, mother." I back out of the room — if I show her my back, it will seem like I am opposing her authority. The door closes silently behind me and I am back in the hallway. The maid is no longer there, but that is fine, I know my way to the kitchen perfectly.

When I was little, my mother would get angry at me all the time, so I would take most of my meals with the staff in the kitchen; they were always nicer. Even when I was not eating, the kitchen was my favorite place to go. But since marrying Gevan, I am allowed to spend most of my nights at his place. Assignments during the day and sleeping at Gevan's flat are better than hiding from my mother in the kitchen. Those days were simpler, but now I have more places outside of the house to go to to get away from my mother.

The door to the kitchen sometimes gets stuck because of how old it is; the one time that I am in a hurry, it gets stuck badly. I put down the glass and put both of my hands on the door and try tugging on it with all of my strength. Surprisingly, it does not open — I am very strong, I go to the gym at least 5 nights a week, and I always lift heavy weights. The door only opens when a server comes out of the kitchen and bumps into me.

He looks up and spots who it is. "Victory, is that you?"

"Hi, Stevan. Long time, no see. How are you?"

"Fine, I heard you got married to another spy."

"Yeah, his name is Gevan, he was a part of The Circle...but his father was a member of The Unknown; the gate chose him to be a part of his father's group." Stevan and I used to play as kids, we were the only ones in the house then. The other spies my age lived in other houses that belong to The Unknown. "So, your day never came, you still work in the kitchen?"

"Yeah, not many people in my family were spies; they haven't been for generations — I think the genes got replaced."

"But were you not recently on a mission at a science facility? I thought I heard about it on the spy news."

"Yeah, but they only used me because my creation was accepted into a contest that the Science Centre was doing."

"What did you make?"

"Some kind of satellite gadgety thing, no big deal."

"But I heard that it won."

"Yeah, it did. But the small amount of prize money went to my sister."

"I heard that she fell ill, how is she doing?"

"She died last month."

"Oh, I am so sorry, I did not know."

"Not many people ever do."

I feel so bad now. We were inseparable as kids, and now I do not really know him. I guess when I was old enough to go on missions, it took all of my focus, and everyone from my childhood became less important. "Do you want to grab lunch sometime and catch up on everything?"

"I don't know, my work here piles up."

"It could be on the next holiday." Suddenly, I remember more about him and snap my fingers. "Hey, is not your birthday coming up soon? I could get my mother to give you the day off and we could hang out."

"I don't know. If we do that, everyone else would be given my work. I'd rather not."

"I insist, come on. Please, Stevan. It has been ages since the last time we hung out, I miss it. We had such fun."

He seems actually to be considering it. I have hope. Please, do not let my hope be in vain.

"Ok, but I can only take a few hours off, not the whole day."

Yay! I think that this is a good omen for everything else to come. "Awesome! I will go and talk to my mother right now."

I turn to go and as I do, I see the glass on the floor and remember why I came to the kitchen. "Can I get into the kitchen? I promised my mother that I would take this glass to the sink and wash it."

"You mean your mother ordered you to do it?"

"Well, yeah. But I still have to do it either way."

"I can do it for you; I have that exact glass already washed and dried."

He goes back into the kitchen and comes back out with a clean glass that looks just like the dirty one.

"Thank you so much. Oh…my…god, you are a lifesaver. My mother hates it when people take a while, and cleaning that glass would have taken me longer than she wants to wait."

"No problem, anything for a childhood friend. Plus, you are getting me time off of work."

I take the glass from him. "See you then. Bye."

"Bye."

I turn around and walk as fast as I can to my mother's study. I check my watch, it has already been 20 minutes, I talked to Stevan for a while. My mother is going to be so mad — still. I hope she agrees to let Stevan off for a few hours, I already told him and got his hopes up. I forgot he still worked here, I thought that he had changed jobs.

When I get to my mother's office, the occupied light is on, which means she beat me here. That is not good, she usually gives you a head start and if you arrive after her — let's just say that it does not end well. The only thing to do now is: knock on the door, accept all three punishments, and hope that she is not terribly mad.

I knock and not even a minute later, the door clicks open. I step inside to a neutral scene: my mother is behind her desk — no weapons in sight — and she has a slightly less angry air about her.

"I'm sorry, Victorious. I might have gone a tad bit too far. You know you can have friends over, but you can't let them trash the place. And I have to lock everything up before they come. I won't punish you for that. But you were late coming here. No dinner tonight."

She never admits she was wrong, what is happening? Did

a little bit nicer version of my mother take over?

"Um. There is something else."

"What is it?"

"My report from the mission."

"Oh. How did you do? Did you find the girl? Did you bring her here?" She gets an almost excited look about her.

"No. I could not find her. I swear, I looked for a whole day, and nothing. I do not think that she is in the hub of Musalin. She might be in the country or islands for all we know. A day is not enough time to look for her."

Her face turns as red as a tomato. This is not good — red is the last color one sees before bad things happen and one is severely punished. I have only ever heard about my mother turning this color.

"I am freezing all of your accounts; you will have no cash, no credit cards; and you are to be locked out of Baker St for 3 whole days, starting tomorrow! Maybe that will give you time to think of where a little nobody who escaped from the Devil is hiding out! Get out of my office and Baker St at once!"

I stand here dumbstruck, it is all that I can do. This is one of the worst punishments ever. What is happening? Why is she suddenly being so mean to me...What?

"I will not order you twice!"

My feet move; I do not want a worse punishment than this. I back out of the room and run from the house as fast as possible. I did not even get to ask if Stevan could have his birthday off. Why does this day keep getting worse? First, I have to witness a horrible act; then, Gevan is becoming a different person; and now I have failed my mother and she hates me. What the heck?!

After the gate closes behind me, it beeps and flashes red; when I try to get back in, it does not open. My mother said it would not start until tomorrow, though.

Well, what am I supposed to do for three whole days? Gevan's flat is on the other side of this gate. She probably turned my phone off; I have no way of contacting him.

I check my pockets for my phone, pull it out of my left pocket, and try to turn it on. Yep, she turned it off, it will not turn on — it was at 90%. She said that I would have no cash, but I actually have some in my pocket. I have 300 in Musalin's currency. That should be enough for a hostel for three nights and some food.

The cheapest hostel is in Potter's Town, but Gevan said that it was closed. But then again, he has been acting differently lately, so maybe Potter's Town is not actually closed. And even if it is, it cannot all be shut down. The hostel is on the farthest end from the hub of Musalin, it is probably still open.

I do not feel like walking all the way there. Cabs will be impossible to get at this time of day. The only other option is the subway. The subway is not the cheapest option; I wish I had my bike — but, unfortunately, it is in Gevan's flat.

Maybe I can afford it. The hostel for three nights should be one hundred and fifty, which leaves one hundred and fifty for everything else. A subway ticket for five uses is fifty, I think. So that leaves one hundred for food — looks like I am going to have to go to cafés and diners that are not that expensive. I can do this, it is not going to be a punishment as my mother intended it to be.

Now, I have more time to get Iris ready for The Unknown…and I finally have a break from my mother, she was getting more demanding with Iris escaping from the Devil. She never lets me go a single night without a mission, not even when she specifically told me that I could spend the whole night with my friends.

This is why they started hanging out without me and all have inside jokes that I do not know. I have not hung out with them for real since school. When school ended, I became a full-time spy. No wonder Iris did not want to be one, you do not really get to live a normal life.

There is a subway entrance only two blocks from Baker St, I have no trouble finding it. At least something is going right for me. I do not want the same thing that happened to Iris to happen to me, Gevan will not be there to save me.

I have not ridden the subway in ten years; I only ever walk, bike, get driven, or drive my own car. The subway is dirty and not safe — not even for someone who knows how to kill and take down all types of people. Wow, there are a lot of stairs, 3 sets just to get to the level with ticket sellers. And even more to get to the level that the actual trains are on.

There are so many kiosks that sell tickets, they sell different tickets for different tracks. I need to find the one that goes to Potter's Town, if I remember correctly, I think it is the B-track. I see the kiosk that says B-track, it has a list of destinations that it stops at. I run my finger along the alphabetical list until I get to the Ps: PO, Pott, there it is: Potter's Town. The kiosk is a machine — just like everything else in this world — I press the button for buying a ticket. It says to put a fifteen bill into the slot; I only have a fifty, hopefully, it dishes out change.

I put the 50 into the slot, a ticket pops out of another slot, and I hear paper coming out of a third slot. It gives me back 35 in three 10 bills and a 5 bill; I put them in my pocket with the rest of my cash, grab the ticket, and head down all the rest of the stairs to the platform with the trains.

The lanes for the different tracks all go in order. A is a few feet from the stairs, there is a stairway going up and over and Track B is on the other side. I go up the stairs and end on a platform with dirty, poor-looking people. I wonder if they are going to Potter's Town — it is a big deal amongst the poor.

But there is a clean-shaven young man not far from the stairs; he does not look like he has done much work in his life. Who is he? He looks in my direction, causing me to gasp. It is the Prince, he is disguised...but it is for sure him. Why is the Prince taking the subway — in a disguise, of all things — and where is he going? I want to ask him, but not with all the ears on the platform. Maybe I can ask him on the train.

I grab a newspaper from a stand and sit on the closest bench; the train is not supposed to be here for a half hour. I look at the Prince again before opening the paper; he seems to be debating something in his head. A minute in, he comes over to me and starts talking.

"Feasgar math. Dè an uair a tha e?" Where did the Prince learn to speak Aed? They do not teach that at royal school, they only teach Sirapian and Mlohkcotsian — the two most used languages after the common language. Maybe I can ask him what he is doing here in Aed, not many people are bound to understand it — in fact, I thought it had gone extinct.

"Tha leth uair a thìde ann gus an ruig an trèana."

"Mar sin tha e 3:30, taing."

"Gabh suidheachan, Prionnsa, gheibh thu sgìth."

"Ciamar a tha fios agad gur mise am prionnsa?" Uh, oh. Maybe I should not have made it clear that I saw through his disguise. I have been with The Circle long enough to know that he has no idea that the spy organizations exist.

"Tha aghaidh sònraichte agad."

"Ach chan eil mi a 'coimhead mar an ceudna."

"Look, I am a makeup artist who can detect when people are wearing disguises. Can we please stop talking in Aed? I am tired, I just want to get to my hostel in Potter's Town and get some sleep. Ok?"

"Chan urrainn dhomh."

"Common language, please!"

"Ok, fine." He has taken on a different accent than his real one. Boy, is he really getting into character. "Most of Potter's Town is closed for renovations; apparently, the Prince wants all of Musalin to look nice and fancy."

"I am sure that my hostel is still open, it is on the outskirts of Potter's Town."

"Do you mean Riki's?"

"Yeah."

"It's still open, but it's no longer a run-down hostel — it was the first to be renovated."

"Is it still cheap?"

"Yeah, that's where I'm going, I booked a room there months ago."

"For how long?"

"About 2 years; as long as the renovations will last."

"That must cost a fortune."

"Not as much as most people's rents cost."

"I would not know, my flat has been paid for."

"I wouldn't know either…if I hadn't done research."

"If I close my eyes until the train arrives, will you tell me when it gets here?"

"Sure thing."

"Can you also make sure that I do not get robbed?"

"Yeah, I'll be right here." He sits down on the bench, takes the newspaper from me, opens it up to the sports section, and starts to read.

"Yeah, go Robins!" He accidentally says without his accent. He does not seem to catch his slip and keeps on reading. Nobody looks over here though, they are all too busy with home and bed on their minds. I would love to go home. Gevan would have made lunch, and Roxie — my poodle — would be on our foam-mattressed-king-sized bed, waiting for me to go to sleep. Oh, how I long for my comfy bed. At least this bench is comfier than one would think. I let the sound of the Prince flipping the newspaper's pages be the noise that slows my mind by focusing on it; within seconds, I am fast asleep.

CHAPTER TWENTY-ONE

Jezebel

When I open my eyes, I find the car standing still and nobody else in it. Where are we? Where did they go? Why did they leave me all alone? Who are they really? For no reason, I just have a heavy feeling, one that makes me nervous and uneasy.

But I'm not fully worried, now I have time to collect myself before — if — they come back. I still have a really bad headache, I think it's because of my body fighting the information overload — it's definitely not due to lack of sleep, I actually feel completely rested.

Ok, so what now? Earlier was horrible and I don't want to have a repeat of it; but if the Devil were to catch me, it'd be even worse. I don't see many options: I've no money, no relatives, and no idea of where to go without any documents; the safest choice is to just trust Trus and hopefully be given a mission and a new identity. But is he coming back? I don't even know where I am — the windows are completely black, so I can't see the outside.

I grab the handle on the door and try to open it, but it won't budge. Why would they lock me in here?! I'm officially starting to freak out, only kidnappers want to lock people in cars. What if it wasn't my body fighting the information, what if Trus injected me with something? What if he's pulling a Gevan — fake saving me to get me to trust him?

Whether I can trust him or not, I need to get out of this car. I'm vulnerable in here; not knowing your surroundings gives you a disadvantage. If I need to run, I have nowhere to run to. It'd be better if I could see, it's pitch black with the windows covered. I feel around on the door for a different way of opening it. I find a thing that's similarly shaped as to what I thought was the door handle, except this one's bigger and thicker, I try it. The door opens.

When light comes pouring in, I can see that there are 2 door handles — the first one that I tried must be for the window. So I basically freaked out for nothing; Trus isn't trying to kidnap me, I just don't know how a car works. Well, I just got the information from the gate, and not all cars are built the same? I feel so embarrassed now, it doesn't matter if nobody saw my mistake. I saw it and I can never get mistakes out of my head, even ones that saved my life.

I step out of the car and find myself in the middle of a gigantic blacktop surrounded by the largest house I've ever seen. It's even bigger than the Devil's house — and his screamed money. I don't see any woods to run into and hide — I don't see much of anything at all; there are no other buildings in sight, just barren ground on either side of the house.

The sun's blazing hot; the front of the house is in shade. I close the car door and go to the porch. I still don't see anybody, they must be inside. I turn around to look at the sights. What I thought was barren, is actually beautiful. The house — as big as it is — is tucked away in rolling hills. They're green, luscious, and just about the best thing I've ever seen. The spies never get out of cities, so the gate has no breathtaking sights such as this.

This is my own memory that'll possibly be inserted into the gate; if Trus is still here, he's going to take me back, which means back to Baker St. All of the spies are on Baker St, even The Red List — I don't see how bad can live with good right next door, maybe they don't even know that The Circle's there and vice versa? They definitely don't know that The Unknown's there — hence the name, it's unknown by everybody, even some of its operatives, like my father.

Enough thinking, I need to confront the rest of my future; thinking's just stalling. I don't really want to join the spies, it doesn't seem like my cup of tea. I'm a shy girl who can't stand the idea of killing or lying to people — that last one's a lie. I love nobody knowing who I really am; it's fun to be someone else, someone who wasn't tortured or secluded her whole life.

"Jez," a voice inside of me nags.

Right, inside. I turn around, take a very, very deep breath, and open the door. Upon entering, you're faced with a cozy living room — totally not what one would expect. I expected a giant lobby with the most beautiful grand staircase. A lady — the driver? — is sitting on an L-shaped sofa and Trus is standing next to a desk with a laptop on it. I'd never seen a laptop before, it looks just like the high-tech ones in the pictures from the gate. Will I get one? That'd be awesome!

Neither of them seem to have noticed me — weird, they're both spies, you'd think that they'd be more observant. I clear my throat.

Trus turns around, "Adelia, did you hear something?" He's looking right at me, yet he seems not to see me.

I'm so tired of all this nonsense. "I'll talk in Brilla, I'm ready to cooperate."

"Nej, det finns ingen här att göra ett ljud."

"Except for Jezebel, but I haven't heard the door open — she should still be in the car. Would you go check on her? I'm about done setting up the connection to Soppy."

Adelia gets up, she would've walked into me on her way out the door if I hadn't moved out of the way. Sheesh, people are so rude. I'm right here, why would she have to go and check the car?

"I hope she hasn't tried to escape," Trus whispers.

"Escape, what're you talking about? Trus, I'm right here!" I go up to him and wave my hand in between his face and the laptop's screen. He has no reaction. Now I'm starting to get mad. "Stop pretending like you don't see me!"

Still, he has no reaction. This isn't fair! I was having a nice time feeling rested and enjoying the beautiful sights, and now this? Come on! I go to sit on the sofa and wait for him to finally notice me.

A scream comes from the direction that Adelia went. Trus stops what he's doing and rushes to the door while shouting, "What's wrong ailedA?" He grabs his gun out of his pocket on his way out the door.

Why's he grabbing his weapon, why did he use code and not say the lady's actual name? Is the Devil here?! I jump up and hide behind the sofa — not the best hiding spot, but I don't want to get lost in this strange house.

They're outside for a while before I realize it's safe to stop hiding behind the sofa. I didn't hear any gunshots, so why wouldn't it be safe? I hear rustling coming from inside the house, is this place haunted? My headache's starting to come back; I don't like ghosts. I hear more rustling. That's it, I'm getting out of here!

I run to the door, open it, and don't stop running until I reach the car. Trus is standing right next to the open car and is looking at the spot where I was sitting. But Adelia's reaction to what she saw is worse, she's crouched in the middle of the pavement crying, with a horrified expression on her face — I think her emotions are confused as to cry or scream.

What's going on? First the thing in the house, and now this? Why are things becoming even weirder? I can't see what's in the car that would make them act in such a way. Trus leans into the car and pulls something out. I see a limp hand and stop looking. I don't know what I saw...but I'm getting scared. I just came out of that car, I'm a physical being. I can touch things: I opened the car and house doors. Please, don't tell me that I'm dead. I **just** started living my life.

I feel tears come to my eyes; I need to look and confront my fears. Trus walks by me, and in his arms, is my limp body. It's breathing, right?! I didn't come this far just to be dead. There's been more than one person that got all the information from the gate; they all lived, what's so different about this time? Why am I dead? I'm getting all hot and flushed, I'm full-on freaking out now. Dead people can't feel heat, can they?

Perhaps, I can spirit walk. I feel something warm originating in my chest, gaining hope's a lovely feeling. Some shamans did it in my fairytale book, maybe the gate gave me a special ability. Trus did say that it has been updated recently. Maybe it advances more than just memories and fluency in languages, maybe it twists the mind and allows for supernatural beings. But I don't want to walk the spirit world, there are spirits, and I hate spirits! They just haunt you and make your life worse; luckily I've never had experiences with them, but people from the gate have. Their experiences have terrified me enough for a lifetime.

Maybe I actually did die, of horror. The memories of the spies might not've been an overload, but they might've given my system enough fright and terror for a heart attack. I should stop freaking out and wait to see if I get pulled back into my body like the last 2 times.

I follow Trus and my body back into the house. It takes a few moments for Adelia to control her emotions; she doesn't come into the house until after Trus has laid my body down nicely on the sofa. He has laid it as if I'm just sleeping and about to wake up — maybe he knows that I am spirit walking? Adelia closes the front door behind her and sits as far away on the sofa as she can from my body. Trus goes back to setting up whatever it was that he was working on.

"Vart ska vi begrava kroppen?"

"We don't know for sure yet if she's dead."

"Men hon andas inte!"

"I know that it appears that way, but she might be breathing in another form. She possibly traveled far from here. I have heard of a few shamans, but they went on voyages to be able to enter the spirit world. Maybe Jezebel's voyage happened in the Devil's house and the gate brought it to the surface."

"Skräp! Det är en förbannelse!" She spits onto the ground. "Vi borde aldrig ha plockat upp henne."

"We work for The Circle. Soppy would punish us if we left her niece to die. Jezebel was having a seizure due to the gate, it would have killed her if I hadn't given her the injection. She should hopefully wake up soon. If not, Soppy will no longer be the nicest spy leader."

"Du har rätt. Förlåt, jag har aldrig sett en död ung flicka förut."

"It's all right; she's not dead, her body is just in a coma until her spirit gets back."

Adelia seems very skeptical. "Vad du än säger." She looks like she believes that she's talking to a crazy person.

I hear a beep and look over at Trus 'laptop. A white light's coming out of it and a video appears with a person in the center of it. I go closer to get a better look so that I can identify the person, it really is Soppy! She's the one who gave me the water, but I got bad vibes from her. Looking at her now, I've no idea what gave me bad vibes, everything about her screams good and nice.

"Hullo, Soppy."

"Trus, you know that you don't have to use my code name when you are in a secure location."

"I prefer Soppy."

"Whatever. Hullo, Adelia, how are you?"

Adelia seems about to explode with something. She looks very troubled. "Hon är död. Hon är död!"

Soppy turns back to Trus with a suspicious look on her face. "Trus, what is she talking about?"

"Um, well...you see." Apparently, he's not so confident about me just taking a spirit walk.

"Trus, out with it. Report!"

"Yes, madam. Jezebel might be dead." Trus seems to shrink even though he appears older than Soppy by at least a few years.

"Trus, what did you say?" Soppy seems to be trying to hold in her emotions. I can see sorrow and anger warring in her eyes. Adelia just keeps repeating "Hon är död. Hon är död!" under her breath. I guess my death really shocked her? Well, it's definitely shocking a lot of people, I can't believe I'm so popular.

People love me? Not just my dead mother's love has brought me this far? Do I seriously have a different reason to live than just wanting a normal life?

I go to my body lying on the sofa and try pinching it. "Come on, body! Wake up, wake up, wake up! S'il vous plaît?" Nothing works.

"Trus, take me closer to the sofa — I think I just saw a flash of something."

"Ok, but be prepared for the sight you're about to witness." Trus picks up the laptop and points it at my body.

"No, Trus. To the figure standing over the body."

"There's nobody there."

"Just do it, please."

"Ok." He points the laptop away from me, far to my left.

"More to the left, Trus." He moves it closer in my direction. "Stop! Right there, Trus." The laptop's pointed right at my face now.

"Trus, you really can't see her?"

"No, madame."

"She's right there, is that Jezebel?"

"What does she look like?"

"Like the body on the sofa, except, she's closer to transparent and looks worried and scared."

"Yep, that's her."

"Why can I see her and you can't?"

"Because you are her family; only family can see those on spirit walks."

"How can we get her back into her body? She won't be stuck this way forever, will she?"

"I really don't know. The last shaman was ahead of my time. There might be a notebook or two of his in this house that will be instructive for future shamans."

"Get looking; I already lost both sisters to the Devil. I won't lose my niece too." Both...how could she have lost both to the Devil? He only took my mother, there wasn't another person being held hostage in that house. The screen fizzles. "Trus, what is going on?"

"I don't know."

"Well—" The screen cuts out and Soppy's no longer here. The room's starting to grow cold. It's creeping in, I've no idea what's happening. I'm starting to shiver on an uncontrollable level. Trus and Adelia are feeling the same as me but on a smaller level. They don't feel the cold as much as I do, but they're starting to get goose pimples.

"Adelia, do you feel that?"

"Ja, tycker du att det är ett spöke?"

"What else would it be? Jezebel is on a spirit walk...So, of course, they would be attracted to her."

"Jag gillar inte spöken. Ska vi gå?"

"No, that might make them angry. And we shouldn't leave Jezebel here all alone. If we took her, they would just follow us."

"Okej." She lays back against the sofa and closes her eyes. She holds up her arms in an x position against her chest — to ward off the spirits?

Well, if the spirits are here for me, I might as well get this over with. Maybe they're holding me back; once I'm done talking to them, I can go back into my body. I heard the first noise come from the hall at the back of the living room. I don't want to go that way, but that must be where their presence is strongest. I hear more rustling; the closer I get to the hallway, the more it sounds like someone whispering. When I'm right in the doorway to the hallway, the lights flick on. I hear startled noises coming from the living room.

"De är här. Gudar räddar mig," I hear Adelia exclaim. She sounds very jumpy and scared.

"Don't worry Adelia, they aren't here for us. They only want to talk to Jezebel. It's a spirit walk, spirits are the nice ones — they've already gone through the light and have no unfinished business." Trus isn't doing a convincing job of comforting Adelia, he sounds terrified.

"Hullo, is anybody in there?" I don't enter the hallway just yet. I don't want to talk to anybody. Jez, stop freaking out, you have to get this over with. Shut up, voice in my head! I don't want to do this, my headache's back and there are tears in my eyes. I rustle up my courage and put one foot into the hallway. As soon as I do that, my head starts thundering, and I get this eerie feeling of being watched.

"Hullo?" The cold becomes so bad that the air starts to frost up. On a cold wind comes a smell, it smells just like the perfume bottle that I slammed over the guard's head. "Mum?" I whisper. The door to the living room slams closed behind my back; something touches my arm and pulls me more into the hallway. The lights shut off abruptly. I jump and run. I see a door at the other end of the hallway; before I can go through it, it slams shut in my face and locks.

I'm really scared now. If it's a spirit or my mum, why are they so angry and doing this to me? Maybe it's an evil spirit. I press my back against a wall, close my eyes, and slide down so that I'm sitting on the floor. My heart's about to race out of my chest. I try to slow my breathing and calm down, but I can't. I'm shaking now; I've seen hauntings, but this is worse.

I feel a hand touch my head and pull away swiftly. The eyes watching me seem farther down the hall, closer to the living room. I put my arm out and grasp for something, anything I can use to ward off the spirit. To my left, my hand hits an object, I pull it to me and open my eyes a tiny bit. I close them right back up and throw the bottle, it's my mother's perfume. What's it doing here? I slammed it against that guard's head in my escape from the Devil's house.

I think it's my mum, her perfume's a way to tell me that she's here. Maybe she didn't mean to scare me, maybe being a spirit makes one that way. Well, the only way to find the answer is to stand up and confront her.

I try, but I can't — it's too hard, I'm too terrified. Maybe if she knows that it's me — her daughter — perhaps she'll stop being so scary?

"Mum?"

"It's me, it's Jezebel," I say louder. I wait for a response, anything. I see light through my eyelids. I open my eyes, and the lights have come back on. But that's not all, before my eyes, a translucent shape appears.

"Jezebel?" Her voice sounds like that windy voice that I've been hearing for years, but I stopped hearing it when I escaped the Devil's house. It's just been my voice in my head lately.

I stand up on shaky legs to talk to her. "Mum, why are you doing this?"

"I didn't know who it was, nobody but the Devil can enter the spirit world."

"Why are you here?"

"The light took me, but I wanted to get back to you."

"Why am I here?"

"I don't know."

"Do you need to tell me something?"

"Maybe."

She walks away without her feet touching the ground — is she floating? "Well, what is it?"

She floats back to me in a rush of wind, puts her hand against my head, and pulls my hair up. "How am I to know it is really you?"

"Mum, you're hurting me."

"Answer me!" She's getting mad and I can hear a very loud rumbling.

What do I tell her? What am I to know that the Devil doesn't? I guess that I should speak from my heart and say the first thing that comes into my mind. "Theo's meant to be a great king. I hope The Unknown don't have plans for him as they did for his father," I say in a rush. My head's really starting to send pain throughout my body, making it hard to think.

She lets go of my hair and cups my face in her hands. "It really is you, my little Jezebel." She leans her forehead against mine. For a spirit, she's strangely solid. She holds my face against hers, and we enjoy a mother-daughter moment. We've never had one like this, for the last one, we had fear of the Devil's consequences looming like a shadow over our heads.

After a little while, she pulls away and sits down; I also sit down. She gets a focused and serious look on her face. "We don't have long, I need to tell you the truth."

"Quelle vérité? Je connais déjà beaucoup de grâce au portail."

"I can tell, you speak perfect Sirapian. But this truth has been kept from the gate because of its harm to high-up people. And it would be better if you left all comments and questions for the end — it will go much faster this way."

I close my mouth and silently vow to keep it shut until the end. I'm willing to comply because I'm with my mother, this is one of the best times of my life — it even beats escaping the Devil.

"You must remember what I am about to say, it will help you in the future." Oh, great. My memory sucks, there's no way I'll remember everything that she says. "There are 3 main groups of spies in the spy game: The Red List — Villains and evil people. The Circle — good people and protectors of world leaders (Royals). And The Unknown — so-called that because they are the balance; nobody knows about them, they are to always stay a secret from the other two groups and everyone else. The Circle and The Red List have a sense that there's something out there besides them, but they never find any evidence — they must never find any evidence. The Unknown keep the balance; they make sure that The Red List doesn't wreak too much havoc, and that The Circle doesn't become evil to stop The Red List. The Unknown is supposed to be neither good nor bad, they aren't supposed to take sides, all they used to care about was balance. If it meant fighting The Circle, then they would help The Red List and vice versa. But, my sister, Siria-Mae, was influenced by the Devil and so The Unknown is off course." I know I wasn't supposed to say anything, but I have to get it out before I forget my question.

"Was I in Siria-Mae's house before? I thought I was in Soppy's house — the leader of The Circle — but I got really bad vibes, which made me think she was evil, but then I just saw her on Trus 'laptop and all I got were good vibes."

"I have been following you for a day. After the gate processed you, you were in Siria-Mae's house. But, there you met my other sister, Melina."

"But why did she ask me to call her Soppy? I overheard Gevan — a spy for The Unknown — call his leader Soppy."

She sighs. "It is all very confusing to one so young. I wish I could have been there showing you the ropes. The simplest explanation is that my sisters and I all used the code name Soppy at one time or another. We used to be very close until Siria-Mae changed, at the time we didn't know why — I think that Melina still doesn't know why. I only know because of being tortured by the Devil. Apparently, years ago, Siria-Mae was the Devil's lover and he turned her."

"Oh. I get it, does this mean that Victa's father is the Devil?"

"Yes, now can I get back to telling you the truth?"

Whoops, I'd say sorry, but I don't want to waste any more time. I nod my head for her to continue.

"The Unknown's first headquarters are still used to this day, located in the very first house that ever stood on Baker St — house #42." I already knew that, my father told me to go to that house; from there I figured out the truth. "Siria-Mae, a.k.a. Soppy now leads it, but it was supposed to be me. Our ancestors helped to form it, along with your father, Drew Arch's ancestors. It passes onto the eldest child of both families, I am the eldest and Drew is the only one left of his family—"

"Mum, I have to tell you: Drew's dead." Well, the man that she knew. And who knows what happened to him after the Devil regained consciousness. I can't let her continue to think that he's still alive.

"What? Your father is...is dead?" I can't explain the emotions that I see coming from her, but if she were still alive, I believe that she would've died of heartbreak.

She doesn't say anything for a while, we need to get back to talking. I've no idea how long I can spirit walk without actually dying. I'll be lucky if I can go back into my body — I've been out of it for so long. "I'm sorry about Drew, but can you get back to telling me the truth, s'il vous plaît?"

She pulls herself together and puts a calm mask on. "Time is of the essence. You are the heir to The Unknown, you are the rightful leader of it. You need to know the truth about your late father. He didn't know that he was a part of The Unknown; he thought his whole family was evil and a part of The Red List. They were actually working undercover for The Unknown, they were keeping the balance within The Red List. On your father's selection day, the signs for both The Unknown and The Circle appeared on his forehead. He had no idea what The Unknown's sign meant, so he joined The Circle. Now, back to the spy organizations: The Unknown has been around way before both The Circle and The Red List. There has always been a need for balance, which means there has always been a need for The Unknown. The Red List and The Circle were formed for people's own gain, they never really needed to be formed."

She gets a scattered look about her and stops talking. She looks at me and acts as if she just spotted me; as if she doesn't remember us talking for like an hour. "Hullo, who are you?" She's talking in a kid's voice.

"I'm Jezebel."

"I've never met a Jezebel before. Are you my cousin? You look just like my mother, are you an Atributous?"

"I don't know what that is, I'm sorry."

"It's my family's name — it's our legacy, silly."

"Where are your parents?"

"My Mummy's right there." She points to her right, but she realizes that she doesn't know our surroundings. "Where are we?" She sends a quizzical look my way.

"I don't know either, somebody's huge house. Are your parents here?"

Something dawns on her. "My Mummy just died, she was on a mission and came back in a wheelbarrow." Her eyes start to fill with tears.

"And your father?"

"He left without a word after Siria-Mae was born. My Mummy said that 3 girls and a spy as a wife was too hard a life for him. But I never believed her, my daddy was the best. He loved it when he got to take time off of work to stay home and watch me and Melina when Mummy went on a mission."

I need to distract her, to make her forget her sorrows. "How old are you, sweetie?" What am I doing? A grown woman is a spirit and acting like a child; she's dead, what I'm doing is pointless.

"I just turned 10, Melina is 9, and Siria-Mae is 4. It's almost Siria-Mae's birthday, I don't think we'll be having much of a celebration. As the older sister, it's up to me to take care of them. Grand-Mamma is too busy running The Unknown to focus on us, we have to live with her now that...now that—" She starts to blubber.

I know that she's a ghost and my mother, but I can't just leave her crying; I itch to comfort her. I go over and hug her. "It's ok, you'll be able to handle it." She must be going through her memories, she said she came back from the light to look for me. All of her must be coming back piece by piece. I wish she had stayed in the light, she didn't have to come all the way back and suffer just for me.

She stops crying. "Thank you." She sniffles and disappears. That was very weird — one second I was holding her, and the next, I'm holding nothing but air. The lights in the hallway become brighter, and the doors at either end of the hall unlock and open. A wind tunnel comes through the door to the living room, it's coming right at me. I try to run to the other door, but before I can, it sweeps me up; I see nothing but darkness before losing consciousness.

CHAPTER TWENTY-TWO

Victa

I am awakened by rhythmic movement; I fell asleep on a stationary bench, how am I feeling movement? I open my eyes and have the vantage point of someone being carried. What the heck? I would slam my arms into my captor, but my limbs still have that heaviness of sleep in them.

Whoever is carrying me, carries me through a set of doors and onto a train. I look up at the person — oh, it is the Prince, not a captor.

"O, hullo. Bha mi a 'smaoineachadh gu robh thu fhathast na chadal."

"I am too tired to understand — in the common language — what are you doing?"

"You were sleeping and you just looked so tired. It seemed to be a healing, deep sleep. So, I thought I'd bring you onto the train. I was away for a little while and hadn't been to the gym, so I also thought it'd be a good workout — not that you're heavy, you aren't."

"Thanks for the consideration?" I am still a little weirded out, how did I not notice right away? "Can you please put me down now?"

He stares at me for a little while before my words seem to sink in. "Right, sorry. I got distracted." He sets me down on a seat and remains standing. "So, why are you going to Potter's Town? Not many people know about the renovations and how Riki's is now a nice place to spend the night."

There is no reason to lie to him — nobody here should know what I am talking about, nor will they exploit it. I will just leave out anything to do with espionage. "I am not allowed to go home for a few days."

"Why, did your boyfriend kick you out?"

"No, I do not have a boyfriend."

"You don't?" He gets a hopeful look about him. "Do you want to grab a coffee with me later?"

"Sure, as friends. I am married." I hold up my left hand... which is empty. It usually holds my engagement ring and wedding band, but I took them off for my mission with The Circle — right, the person I am portraying does not have a husband.

"Right. You just don't want to date a Prince." He sighs in a depressed manner and sits down next to me.

"That is so not true. I think that the girl for you is out there, but I seriously am married. His name is Gevan and he is the cutest thing; he makes the best Lamb Salad with Fregola and Braised Leeks with Mozzarella & Fried Egg. I took my rings off because I was cleaning the whole flat — I did not want to lose or mess them up. Then I got locked out of our flat and he will not be back for a few days."

"You don't have a spare key hidden anywhere?"

"Do you?"

"I see your point. But would you really like to be friends?"

"Yes, I would. But first, can you help me find Riki's once we arrive in Potter's Town? I have not been in a while and with the renovations, I might not be able to find it."

"Sure thing. I saw that you also had a book, can I read it?"

"I do not have a book." I look down; somehow I have my purse and a book. What the heck? "Did these just magically appear?"

"No, you had them when you sat down on the bench."

"Huh." I pick up the book and look it over. I do not see a title, but it has a bunch of fairytale characters on the front. I shrug. "Here." I hand Theo the book. "You can keep it."

"Awesome, thanks." He studies the cover; the longer that he looks at it, he acquires a disappointed look. But then the cover comes off and he becomes excited again. "Did you think that this was a fairytale book?"

"Yeah, why?"

"It's not a fairytale book, it's a rare edition of the adventurous short stories of Kevin Mihern — there's only like 3 in existence!"

"That is great." I do not really care. All that I can think about is the fact that I failed my mother and am not allowed on Baker St. I have never let my mother down. I did not even know that the gate could lock residents out — it has never happened to me before. And how did my purse get here? I left it on my mother's table.

What is even in my purse? A stranger must have given it to me, but how could a stranger know the exact purse that I usually use? However it got here, there has got to be something major in it. I need to look very carefully to make sure that nothing bad was placed in it — if a bomb is in it, one does not want to go digging around carelessly.

There is only one object in the purse — not even my wallet? I pull out the object: it is flat and the front mirrors its surroundings. It is not exactly a phone — it is too thin — but it does have a screen and a button. A bomb going off is the only bad thing that could come from me pushing the button. I lift the device to my nose — the gate has made it so that not only dogs can sniff out bombs, humans can too. It took a lot of programming to make the gate only be able to give the scent of a bomb, and not heightened smell — that would make the stinky side of life really bad. It does not have a trace of the chemicals used in the known bombs. If it is not a bomb or a detonator, then what is it?

There seems to be only one way to find out what it is... I must push the button. But what if I am wrong, and it is a detonator or a bomb? I could possibly set off a chain reaction or kill a bunch of people.

It does not have the chemicals, though. I push the button. The screen lights up and a person appears on it. It is a woman that I have never seen before. Her eyes are closed, but I am unsure as to whether she is sleeping or not. I do not want to disturb her, but I want to know what is going on. Before I can say hullo, a hidden compartment comes out that contains headphones — but how? The gadget is too thin to hold a hidden compartment. I put the headphones in my ears and the hidden compartment closes on its own.

The lady opens her eyes and begins to speak. "It is time."

"Hullo?" She does not look directly at me at first, but when I speak, she looks dead center at something — there must be a camera on her end.

"Are you the one called Victa?"

"I am, who are you?"

"It is not important. We are looking for ones to make the world as it should be. We have been studying you for quite some time, and we believe you are just what we are looking for. If you are going to join us, there are certain rules you must follow. Are you ready to listen and accept?"

"Who is we?" One cannot be too cautious. The Unknown is supposed to be the balance, we make the world as it should be. Who is this lady and how psycho is she?

"That is confidential. You will find out once you accept."

"Can I listen to the rules and not accept?"

"That seems fair, but you must not record our conversation or share it with anybody — especially not your mother, Gevan, or anybody a part of The Unknown."

"How—"

"We know all about you. As I have said: we have been studying you for a long time and have done our research. Do you wish to hear me out or not?"

"What is wrong with The Unknown? Do we not put things as they should be?"

"They used to, but recently — cough, your mother, cough

— the system has been corrupted and is no longer about balance. We will right those wrongs, uncorrupt The Unknown, and bring it back to its former glory. We need your help to do so."

"Why me?"

"You are the heir to The Unknown. You can help us from the inside."

"And what if I choose not to help you?"

"All of your memories after the gate rejecting you will be erased; you will eventually be killed once people figure out the truth."

The lady's voice stays the same — no emotion — and she does not appear to blink. Should I trust her? I have been getting some negative vibes lately, and that business with the king proves that The Unknown is doing things that we should not be doing. What harm could come of this? I do not think much could, the world might become worse if The Unknown continues this way.

"Ok, I shall listen."

"You must take a serum that gives the gate false memories; you must never let your guard down nor let your mother or Gevan get suspicious. You must act normal and fake it all. You can only give information that you uncover to your assigned contact—"

"How will I know who my assigned contact is?"

"There will be a meeting place and a code that must be said correctly by them every time. You must always avoid the cameras when on a mission — your mother can not know where you go. You may have to stay for long periods of time away from your family, sell it nicely, and make it believable — your mother will know right away what's going on if it's not believable. And when all is said and done, you must go through tests to ensure that you have not been corrupted through the many trials and missions of un-corrupting The Unknown."

The rules seem pretty reasonable for un-corrupting The Unknown. I **do** want it to be good, like when my great-grandmother ran it. If I agree and un-corrupt The Unknown, there will be no more unnecessary killings in cold blood, we will take no more sides, and officially be the balance again. It sounds too good to be true.

"Did you ever say what the code was?"

"No, I don't believe so."

"Is that the code?"

"No." It is though because she is nodding her head.

"What is the catch?"

"Except for the trials and tests at the end, there is none."

That is not bad for something that sounds too good to be true. "Are you recruiting others?"

"That's confidential." So they are. Will I ever meet the others? They might be my assigned contact. I think that I am willing to accept. I will fail my mother even more, but I will be proud of myself because I will have put the world back as it should be.

"I accept. When does my mission start?"

"You will be informed at Riki's in Potter's Town. For now, fulfill your duty to The Circle and make sure that Prince Theo isn't harmed or killed."

"I will."

She blinks and the screen goes black. That was really weird. In all of my 22 years of life, I have never had anything like that happen to me. Who is this group? Is that lady really not a psycho? I have not fully made up my mind about the organization; once I get my mission and information from them, then I will make my final choice.

When I come back to the world around me, nobody has changed or experienced something weird like I just did. I take the headphones out of my ears, put them back in the hidden compartment, and put the device back into my purse. Theo is deep into his book. As I go to ask him how much longer, he slams the book shut and looks at me. "Done."

"You are done with the whole book?"

"Yeah, it was an easy read."

"It looks like there are 400 pages."

"They're all short stories: fast to read quick-paced adventures. Also, I found this in the pages." He hands me a bookmark. The bookmark has a name on it — Jezebel. Who is Jezebel, is that who the book belongs to? I have never met anybody named Jezebel; it does not sound like a common name.

"Thanks. So, how much longer until we get to Potter's Town?"

"We're about there." He checks his watch. "The train has been going for about 30 minutes, trains don't take much longer than that. Also if you look around, everybody else is waking up from dozing."

I do look around. The first time I looked, I thought that they had not changed from when we got on…but they must have taken a nap because most of them look tired and are wiping the sleep out of their eyes. The train's conductor comes into the car. "Almost to Potter's Town everyone, look alive. It is our last stop, so all of you must get off."

A young man stands up and puts up an argument. "I thought this train doubled back to Musalin Centre. I've been on since the last stop, the directory said that it doubled back."

"Well, we don't."

"I ride this train a lot, you don't look familiar and I know for sure that it doubles back to its starting point at this time of day."

"I…uh."

"**You** get off this train, I don't even think that you are the real conductor." He looks around for backup but nobody else cares, they just want to get off at Potter's Town and go home.

"Guys, you ride every day also; you know he's not the conductor." They all seem not to hear him.

I turn to Theo. "Theo, do you—" Theo seems frozen with one arm still outstretched to give me the bookmark and the other checking the time. I try to knock some sense back into him; no matter what I do, he stays stuck. I look closer at everyone else on the train, they are stuck in their last movement positions too. The only 3 who are not affected are the young man, the conductor, and I.

"I've had enough of this. Come with me, young man." The conductor grabs the young man by his collar and drags him off. As they leave, everyone becomes unstuck.

Theo catches sight of the young man before he disappears. "Bryce? Wait, conductor, what's happening?" Theo tries to go after the conductor and the young man but the door shuts behind the 2 and Theo is unable to open it. I go over to him and put my weight into helping him, but neither of us can get it to budge. I stop trying to open it — it is not going to open until the train stops. Theo keeps at it, he seems to be losing energy, yet does not stop. I put my hand on his arm, "It is no use; leave it, Theo."

"But, he...I can't just..." Theo seems at a loss for words.

"We still have a few minutes until we arrive, how about we sit down and you tell me why that bothered you so." I gently lead him back to our seats and we both sit back down.

"So, who was that?"

"Bryce."

"Who is Bryce?"

"He's my only friend and somewhat of a bodyguard. He always has my back. I thought he went to sleep; apparently, he didn't, and ended up on the train with me."

"Why were you frozen in time?"

"I wasn't."

"Yeah, you were. You gave me the bookmark and told me that everyone was waking up, then you got stuck and a whole scene happened with you just sitting there, not being fazed by anything."

"Oh, I don't remember that. All I know is I was talking to you one second and then the conductor was here dragging Bryce off of the train."

At that exact moment, a voice comes on over the speakers. "We are approaching Potter's Town station. Everybody getting off at Potter's Town, grab your belongings, and prepare to get off. Everyone else, our next stop is the Brocha platform, and then it's back to Musalin Centre." How come this voice says the exact opposite as the conductor? Maybe the young man was right and that guy was not the conductor.

"Theo, did the conductor ever come by?"

"Yeah, when you were wrapped up in your phone. I showed him your ticket and he passed on to the next car. Is that a new version of the Dickery phone? I know that they are coming out with a new one, but it's not out to the public yet. I really want it, it supposedly has a function where it donates to charity with every 1000 steps that it tracks. Do you know someone on the team who gave you a prototype to try out? How much do they give for every thousandth step?"

I should not have let him see the device, it needs to stay secret — I need to think of something fast to distract him. "No, it is not the Dickery V6, it is my music player. What is your favorite band? I prefer EcI9."

"They're good. But I'm not into country rock; I like pop. I don't have a favorite band, but I do have a few favorite singers: Eramotla Ytsirhc, Dirgis, Yer Led Anal, Nareehs De, and Notlob Nhoj. I can never decide between them, all of their voices are just so good; each one has their own unique sound. Do you have— Hey! That's not nice; you are distracting me, what really is that device? I'm interested in how different technological devices work and have studied them all, so I know it's not a music player."

"All right. It is a new prototype from a home security business, but do not tell anybody."

"Ok." He does not look convinced. "Why can't anybody know what it really is?"

"Because if thieves and robbers got ahold of it, there would be no houses that they could not get into. The criminals would be on top; that is not a world that I want to live in, do you?"

"No, I don't." He face lights up with excitement. "I'll keep it a secret, my lips are sealed."

"Thank you." The train slows down and comes to a stop.

"Looks like we have arrived."

"Yep, looks like it." Now, all we have is awkwardness. I should have waited to use the device once I got to my room at Riki's. But I did not know whether it controlled a bomb or not, I wanted to get it over with right away. Oh, this must be why I am not usually assigned big, important missions: I am too impatient. Yeah, that is not a good quality for a spy.

We stand up, go to the door, and wait for it to open. A few moments after the train comes to a complete stop, the doors slide open. I let Theo go out before me — he is the one who knows how to get to Riki's from here, I am not sure if I have ever used the train to get to Potter's Town. He takes the lead and I follow him up just 1 small set of stairs — Musalin Centre must be higher above ground than Potter's Town. He stops me before we are outside and turns around to talk to me.

"When we get outside, you have to be alert at all times — construction is not going as great as I planned and things might be unstable and fall onto your head. Also, you are going to have to walk fast and avoid obstacles on the road."

"I can do both of those things, but why do we have to walk fast?"

"Even though it is becoming a nicer district, beasts — both animal and human — still roam the streets."

"All right, shall we go? I have somewhere to be at a certain time."

"No, we can't."

"Why not?"

"We have to give our tickets to the people who run this station. If we still have them, they will think that we will use them many times and not pay. There's no way to tell if they have been used, they are not specific to times."

"I do not remember there being so many rules."

"People had begun to take advantage, I applied the rules and now the train stations have more money to employ tons of people. That means fewer homeless people — with jobs comes the ability to pay for places to live and food to eat. That's my goal with all of these renovations: to make Musalin great."

"That sounds naive. No region as big as Musalin will ever be perfect with zero problems; there is no such thing as that in the world. It is the nature of people that makes it impossible." Like with my mother. There are plenty of houses on Baker St. that are in disrepair and empty, yet she forbids anybody who is not a spy or related to one from living there. She also never lets us donate to charity — our accounts are full enough to support at least a thousand orphans for their whole lives.

"Come on, the checkout station is right before the door. Also, keep your head down — you have the look of a pampered rich person who has never worked. You will be a big target for pickpockets." And he does not? I worked in the streets for years during my initiation process.

We walk the rest of the way to the doors; a man at a desk takes our tickets, punches a hole into both, then hands them back to us. As we are leaving the station, there is a question that I just have to ask Theo. "Why did he punch a hole in our tickets and give them back to us?"

"I don't want to make people angry; if you use the trains twenty times and have the tickets to prove it, you get 3 days' worth of free rides to your destination."

"That is smart." No, it is not, he should have just made tickets that show times, dates, and people's names — people can still cheat the system by stealing those tickets or forging them.

We finally exit the building and are on Stanton St. — it looks completely different, there are actual paved roads. Stanton St. used to be a dirt path with human waste and rubbish piling up on either side. Also, there were no buildings except for the train station, you used to have to walk for three blocks before coming upon houses and businesses. There is no more rubbish; cafés and restaurants line one side of the street, while houses and shops line the other. I would love to live here. Maybe Gevan and I can buy a house and make it a home for some of the homeless children that we find, each one of them will either have their own room or share with another kid.

"Catch up." Theo continued walking while I stopped, stuck in my head.

"Sorry." I rush to catch up with him. We do not talk much on the way to the hostel. Theo was right though, I hear many noises coming from the alleys. I walk with my head up until a strange man with haunted eyes looks at me — that is enough to convince me to walk with my head down. I only look back up when we reach a street that is less dark and gloomy, the light from the sun shines brightly down and is reflected by all of the windows of the shops. But the most beautiful building on the street is what used to be a run-down hostel. Riki's looks like it came right out of ancient mythology, with its pillars and architectural design of stone.

"Breathtaking, isn't it? I made sure that only stones mined in Musalin were used; I tried to make them different types, but have them complement each other."

"It is marvelous."

"I used my mythology books as examples. I just love the way that the ancients saw architecture."

We go through the doors and the inside looks as different as the outside does, it does not just have a little bit of class, it is all class now. Riki is a very classy guy — just because he had a run-down place, did not mean that he wanted it to look like a complete dump.

"Did you give Riki full reign of the design?"

"I wouldn't wish for it to be any other way. You'd think that it would be too much class, that it would be overdone—"

"But it is perfect."

"You took the words right out of my mouth." I smile, he is going to make a great king. He is almost of age, the ruler has their coronation 6 months after their 19th birthday. I shake my head to clear the wonderments of the new hostel — I have places to be.

The desk is halfway into the building, I go to it and the man behind it looks familiar. Surprisingly, there is no line, so I go right in front of the man and ring the bell.

"Hullo, how's it going?" When he looks up, his face becomes full of shock and then changes to excitement. "Victorina, E don te. How una dey?" I forgot that most people in Potter's Town speak broken common language.

I am a little rusty, so here goes nothing. "Fire?" Did that sound as bad as I think it did?

He clears his throat. "You not good at pidgin. Me let try yours. I practising. Good see Victorina. How you?"

"I am doing well; you have improved greatly in your common language."

"I've been teaching him." Theo comes to the desk and holds out his hand to Riki.

"267. Clean." Riki hands Theo a room key.

"Later, Victorina — cool name by the way."

I nod my head to Theo and go back to my conversation with Riki. "Your place looks amazing."

"I thank Prince, he me a chance."

"Are there any rooms left or have they all been taken?"

"Few take. No people come, P-Town still renovate."

"After renovations, hopefully. It will compliment your place and look just as beautiful."

"Thank. Here room. Best fo 'Victorina." He hands me a key that says room three hundred.

"How many floors are there now? I only remember there being a hundred rooms."

"400 room, 12 floor, 33 room each floor, this floor has 4 room."

"Oh, so this is the ground floor?" Why am I still talking to him? I have important things to attend to, I need to meet Iris and then start my mission for The Circle.

"Ye."

"It was nice catching up with you, bye."

"Be."

I go in the direction that I saw Theo go in. He entered a hallway and at the end of it, I find a set of stairs. Do I seriously have to walk up more than six sets of stairs? I am really tired; the clock on the wall says that it is sixteen-twenty, which means I should be able to catch a few hours of sleep before I have to meet up with Iris.

There is no point in complaining, just think of it as a good workout. I push open the door and get started on the stairs.

At the door to the fourth floor, I look up and all I see are endless stairs. Next to each door, it states the range of room numbers, I compare it with my room key. The range is one-hundred and four to one-hundred thirty-six. My key says three hundred — many more stairs to go. I walk up four more levels; I guess at every four levels, I will take a break.

The eighth floor only goes up to room two-hundred sixty-eight, I still have forty-two more rooms to go, maybe it is on the tenth floor? I hope that it is as good as Riki says — otherwise, all of these stairs are not worth it.

Finally, I made it to the tenth floor! Wait, what is the range for this floor? It starts at room three-hundred and two? What! But I counted how many rooms were left? What number did I count? So the eighth floor ended at two-hundred sixty-eight, which leaves only thirty-two more rooms to go; my room is on the ninth floor?! I got As in maths, wow, I must be really tired if I screwed up a simple subtraction.

I guess it is back down the set of stairs that I just came up. The door to the ninth floor is just a regular hotel door — I guess it is a hotel now and no longer a hostel. The hallway looks endless from this vantage point; the first room on my left is two-hundred sixty-nine and the room on my right is two-hundred seventy. My room will be all the way at the end of the hall, on the right.

After all of my troubles, I arrive at my door very sweaty and overheated — I feel so overheated that I could throw up. Hopefully, my room has air con. The lock is not a key lock, even though my key is an actual key; the lock has to do with numbers. Is nothing going right? What else could go wrong? First my mother, all those stairs, and now a lock that has nothing to do with my key.

Oh, wait. The key has numbers on the bow. There are six numbers on my key and the lock needs six numbers, except the numbers on the key are backward. My eyes are barely staying open, I am sick of dealing with all of this, maybe I will just sleep in the hallway. My eyes close for a brief second and I shake my head to open them back up. I realize my mistake and turn the key over. I type in the no-longer-backward-numbers and the door unlocks. I go in and the door closes behind me. I enter a little hallway and that is as far as I get before my knees buckle and my legs fall out from under me. I do not feel pain as I hit the ground because my eyes close and I am fast asleep before the pain hits.

...

I wake up what seems like only minutes later, but the clock in the hallway tells a different story. It is 3pm. I do not know why that seems bad — if I was tired, I slept until I was no longer. But then the fog of sleep leaves my mind and I start freaking out. I was supposed to meet Iris yesterday! I cannot get the underground train — it would take too long. The best course of action is to run all through Potter's Town and get a taxi from Sweets Corner. No taxi would dare to enter Potter's Town before the renovations, they would only go as far as Sweets Corner — I think that the same goes with renovations, it is even riskier with all of the construction materials and unstable buildings.

I arrive at the corner at 15:30. There is no way Iris is still there, hopefully, she left a way to contact her with the chef. There are people in a crowd and many taxis; none of the people are trying to get a taxi, instead, they are surrounding something. I go closer to see what they are surrounding, but I still cannot see because there are so many people. There is a lady at the back who does not look as focused on the thing ahead as the rest. "Excuse me," I tap her on the shoulder, "What is everybody trying to see?"

"The Royals are setting up a concert to make everybody excited for an announcement that will be played on the signs this evening. Everybody wants a good spot."

"Who is playing?"

"Nareehs De was originally the only one to play, EcI9 was added to the set last minute."

"Thanks." Theo must have added EcI9 just for me. He did say that he wanted to grab a coffee; walking by Sweets Corner with our coffees and hearing EcI9 must be his way of thinking that I will automatically be his friend. We hear my favorite band and bam: it is fate. But it is our friendship that would start, not our romantic relationship — he knows that I have Gevan. I wish that I could stay here and wait for EcI9 to come on, but I have work to do.

I force my legs to the end of the sidewalk and force my hand to hail a taxi. One comes over not long after I start hailing. I get into the back of it. "Town Centre please." The driver turns the radio up and starts in the direction of the center of town.

I have paid the driver and am on my way to Krystal Café by four o'clock. I hope there is a way to find Iris. Please Gods. I cannot fail my mother anymore, this one time is too much for me.

In no time at all, I am outside the door to Krystal Café and go inside. There are fewer people than there were yesterday.

The booth that I always sit at — the one where Iris and I agreed to meet — is empty. I go and sit down. A waiter comes over and asks if I want to order anything. "Can I speak to the chef?"

"Oui, Madame. Elle est dans la cuisine."

"I am just allowed to go back there?"

"Elle t'attend." How did she know that I was coming?

"Merci." I get up, head to the kitchen, open the door, and enter the kitchen. It is not as impressive as the one back home, but it is pretty big.

"Jimmy, l'ordre du tableau cinq est prêt."

"It is not Jimmy. I heard you were expecting me?"

She turns around; once she spots me, she stops what she is doing. "Victa, darling, I was expecting you." She has a very thick Sirapian accent.

"I am sorry, but do I know you?"

She pushes a button on the wall before answering. "No, I don't believe so. But I know you."

"How?"

"What j'ai juste dit. Did tu écoutes?"

Oh! She just said the code word that the lady from the device gave me. "What happens now?"

"You are to come here every week for a complimentary meal — your husband set it up." She emphasized "every week" and "husband": a good spy meets with a handler and reports, and I am not supposed to tell Gevan anything.

"Was there a girl here? She has long black hair—"

"The girl that was here with you yesterday?"

"Yeah, have you seen her?"

"No." I sigh with exasperation. If she did not come back, then how am I going to find her? I have nothing in which to utilize in tracking her; I do not even know if her real name is Iris. And my mother has all of her documents. "But I did put a tracking device in her food yesterday — I put it in her Crème Brûlée." Awesome! "She did not swallow it, though." Crap. "And then I put it on her dress, a little bit was peaking out of her coat." She is really bad at getting to the point.

"You know, you could have gotten that out faster and better."

"I know, I just loved the look on your face as it changed from one emotion to the next rapidly." Her laughter is as grating as nails on chalkboard. I am just going to let her have this moment, I will wipe that smile off of her face with all of the intel that I give her.

"Is that all? Can I go now?" She stops laughing.

"Oui, you are dismissed."

I leave the kitchen and the café. I can get breakfast at a better place, one that does not have a rude lady who I now have to work with. I have no idea why Iris never showed up, she seemed like the kind of person to stick to her word.

I hear a buzzing noise come from my purse, I get the

gadget out and press the button. The headphones compartment pops out, I put them in and the screen starts up. The screen is divided into many parts: one is a live feed, one a map with a dot, and tons of other stuff that I do not care about. It looks like Iris is still in Musalin, but she is in an unmarked portion of it. That is where I am headed then, I hope that Gevan does not become too worried.

What about my mission for The Circle? I almost forgot about that. I will have to put finding Iris on the back burner — my mission for The Circle comes first. I can do the mission without both my mother's help and the use of Baker St. What I first need to do is some research at the local library. I go to the main street to hail a taxi. A taxi comes right over and I jump in. "Library, please." I close the door to the outside world.

CHAPTER TWENTY-THREE

Jezebel

The first thing that I smell as soon as the blackness starts fading away, is something burning. "Gå bort spöken. Vi välkomnar dig inte. Gå bort spöken. Du är inte välkommen här." At first, I thought I was hearing someone breathing or some other sort of noise; but as the blackness fades, it becomes clear that someone is chanting. It's Adelia, she just keeps repeating the same phrases over and over and the smoke smell becomes stronger and thicker with every phrase.

I can't breathe due to all of the smoke, I start to choke and lift my hand to wipe it away from me. My other hand goes to cover my mouth so that I don't cough on anything or anyone.

"She's awake. It's a miracle! I was afraid that you had died. I knew that you might have been on a spirit walk, but it's so rare that I just couldn't fully give hope to that being the case." I haven't opened my eyes yet, so I can't see how he looks. But with the way his voice sounds, Trus must be very worried.

"What happened?"

"Did you talk to spirits?"

"My mother...I saw my mother."

I hear a snap of fingers. "I should have known it was her. She had information that she was never able to tell you due to the circumstances of your birth and growing up in the Devil's house."

This whole time, Adelia has been mumbling "Gå bort spöken. Vi välkomnar dig inte. Gå bort spöken. Du är inte välkommen här." Over and over.

"Adelia, you can stop now. The spirits are gone; Jezebel is back from her spirit walk. It's all good."

I finally open my eyes. If I'm not willing to see the sight that my "back from the dead" act will bring, then I won't be able to complete my mission: Get rid of my mum's sister, make The Unknown the balance again, and live a normal life.

"What's all of this smoke?"

"It's sage. A superstition is that if you burn sage, you can ward off the spirits."

"What happened while I was out?"

"We drove for many hours to get here and then all of our devices wouldn't work once the spirits came. So I've been sitting in the freezing cold waiting for you to wake up; while Adelia has been freaking out. Only a few minutes ago did she decide to burn sage."

"Exactly how long have I been out?"

"About 12 hours — hey, you're speaking the common language, why are you talking in that all of a sudden?"

"Before I knew that I was on a spirit walk, I decided that I'd cooperate with you and only speak Sirapian in public."

"You do realize that the Devil can't track you by your Brilla accent?"

"Why's that?"

"You don't have a Brilla accent; you sound as if you were born and raised in Musalin."

"That's awesome! But I'd feel more comfortable speaking Sirapian."

"Let's wait to decide anything until after we get your mission from Soppy."

"I know that she's not the real Soppy, my a— my mum was. So what's her real name?" I know that it's Melina, but I can't seem to have gotten confidential information from out of thin air. How could my mother speak to me and tell me everything? They barely believe that I was actually on a spirit walk.

"Not many people call her it for protection, but it's Melina

Atributous. She's your aunt, Linris 'sister. Ever since I told her about you, she's been really happy. For a while, she was sad because she had no idea what happened to Linris. Then she found out and became even sadder knowing she'd never see Linris again. But her spirits soared when she heard about you."

"Why did you have your laptop running?"

"I was setting up Facerina before my laptop crashed — it's how most of our missions are given to us. Most agents are in other countries or just unable to meet on Baker St. Facerina is a secure network where Melina gives us our assignments directly, without any letters that could be intercepted by The Red List."

"So the bad guys are The Red List?"

"Yeah."

"Why?"

"Well, they..." He racks his brain for the answer. "I don't really know, it's always been this way: The Red List doing bad things and being the villains, while The Circle opposes them."

"What if what they do is actually good and not bad?"

"All they ever do is bad stuff."

"What if it's good for the future but just seems bad?"

His computer clicks, "Oh, look. Our connection is back. Soppy's going to want to talk to you in private."

Humph, saved by the click. He's going to have to give me an answer later, he can't just say "because that's how it is". There has to be a reason why they act the way that they do.

Maybe The Circle and The Red List used to be a part of The Unknown. What if the person who started The Circle didn't want to be the balance of good and evil, they just wanted to be good; they went out on their own and created The Circle.

And another person who was a part of The Unknown had an evil mind and had been kicked out. Then, they had vengeance and hatred on their mind, so they started The Red List. But that idea won't help me with my point of The Red List doing more than just bad things. Maybe there's no answer except for what my mother said: they were both created for personal gain.

"Hullo, Trus? Is it working now?"

"Yes, lady. Jezebel isn't dead; she would like to talk to you."

"Good, put her on."

"Come here." Trus motions me over, pulls out a stool, and places it in front of the laptop. "Adelia, let's give them some privacy." He pulls the still-shaking Adelia with him into a different hallway off of the living room.

I'm not sure if I'm ready to face Melina. I just spoke to my mother's spirit, you could say that I'm a little shaken up; speaking to Melina will be even more upsetting. I don't know her, she doesn't know me, the only connection that we have is my dead mother. As yesterday's events have shown me, I'm not yet ready to enter the world.

Best to just get it over with Jez. You won't be as sick to your stomach if you worry less and are done with it. Sometimes I hate that voice in my head. Worrying is safe and comfortable, it means stalling and not facing my fears. But the voice does have a point — it's always right.

I take a shaky breath and go into the eyesight of the laptop. Once Melina has a full look at me, her sadness comes in full force. She gasps and covers her mouth with her hand while her eyes fill with tears. "My darling, I can't believe that you are alive." I don't move any closer; she's a stranger whom I want nothing to do with. "Jezebel Iris Arch, your father did say that you are so much like your mother. A fighter's spirit. If only she could see you today, all she ever would've wanted for you was a normal life — your escape from the Devil brought just that. You don't have to look so scared or be so shy, I'm your aunt. I don't want to hurt you, I just want to help you figure out what you want to do with your newfound freedom."

"Comment allez-vous m'aider?" I've reverted back to my comfort language. I guess for someone who went through all that I did, I'm still a frightened 18-year-old who's way out of her comfort zone.

"Are you only trained in Sirapian? Well, that's not a problem, I understand it perfectly. I even went to university in Sirap. I can help you with all manners of things. Why don't you sit down so that we can talk easier?"

I don't really want to, I'm fine where I am. But I don't want to be rude — she asked politely. And she kind of didn't give me a choice without seeming very rude and mean. I sit down with the feeling of resignation heavy in my gut.

"That's better, now I can see you more clearly. You are the cutest thing, you look exactly like Linris and Arch. You are even staring at the screen while clenching your hands — that was always a sign that Linris was nervous and just wanted to get something over with. I remember one time, when she was meeting with our grandmother, she made Linris sit out in the hall for hours. Linris was so scared about what would happen, she had no idea why our grandmother wanted to meet with her. Linris sat in that hallway, staring at the door to our grandmother's office for hours, clenching her hands all the while. It turned out she just had to talk with Linris about her grades in school — which were excellent — she wanted to have Linris celebrate, but she forgot about Linris and got lost in a stack of paperwork."

"Um. Pouvons-nous arriver à la partie où vous m'aidez? Désolé, pas de manque de respect voulu." I say with a waiver in my voice. She's just my aunt, why are all of my words coming out like this? Why does she affect me so?

"You don't have to apologize, my dear. The day is new and you probably want to have fun; I won't hold you for long. The only way I can help you is if you help me. The Circle's rules don't allow me to do so otherwise. I have a mission that needs to be done — but only if you are willing."

I clear my throat, I need to speak the common language. If I can't speak it with my own aunt, I won't get very far in this world. "I'm willing, what's the mission?"

"As you know by now, The Circle mainly protects members of the royal family or people of importance. Well, ever since the king was killed and the Devil stole your mother, we could never find a good replacement to take care of the Prince."

"What about his current protector?"

"He's good at it, but his heart's not in it. He desires to protect the palace and I believe that that is what he was made to do. But we can't just leave the Prince with no one to protect him."

"What do you wish of me?"

"I would like you to become a regular about the palace and get Theo to trust you. If he likes you, we can eventually replace Bryce with you."

"That's all?"

"It's a lot to ask because it's kind of a job for life."

"But I still get to have a normal life, right?"

"Yeah."

"I'll do it." I've no hesitation. My new rule is a normal life no matter what. It may seem dumb, but all I dream about/want is a normal life. People do what it takes to achieve their dreams; I'll do whatever it takes to have a normal life.

"Good. You start on Monday."

"What day's today?"

"Today is Saturday."

"Will I need to be prepared a certain way for Monday?"

"I was just about to get there. Yes, you will need to be given a complete makeover because Theo has probably seen what you look like, right?" I nod my head. "You will have all new papers and a brand new identity. You will get to choose your name and everything. I will send my best team over right away. I look forward to your reports. Every day you will meet with Trus and when he deems it proper, you will meet with me. Do you have any questions?"

I'd ask her about Siria-Mae, but my mother told me enough for now and I don't want Melina to get suspicious about me. Besides, I met her at Siria-Mae's house; what if Siria-Mae has turned her to her side and she'll destroy anybody who opposes Siria-Mae — even me, her niece?

"No. I can't wait to start working for The Circle, I believe in your guys 'cause. Thank you for allowing me in. Have a nice day."

I go to shut off the program but she stops me before I

finish, "Can I speak to Trus?"

"Sure." I get up and go in the same direction that Trus and Adelia went in. There's no door in this hallway — I prefer this hall, you can't get trapped with scary spirits. A few rooms are leading off of the hallway but they don't have doors and all seem to have tons of light streaming in. I hear voices coming from the room at the end. The room at the end's a gigantic kitchen.

Adelia's sitting on a bar stool at the counter eating something while Trus is preparing food. They appear at ease and are chatting carelessly. I hate to break this up, but I want to get all of this over with and get on with my normal life.

I clear my throat before speaking, "Hullo."

They both turn to look at me, Adelia keeps eating. "How did it go? I'm making a snack, I hope that you like celery and peanut butter."

"Soppy wants to talk to you." Don't say anything else, don't make it personal. I don't want/need friends; I need to get this over with and get a normal life going so that I can have fewer worries about the Devil finding me.

"Ok." On his way out, Trus hands me a plate with green things on it — celery — and a brown thing in the middle of it — peanut butter.

I take the plate and sit on a stool a little ways away from Adelia. She's staring at me but still eating. "Hullo." Should I be polite? Should I just stare back at her? I don't know what it's like to actually have a normal conversation with someone. "So… do you like Musalin? This house is in a breathless location and I can't think of anything more beautiful." Just because I said that it's not personal doesn't mean that I can't discuss things that could help me with my mission to pass the time.

She stops staring at me but takes a few seconds to answer me. "It is very beautiful. One of the best sights in all of Musalin." So she does speak the common language, I didn't think that she did. She actually has little to no accent, but it doesn't seem like the common language is her native tongue.

"Are you from Musalin?" She ignores my question and

pulls something out of her pocket. She unwraps headphones from around it and pops them into her ears — it must be her phone; sheesh that's kind of rude. She doesn't even want to talk to me? Why not? She could of at least told me that she wanted to listen to music, instead of ignoring me.

I get it though, I mean who'd want to hang out with the girl that spirits are drawn to? I wouldn't want to hang out with a person like me if I were her — what if the spirits then started following me around?

I could bring about bad luck to anyone who talks to me; spirits are never considered good luck. And she's pretty superstitious, which makes her frightened of spirits, so it makes sense that she doesn't want to talk to me. What if I'm not even a person?! Who knows, I could just be a physical spirit. "Am I real?" I look down at my hands and pinch my arm — is that just supposed to wake you up from a dream, or does it indicate if you're a real person?

"Of course you are real." I didn't hear Trus come down the hall. Startled, I look up at him, he's leaning against the door frame with a tired look on his face. He sighs and comes fully into the room. "Don't mind Adelia, she's not really a people person."

"What's her deal?"

"It's not my right to say. The team that Soppy sent is almost here." As soon as he finishes speaking, the doorbell rings. He grabs an apple off of the counter and goes to answer the door.

Within minutes, there are people everywhere and no empty space. Things are set on all of the counters, racks, and stands are set up on the floor, and every station comes with at least 2 people.

So many people, too many. The walls are closing in and my vision becomes cloudy — what... is... happening? Is this house booby-trapped?! Are we all going to die?! My breathing's starting to escalate and all I can do is fall into a huge freakout.

"Jez...ok? Come...you...need." Trus 'face is swimming in my vision, his words fade in and out. He pulls me out of the kitchen and through a door at the back of the house.

The door closes behind us; my vision's too blurry for me to notice our new surroundings — good way to be vulnerable. There's nothing wrong with the house, the problem's with me. Now they won't want me to be a spy, spies can't get vulnerable and have such a huge freakout amid tons of people. My stomach's in knots and I feel just so sick and miserable. Why's my life so horrid? Why's everything — even my mind — out to get me? Why me?!

Stop freaking out. You didn't escape the Devil just to lose your sanity. It's fine, you're fine, everything's fine.

I actually didn't need that calming voice in my head to speak. With fewer people and commotion, it's getting easier to breathe and my vision's clearing up.

Once everything's back to normal, I look up — I can't let myself continue to be vulnerable, I need to know my surroundings. Trus is standing patiently in front of me, but behind him's a sight I've never seen before. The house's garden is as beautiful as the front, except it's all man-made beauty, not nature's. There's a lot of fine, awesome-looking furniture and tons of fake rock piles; the most impressive piece is the giant waterfall running from the top of the rocks into a pool. Ok, identification of surroundings — check — now back to the problem at hand: me.

"What's wrong with me?" Wow, my throat's really dry — is there anything I could drink?

"Nothing's wrong with you—"

"Th..." I clear my throat. "Then what just happened?"

"You had a panic attack, it's normal when one is so overwhelmed and in uncontrollable, unfamiliar surroundings. Have you ever had one before?"

"No, I don't believe so." But then again, I have a bad memory. Also, I don't believe that I've ever been around so many people in that sized space before.

"Ok." He seems to be thinking something through. Trus has a very unique deep thinking face. "Why don't you wait out here and I'll call you in when it's time."

"Thank you." Trus is the nicest guy I've ever met. I wish he had been my father, he would never have let me and my mother get taken by the Devil. Also, the gate only has good intel on Trus; he has never killed a person for a mission — almost all of the spies have.

Trus goes back inside and I have no idea what to do. What do normal people do? What do they do in a garden like this? My life since escaping the Devil has had a purpose; every second I had something to focus on. Now I've nothing to do. Hours always ticked by at the Devil's because I was either sleeping, cooking, or reading. There's a pool and waterfall, but I don't have a swimsuit. I really want a drink, maybe there's something around here that holds one.

All I see are chairs, sofas, and tables, but maybe there's more than meets the eye. Aha, I was right! Underneath one of the tables is a little cooler — it must have a drink in it. I go to the table, kneel down, and attempt to pull the lid off of the cooler. But the lid won't budge, it seems to be stuck to something. Maybe if I lift it off of the ground, it'll open. Ok.

I can't even lift it off of the ground! What the heck?! Why is this thing so heavy, and why does it seem to be anchored to the ground?

I just want some water! I'll not let a cooler beat me! I reposition myself so that all of my weight can be put into lifting it. I grip the cooler as tight as I possibly can and count to 3. On 3, I pull the cooler up — it doesn't go far, but it budges a tad. I hear a crunch and feel a resistance on the bottom of the cooler. There's also a different sound in the air — it seems to be coming from my right.

I look up. The waterfall has stopped running. And behind where the water once flowed, the rock is sliding and a sort of door is forming. What the? Should I investigate or should I stay out here and out of trouble?

Jezebel, you're about to enter a cave of secrets! Merci, voice in my head. I get up and go to the bottom of the waterfall. I look up at where the door opened. Ok, so how do I get up there? I guess there must be a ladder or steps? Wait! Are those...I back up to get a look at the bigger picture...There are footholds!

So I just need to climb up the rocks. I look up at the door, it's still opening. When the door opens all the way, will it close back up? If that happens, I need to move fast. I've never rock climbed, but how hard can it be? I put my foot in the first hole and grip the one over my head with my hand. I start a pattern of lifting up one leg, putting it in a hole above me, and then gripping another further up with a hand.

The answer: very hard. My arms are shaking and I'm having a hard time going further up the waterfall. I'm taking a moment to breathe; if I were to look down, I'd probably only be halfway up — if I'm lucky.

You know what, no. No stopping, no breaks. I either go up the rest of the way as hard and fast as I can or I give up and go back to the Devil. There's no whining in the real world, only hard work and pushing yourself past the limits. If I can't climb a freaking waterfall/rock wall, then I can't be a spy or do anything that would've made my parents proud.

I take a deep breath in, start going up the rest of the way with gusto, and arrive at the platform as the door starts to close. Even though my legs are shaking really bad — if I move them even the slightest bit, they'll break — I jump through the door really fast. As if sensing motion, the door whips shut and I would've been crushed by it had I not jumped.

The door opening must've offered the only light in this place; I couldn't even see my own hand if it were right in front of my face. I'm not afraid of the dark; when the Devil got really mad at me, he'd lock me in a very small broom closet — that's why I got so worked up when I thought the walls were closing in, I don't do well in small spaces.

I'm crouching on the floor, whimpering for the door to be opened. I'm trying to see light under the door, but there isn't a crack — if there's space between the door and the floor, something's shoved in between. I'm scratching at the door, begging silently to be released. "I didn't mean it," goes miserably through my head in a silent and sullen voice every second. I've been screaming silently in my head for hours. Time doesn't fly in this closet.

Stop it! Snap out of it! You aren't trapped in the closet, it's just pitch black. There should be a light switch near the door. I feel around for it; my hand touches an oddly shaped button. I try pushing it into the wall, but it doesn't do anything. Maybe it's a twist one, I try twisting it. Nothing happens. What is it if not a light switch?

I walk further into the room with my hands out in front of me. After a few steps, the lights turn on all of a sudden. What the heck? My heart's nearly beating out of my chest. As my eyes adjust to the light, I get a good glimpse of the room. There are a few chairs in the middle, but what catches my eye is to my right. It's a console of some sort. Above it is what I was touching: a bolt, not a light switch.

Then what turned on the light? Don't freak out, maybe, there are motion sensors. Who's freaking out — I wasn't freaking out. I laugh nervously inside my head.

What's this console for? What does it do? I stand in front of it to see what it has to offer. It seems like something's missing from it — maybe it's off and I just need to turn it on? What would you use to turn on something like this?

Maybe the green button that has the word "on" above it, you idiot. Never ask a stupid question until you've scoped out all possibilities — how could I forget one of my few rules?

I push the green button; lights flare to life on the console. About 10 screens pop out, all showing scenes around the house: the garden, the front door, the living room, the freaky hall, and the kitchen. But where's Trus? I don't see him. Shouldn't he be with all the people preparing things in the kitchen?

"Jezebel, where are you?" I hear Trus 'voice, but I don't see him anywhere in the house. I look around behind me, Trus isn't up here either. I look back at the screens and detect movement in the lower right — one of the ones taping the garden. Trus is standing next to the tables and chairs. He looks up towards the waterfall and camera for a split second and then scans the rest of the garden. He seems not to have seen the door — the waterfall must've started back up. Isn't this a safe house for The Circle? Shouldn't Trus know that there's a room up here? He goes further into the garden, searches every corner, gives up, and heads back inside.

If this place doesn't belong to The Circle, then who does it belong to? And why does The Circle use it or even know about it if it doesn't belong to them? Maybe there's a clue in here as to whom this place belongs to. I look and don't find anything. Wait, there's something on the wall — it's covered by dirt. I wipe it with my hand and uncover 2 letters: TU. What does TU stand for?

"Trus always was predictable. He brings every new recruit here." I turn around in a startled jump and gasp. I thought I was alone. I look around again and still don't spot anybody. "But then, no new recruits ever find this place. There must be something different about you. I wonder what that is."

I shake myself out of my initial shock and try to turn the situation so that I have the upper hand. "Who said that?" Nice, Jez, now they know that you're vulnerable while they're in control. Shut up, voice in my head! Obviously, she knows that she's in control.

"I did." A lady stands up and out of the only chair that was faced away from the door.

I back up as far as I can. "W Who are you?" I bump into the console. Does she mean me harm?!

Calm down, take stock of the situation. I breathe in through my nose and focus my thoughts. Is there a way out? All I know of is the way that I came in — even though the door's right next to me, there's no way I can go quickly down the waterfall. I'd only fall to my death — if she didn't catch me first.

I don't dare take my eyes off the lady, she's standing as if she knows what's going through my head. She looks as though she's a predator that has caught her prey. Her voice is familiar, but I don't recognize her face.

"Hello, darling. I have reason to believe that I am your aunt. You can call me Soppy." Oh! No wonder her voice is familiar, she's Siria-Mae! She's the leader of The Unknown. TU stands for The Unknown. I would hit my palm on my face — in a stance of obviously, how could I be so dumb? — if I weren't frozen in terror. What's she going to do to me? Is she going to give me back to the Devil?!

I've never seen her face — she never shows up in scenes from the gate. Her voice haunts many of the spies though. For every misstep in their missions, they have night and daymares about Siria-Mae torturing them for each and every one of their faults.

"What are you doing here?"

"You don't know?" She smiles an indescribable smile — all I can say is that it doesn't belong to a sane person — and pushes a button on her arm, causing the room to cloud up. What's happening? Why does the room appear to be spinning? And why are my limbs beginning to feel heavy? I can't move anything! All I feel is a sense of panic and entrapment before my eyes close and I lose consciousness.

CHAPTER TWENTY-FOUR

Bryce

What to do first? I open my eyes from my slumber and jump right to brainstorming my search for Jez. She's probably still in Brilla, right? But what if Arch had a backup plan in case the one involving us failed — he always was 2 steps ahead of everyone else.

I get up and look at the feed from the cams on my screen: the palace is safe and secure — no strangers or anyone out of place. I go to my dresser and pick out today's clothes and those for my search. Maybe I should search in all of the countries from here to Brilla — just in case she got out of there.

What a silly thing to do when looking for somebody — she obviously couldn't get out of Brilla on her own. But, she wasn't on her own, she had Arch's help. Fine.

I'm just about to freshen up when there's a knock on the door. "Yes?" I swing the door open and am given the sight of Atria with her fist raised to knock again.

"Oh! Good morning. I thought you were still in bed."

"The job never lets one sleep for long." I keep the door open enough so that I can talk to her without anybody being able to look in. "Why are you here, Atria?"

"Because I am your ruler and may do whatever I please!"

Something must have happened — being rude and using her power is her anxiety talking. "What happened, Atria?"

"Can I come in?" I look both ways down the hall and open the door far enough for her to enter. Whatever's worrying her must be serious. I close the door behind her. Hopefully, nobody saw Atria acting strangely. My room is soundproof — nobody will be able to exploit whatever Atria tells me.

I turn back to Atria pacing the room while fidgeting with her hands. "Atria, what's wrong?"

"I...I..." she clears her throat. "I went to check on Theo this morning because we have the town's tennis match to watch; he wasn't in his room." She didn't breathe at all while saying that. As I'm about to interrupt her, she holds up her hand and continues on. "I have already searched the whole palace; he's nowhere to be found. And what makes it worse is that I went to tell Trus and can't find him anywhere either."

"Stop freaking out. They probably had errands to do. Trus did have to report to you know who."

"Yeah, you're right. The match isn't until 2 hours anyway."

"You should rest, you're not completely healed yet."

"Oh! All of this worry about Theo and Trus made me forget my shoulder. But now the pain is back. Why does it hurt so much?"

"Because gunshots do. It would be way worse if anything was hit."

"I know all of this. I just don't want to go, rest, and be alone. I'm not used to being alone. I hate it and the silence. Why can't I run the palace?"

"Atria. You need to trust Theo. He can handle the kingdom. Do you want me to send Lorina?"

"No, I hate that hag. I'll just watch some TV."

"Ok."

She keeps on pacing my room, seeming to have no intention of leaving. I clear my throat, she doesn't take the hint. "Atria."

"I'm sorry, I'm wasting your time. You probably have someone waiting. Little old nobody me will be going now."

"I'll ask Melina to pay you a visit."

"Thank you, Bryce. I'll be waiting for her in my sitting

room. Good day." She walks out of my room as if she is floating.

Ok, now back to getting dressed. If there was a machine that eliminated sleep, I would have it. Sleep takes away too much time from the job. I need to find Trus, Theo, and Jez; work out the plans for taking down The Red List; and get Theo to his coronation alive. I want to take another shower, but sleep took too much time. No shower — I'll have to feel dirty for the rest of the day.

As soon as I finish getting dressed, my phone goes off. "Hullo?" The screen says nothing, so it's either a spy of The circle or Melina. I hope it's Trus — that'd be one less person that I have to find.

"Bryce, are you alone?" A masher's being used — it disguises one's voice. Melina uses it when she's afraid someone's eavesdropping.

"Yes, Madame." I hold the phone against my ear with my shoulder so that I can put my tie on.

"I have a mission for you."

"I was just about to call you. I have a few questions." A few years ago, I never would've thought to talk to Melina like this — interrupting her. But now I know that she is one of the kindest people alive; she doesn't get mad at any of us if we want use of her knowledge.

"Go ahead."

"Do you mind coming over and visiting Atria? She's very lonely. With Theo's coronation coming up, she has fewer duties because he runs more things now."

"I would love to. I was planning on visiting the palace today, I can make it a personal trip."

"Thank you."

"What else?"

"What do you mean what else? There's nothing else." Need to get on with my mission. I don't have time or really care what Trus is up to. I am only responsible for Theo.

"I know there's something more serious you wish to ask. Go ahead."

"Is something going on? Trus isn't here; even if he had reported to you, he would have been back by now. He would never leave Atria alone without a reason."

"The reason has to do with your mission. The Red List is becoming more active lately — I don't know why. I want you to get to the bottom of it." Should I ask her if she's seen Theo around? No, he's my responsibility. If I admit that I've lost him, I'll never be promoted.

"Bye, Madame." She hangs up without saying goodbye. How do I start with this mission? I have to get it over with as quickly as possible so that I can save Jez.

I know that it won't change anything, but I should call Trus. I need to know the information about The Red List. How can I find them when I haven't seen the same as Melina has?

"Hullo—"

"Hi, Trus—"

"Whoever owns this phone is not available at the moment. They will call you back once they are." The call ends with a click. I knew Trus wouldn't pick up — when we are on missions, we use burners. Melina only gives out the number if she deems it necessary — but it was worth a shot.

Maybe Theo will pick up. "Sorry, but this phone has been disconnected." What?! Why has Theo's phone been disconnected? He's had the same exact phone for 7 years, he would never replace it. If Atria has been trying for years to convince him to buy a phone and hasn't been successful, then he is never going to. Should I leave him? I know he's my charge, but Melina gave me an assignment.

He should be fine. But, there have been a lot of strange occurrences lately; what if they captured him? Besides, Melina knows everything that happens — she wouldn't send me on a mission if something happened to Theo.

Where was Theo's phone last? I get my laptop out, log in, and turn on Trincita to track it. "Huh." That's weird, it says that his phone is up, running and that it's in the palace. I bring up the feed from Theo's room on the monitor: his lights are on and I see motion — he must have come back.

Maybe Atria just wanted to use me to get Melina to visit her — no, she would never lie about Theo. Plus, she's not a good actress.

Never mind. Get on with the mission. I've found 2 of 3 missing people, the faster I get this mission over with, the sooner I'll rescue Jez.

So, what's the plan? It's too early for breakfast and I'm not hungry. Maybe a train ride to The Pile. I've been keeping a close eye on it, but I wasn't able to go last night. Where else would the increase in activity be seen? I know that their headquarters are there.

I think I've got my plan. I hear my stomach growl — maybe I should grab something from the kitchen, who knows when I'll be able to eat next.

I make it to the train station 10 minutes before the train leaves. I scan the platform for suspicious characters: to my left, I see people who seem familiar. Why do they look familiar? Do they work for The Red List? I've seen them at events where The Red List has attacked. But I can't know for sure if that's who they are. Besides, they're in conductors 'uniforms — there's no way that agents of The Red List would be conductors.

I have to stop thinking everyone is an enemy — I can't though, that's how I've been able to protect Theo. Stop it. My mind wanders to the new gadget I am working on while the train rolls in.

I get on, sit down, and take my sub out of the bag. I'm so glad that when no big meals are planned, the chef will make anything you want. I would not have wanted goose and mash — they're too messy for a train ride. Emor bread with tomatoes, mayo, lettuce, cucumbers, steak, and light onions is paradise. I take a bite and am literally drooling from it. We have the best sub chef in Musalin; this is the best thing I have ever eaten — it beats yesterday's soup in more ways than one.

I finish my sub, throw the bag away, and get out my newspaper to read while I wait. The train stops at the next stop but nobody gets on. A few stops later though, I move my newspaper slightly so that I can see who gets on.

It's Theo. What is he doing here? This isn't good. What if those guys were a part of The Red List, what if they are here to take Theo? Stop. He's fine. He's got Trina with him, she must be taking over my job of protecting Theo — Finally! I'm being promoted, this mission is the start of my protecting the whole palace!

No, that's not right. There's no way a new recruit would be given the job of protecting the soon-to-be-king. I was only allowed to do it because I have been with The Circle my whole life and I was closest to Theo's age.

The door to the next train car opens and the conductor comes in. It's one of the people that I saw on the platform. I can fully see his face now — it is a Red List agent! Ok, new plan: get the agent away from these innocent people, defeat him, and drag him back to Baker St for questioning.

Well, good news, I got his attention. Bad news: he's much stronger than I realized and he has the upper hand here. But not for much longer, I can't do anything until I get him away from the innocents, but then. Oh, then, I'll show him how my family became one of the best. I have hundreds of years of great warriors and spies in my blood.

Before I can put up just a little bit of a fight — nothing bloody in front of innocents, but I can't give him the whole upper hand — he pulls me off of the train. He doesn't just pull me to another car, no, he pulls me fully off of the train. The strange thing is that the train was going at full speed. How did this happen? One second we were on the train and now we are, what looks to be in the middle of nowhere. How do you go from 574.8 km/h to 0 in a second? It's not possible!

Stop thinking, I need to take this guy down. As tough and strong as I am, that also seems impossible. My arms won't move and I don't feel anything below my head — all I feel is the painful way the conductor is gripping me by the ear. I keep trying but nothing happens, I can't raise my hand to punch him nor can

I raise my foot to kick him in the nuts. He sees that I can't do anything and raises his own fist — but instead of punching me, he injects something into me through a syringe.

What's in the syringe? I hope that he's not poisoning me. I want to go out the way that good spies do, I want to complete my mission — whatever that is. My veins feel weird, the liquid is rushing through them, but I'm feeling a strange reaction. Especially with the veins in my eyes, they seem to be throbbing and getting bigger. With my limited vision, I see a lady coming closer — maybe she can help me. But why does she look kind of like Melina?

I can no longer do anything but think about the agonizing pain that my veins are producing. Before long, they take over my vision and my whole body shuts down.

CHAPTER TWENTY-FIVE

Jezebel

Cold water splashed onto me brings me out of my haze. Siria-Mae's in front of me while I have a vantage point from the ground.

How did I get on the ground? We were pretty high up. Did I fall?! No, no, no! What if something's broken?! I can't feel anything!

Stop freaking out, Jez. You're fine, nothing's broken. I steady my breathing and find that feeling has returned to my limbs. I stand up and face Siria-Mae. Should I talk first or wait until she asks for a response? Power seems to radiate from her. Maybe I should've stayed on the ground. Well, it's too late now — if I move a muscle, she'll probably pounce.

I look into her eyes — bad move, now I'm frozen. I'd remove my eyes, but terror has its hold on me. She takes in a gasping, emotional breath. "You really are her. You're Jezebel, I can't believe you are alive! You have no idea how happy this makes me!" She says in a sweet voice. Who does she think she's fooling? Her eyes are dead — showing that she couldn't care less if I were dead.

She looks at me as if I'm the one acting strange. "Well, aren't you going to give me a hug?" I continue to keep my distance — what if she stabs me as I get closer? Do I speak? What do I even say? Whatever comes out of my mouth could be used against me. Her eyes darken the longer I stay silent.

Maybe I should talk — the sooner I get this over with, the

sooner she'll let me go? "Hello. It's so good to finally meet you," I make my voice sound sugary sweet. Can we just cut the crap? "What are you doing?"

"Nothing, I just wanted to look at you." She grabs my arm — in a friendly way, but her grip's crushing. "Let me show you to your new home." She pulls me into a hallway; as soon as we're out of eyesight, she drops the act. "You are going to do what I say or I'll tell you-know-who." No, not the Devil! "Yes, the Devil. He's contacted me and I have seen his errand boy around."

"What do you want?" I also drop the sugary act.

"Looks like you're not as sweet as my daughter believes." She shakes her head and continues down the hallway, dragging me in the process.

We end up in a room containing a window into another room. Through the window, I see a person tied to a chair. His head's face down, what little I can see of it is unrecognizable. There are bruises everywhere — I'm glad he's not conscious, he'd be in so much pain.

"Who's he?" I know I shouldn't have spoken first, but how could she do that to someone who has done nothing to her? He must've crossed her or something.

"The Circle is becoming too powerful, he is one of the contributors. We need to know how he is so powerful and how to control him. We must conduct experiments to get answers."

"You won't be experimenting on him, will you?"

"What other way is there? No matter the beating, he would not say anything."

"But he's innocent! He's done nothing wrong except work for a different organization. He's not foe, he's just misdirected. I can get him to work with us. You don't need to torture him!"

"Do you know how many people he has killed? How many families I've had to tell of their deceased husband, wife, brother, sister, mother, or father? You don't know the extent of The Circle and its tyranny. How could you, raised as you were. You've no right to say my ways are barbaric. I have grown up in this world; I have seen what happens when one is on the other side. Don't tell me how to run my business. The only reason you're still alive is because you have a purpose."

How dare she! I know everything there is to know about the organizations. She's so sick in the head that she believes she can torture whoever just because she wants to. I'd run and never look back if I could. But if I do, she'll kill me.

Jez, you'll have your moment. Be calm, remember the mission that your mother gave you. Right, I need to convince her of my loyalty, kill her, and end her sick games. *Jeeezzz.* Ok, I won't kill her. But I'll put her somewhere she can't harm anybody.

I'm afraid to ask, but my curiosity won't let it go. "What's my purpose?"

"In due time, you will be the power of this world. You will infiltrate The Circle and take them down from the inside out. Then all that will be left is balance. I will have your assignment ready in the morning."

Siria-Mae leaves through a door that I didn't notice until now — it blends into the wall. She appears again in the same room as the tied-up man. I cover my eyes with my hands — I don't want to see how terrible she can be. I hate gory things! The room's not sound-proof, I hear crunches and pops that I assume must be bones. Siria-Mae whistles and a hand grabs my arm.

"This way, miss." I remove my hand as the servant turns me towards another door. She keeps her head down, but you can tell she has a smirk on her face — she must love the torture and think it's funny how squeamish I am. I'd prove her wrong, but I can only stand gory things when I distance myself.

I hate distancing myself because it's as if I'm not a human being with emotions; the objective is always more important than the consequences. Everything bad that I do, I automatically go distant. I fear that one day I won't be able to stop being distant. I don't want to be turned into a killing machine —

"We're here, mistress." The door's more of an alcove in the wall. The servant leaves without a sound. I don't want to sleep — I'll be left vulnerable and Siria-Mae is not the person you want to show vulnerability to. But if I don't, I'll leave this alcove and wander about, ending in worse punishments than a weakness that can be exploited.

> *"Who are you?" Cruel laughter. "What do you want?"*
> *"You are nothing."*
> *"Stop being a baby."*
> *"It's your fault!"*
> *"Wake him up!"*
> *"I'll protect her...till he kills her."*
> *"NOOOOO!"* The voices and flashes stop.

I wake up in sweaty terror, surrounded by strange surroundings. I look around, make sure nobody's about, sit up, and pull my knees to my chin. *Why don't the voices leave? What do they want? Why do they terrorize me so? What's wrong with me? I can't let anybody see how bad my mind is cracking; I'll never be able to bring down all the spy groups if they deem me not fit to do missions. Remember, Jez: mind on the objective. Ok, I just need to breathe and let the night terrors leave. I can't go out there this shaky.*

Siria-Mae is waiting for me outside of the alcove. She's holding a bag and looks as arrogant as ever. "It's time for your mission. You will contact your servant at the end of the week and give her your report. If you do anything to screw this up, you won't like my ways."

Ugh! Shut up already. Why does she talk like that? Can I kill her yet? Do I really need to work for her to take down The Unknown? No, I don't have to! I can do this without her. Yay, now how do I get out of here.

"Are you listening?" She snaps her fingers in front of my face. I don't have to listen to her, she can't make me — I've nothing that she can use for leverage. I'm alone and have nothing to lose. She should be afraid of me, but she probably knows I won't try anything 'cause she'd kill me. I won't even bother putting up a fight. Does she think that she has my loyalty? How does she know that once I'm out of here I won't go into hiding? I don't want to do her evil bidding —there has to be another way.

"You are to listen to me and do as ordered or I will kill Theo." What, how does she know about him?! Shit is there seriously no way out of this — she's too good at being evil and knowing people's weaknesses. How does she know that I beat myself up for poisoning Theo? I wouldn't be able to live with myself if I got him killed. Fine! Back to Plan A of taking down The Unknown.

"You can't do that, you need him." There has to be a reason why she'd have his name on the tip of her tongue — he must be useful besides terrorizing me into submission.

"We can get what we want without him." She throws the bag of stuff at me. "You know what to do with this. My car will be around back to take you to the palace. Your appointment is in an hour."

"What appointment?" She walks away without giving me any more information. If she doesn't want me to fail her, you'd think she'd give me more information.

Whatever, best to get to the failing part so I don't have to wonder and get super anxious. Plus I don't think she'll kill me if I fail — why am I still alive if she didn't need me?

I take the bag of stuff to a bathroom. It's darker than any I've ever seen; it has the same basic concept: toilet, shower, bathtub, sink, mirror. I place the bag on the counter and turn on the shower before going through it.

There's an array of colored contacts; bleach; hair dye; skin dye; face plasters; and a change of clothes. I'll shower first before I think of how I'll change my look. Somehow, I've days 'worth of grime and dust even though it was only about a day and a half ago that I took a shower.

After my shower, I have no clue what to use for my disguise. I know it should be something simple so that it's easy to keep up — I might be on this assignment for months.

Siria-Mae probably wants me to use everything in this bag, but I'm afraid to use it all. I don't really want to bleach and dye my hair a lighter color — that'd ruin its lovely lush blackness. I don't want to use face plasters; memories of spies having it done to them isn't the same as doing it yourself and making it look believable.

That settles it then, I'll use the colored contacts and hope that that paired with my new haircut is enough of a disguise. There are 21 packs of colored contacts but really only 4 colors to choose from: blue, gold, green, and gray. I feel that the brown of my eyes would overpower both the gold and green; blue's very bright, popping, and distracting...but also attracts attention. That only leaves gray; I put the contacts in and head out the door with the bag in hand.

I get to the car, where an utterly unfamiliar woman's waiting. "Oh, honey. That's not going to cut it, Soppy would have expected you to use everything in the bag. I understand not wanting to dye your hair; I wear wigs instead. But you have to at least use a little bit of face plaster — it will last for months and not come off in the shower."

She opens the back door of the car, motions me in, gets in behind me, and takes out some tools. "Give me the bag." I hand it to her; she pulls out a headband and the face plaster. The headband covers my hair while she lays the plaster down on my face. "Linris was too common around the palace for you not to get noticed," she tells me through a pick in her mouth and a tightly concentrated face.

"There, done." When I go to move, she puts out a hand to stop me. "If you're not going to dye your hair, at least let me style it for you." She pulls a dummy's head wearing a blonde wig out of a cupboard. She bunches up my hair and hides it under a cap before applying the wig.

Once the lady's all done working on my appearance, she holds up a mirror for me to have a look. If I thought I was unrecognizable before...who knew disguises could work so well? "Thank you." I can still see connections to what I used to look like, but other people shouldn't be able to.

"We're almost to the palace." I hadn't realized that we have been driving the entire time she was working on me; I had assumed she was the driver.

"Your appointment is in 30 minutes, you should be 15 minutes early." The woman looks up from her watch and smiles at me.

"What am I applying for?"

"To be the new dishwasher, of course."

"Why don't they have an electric one?"

"There's no room in the old kitchen; for some reason, the Prince doesn't want to spend the money on a new one."

Ok. No more questions, I need to focus. I have to win these people over or else I'll be given back to the Devil, Theo'll die, and the world's balance will be tipped towards the evil side — yeah, no pressure. How does one conduct an interview? What do I say; what do I do? Thinking's making it worse! I'm probably cracking all the plaster by worrying so much.

Maybe...distract myself before finding a conclusion. Ummm, what do I distract myself with? The outside?...wait, that's actually a good idea — I might need to find Siria-Mae's hideout on my own one day.

I turn to look out the window. Before my eyes focus on our surroundings, a blind comes up. What? Why can't I view the outside? In the corner of my eye, I see a hand move away from a button on the lady's side of the car — what, exactly are they trying to hide? I've already seen what they do to gain intel, it's not like I don't already know how bad they are. And we've been driving for a good while — it's not like I'll get much sense of where her hideout was.

"What are you applying for?"

"To be head guard."

"Your name is..." She looks at her sheet before looking back at me. "Linris Oskerti."

"Yes. I was trained under the Rintos in the Sanjria desert. Most of their prodigies become guards here — but you probably already know that."

"What would you offer that the next person cannot?"

"I have been training my whole life — my whole family works protecting this country. I was practically born with a gun in my hand and a royal behind me. I will give my life to protect my charge. And I believe that the Royal Family of Musalin is the only true and pure one of the world — they need every kind of protection to gain the upper hand from all of their enemies."

"Yes, and just like every other candidate has said. But what makes **you** different? Why should **you** be given the highest point without proving your worth through years of experience?"

Why is she making this so hard? Grandmamma said her contact had me for a shoo-in. Is she our contact? There's only one way to find out. But, if I give crucial information away to an outsider, Grandmamma will take my mission away and make me work in the house for the rest of my career. Come on, Linris, just make a decision. Ummmmmmmm.

"The Red List doesn't know my face. They think that my family is all dead. I know all of their moves and the tells of who their agents are. I can protect the king the most — if you give me a chance."

"I see." Uh, oh — did I just give away secrets to an outsider? Grandmamma is going to kill me! She looks at her clipboard and doesn't look at me as if she had really heard a word of what I said. Is this a test?! Did I fail my first test?!

Her eyes become less foggy as she says, "Soppy said you might use that to gain entry. Don't worry, I won't tell her. So long as you keep your word about giving your life for the king, this interview won't ever get back to her. Just be sure never to tell this information to anyone outside of the gate again. Out here, you never know who is listening."

"Does this mean that I have the job?"

"Of course. Your first day is tomorrow. Your quarters will be prepared for tonight. The king is to know of this change in service after you leave."

YES! First mission: accomplished. Melina and Siria-Mae are going to be impressed: my first spy mission at only 19. Will they have their first missions then too? I hope not, I'll never forgive myself if something happened to them at so young of an age. Mother would

not be proud of this. She didn't want me to even become a spy —
she wanted this dangerous legacy to end with her. But I'm doing this
because of her. I want to find out who killed her and take their whole
side down — I bet it was the Red List.

That was weird. Did I just...was that...huh? I think I just
saw my mother's first interview. She wasn't much older than me
— I'm following in her footsteps. I don't care about Siria-Mae's
evil intentions to get me to become a spy; I feel a connection to
my mother that I've never felt before. I'm not sure if I should let
the tears in my eyes say "I'm sad", or let a smile come to my face.

"Ahem." The lady rudely takes me out of my nice thinking
— I'm starting not to like her. I thought she was nice for doing
my disguise, but nobody nice would work for Siria-Mae. "We've
arrived." Didn't need her to clear that up, I just needed her to let
the shades down so I could see the palace.

She has me go to the boot as soon as I get out, where she
pulls out two large duffle bags — are they both for me? "Don't let
security see this one," she holds up the darker one, "before you
pull this strap here." She points to a strap near the top. Why do I
have to do that — what's in it?

She hands me the duffle bags, gets back in the car, and is
gone without giving me further instructions. Guess I'm on my
own from here. Which door do I use? If I go in the front, will
people think I'm Royalty? Servants always use back entrances;
but is my interviewer waiting in the front or back? Usually,
when people come for the first time, they enter via the front
— which is unlocked until a certain time. It's not like anyone
with ill intentions could go through, they get screened before
entering the gate.

I suck it up, pull the strap on the dark duffle bag, put a
confident aura on, and walk up the giant steps to the enormous
double doors. The doors open before I clear the last step. The
light shows a singular man standing there — it's Trus!?

"Hullo. You're quite on time. Nice to meet you — if you'll
just follow me, please." He turns around and leads me to a grand

hallway off of the giant entrance. We take a staircase to the bottom level and arrive outside a closed door. Trus opens the door and gestures me through. I come across a kitchen filled with many people working. What catches my eye is a huge stack of dirty dishes in a sink — do they expect me to work before my interview?

Trus continues through the kitchen and another hallway to a secluded room filled with only 1 table and 3 chairs. He motions for me to sit while he remains standing.

After about 10 minutes pass, Trus starts to look from his watch to the door — whoever are we waiting for? As Trus goes to leave the room, the door opens...in comes Atria. This is starting to go south, there's no way both of them will be fooled by this silly disguise. Why did I ever agree to this? There's no way I'll get the job, they'll either deliver me back to the Devil or arrest me!

"Is this her?" Atria sits down across from me; Trus sits down in the seat next to Atria's. Two against one, can I defeat them with my training if it comes down to it? Probably not — crap. Soppy's going to kill me, the Devil'll capture me, and my mother and father will forever have been sacrificed in vain! My life sucks! Why does this kind of thing always happen to me; why am I a letdown and failure? Hopefully, they'll just quickly kill me themselves.

"Hullo, I am the Princess Regent, Atria." She shakes my right hand and waits for something. Is Trus going next, or me?

She doesn't take her eyes off of me, that's answer enough. "Roma Arch, it's a pleasure, your majesty." I do a head bob instead of a curtsy.

Now, it's Trus 'turn. I already know both of their names, but I mustn't break my cover. "Trus, head of management." His grip's firm, but not brutal. How did he get back here so fast and not look tired at all? He must've had Adelia drive him back all night — she must be unconscious somewhere.

"You wish to apply as the new dishwasher?"

"Yes, madame."

"What qualifications do you have for the job?" I wasn't

briefed. Did Soppy's people give them information — was I not supposed to say my name was Roma?! Hopefully, I haven't already messed it up. I've no choice but to use truthful facts.

"I worked as a chef at my last occupation and was the only person working in the kitchen. I have scrubbed many tough spots on pots and pans; I take pride in spotless, clean dishes."

"Why do you wish to work here?" Why's Atria asking all the questions? Trus watches my every move — does he see through the cracks?!

"I wish to study law and the workings of Musalin's government. This job would give me an insight into how the palace handles situations. Plus, it is an amazing opportunity to work in such a fine place." I hope Trus doesn't detect my accent.

"Hmmph." Did I convince her? My life literally depends on getting this job. "Thank you for your time. If you will excuse me." She shakes my hand one last time, looks at Trus for a few seconds, and leaves. Did she tell him with her eyes to kick me out? Did I get the job?

"You start work in an hour, this is to be your bedroom. I will have furniture brought in throughout the day. Your bathroom is over there—" he points to a part of the wall that doesn't look like a door. "You will find your uniform on the counter. Good luck." He leaves me all alone. Well, good news — I got the job — bad news — I've followed Soppy's orders exactly. I don't want to follow Soppy's orders; I don't want to help her spread her evil ways!

Whatever, there's nothing else I can do that won't get me killed. I press the wall inward and it pops open. The wall closes behind me with a surprising pop. What a room! Everything screams luxury. A beautiful, sandstone texture for the sink, toilet, and shower — is that a jacuzzi?! Oh...My...God! It is a jacuzzi, oh this is going to be awesome!

I instantly find a bikini next to it and get in. The water's warm but not a gross kind of lukewarm. There's a button by my head, I press it and the jets turn on. I dunk my head and soak my hair. Ahhhh. This is the life.

I lift my head out of the water, open my eyes, and spot a mini fridge to my left. So many drinks, but none with familiar names. There's a wide variety of colors; I grab a neon pink one. The cap pops off and there's a weird texture to it. It's silky, soft, a little chewy, and bubbly all at once. What is it and why is it making me feel so light? I finish it off and continue soaking for a while longer.

By the time my fingers start to wrinkle — about thirty minutes later — I get out, dry off, and go to the uniform sitting on the counter.

If the bikini was modern and pretty...my expectations of the uniform turn into disappointment. The uniform's not hot at all, it's very ugly and uncomfortable looking. Why is everyone obsessed with old-fashioned-collared outfits for servants?

It could be worse though, at least it's not a heavy and thick material. And the lack of sleeves will make it easier not to overheat while working with hot water and dishes all day. Why am I seeing positives in everything? Why does my chest feel like it's about to burst from nothing — I don't even feel my anxiety anymore. Maybe I should thank Soppy and get on her good side, she really isn't all that bad.

Brain, stop! What was in that drink? My thoughts are usually more rational. Except for that thing about a bear — and thinking animals are always happy and shelters are always good and not abusive to their rescues. Was there a potion in that drink? Did someone poison me?! Great, the poisoner has become the poisoned.

Maybe, if I think mistrusting thoughts, the poisoning will stop? Soppy's the most atr...beautiful person in the world. She's the spawn of the De...Gods. STOP IT!!! With all my strength, I slam my fist onto the countertop. That seems to have done the trick, happy and bubbly no longer; I see a red haze.

Soppy's the most atrocious; she's a spawn of both the Christian Devil and my old captor. She's the vilest, hated human being I'll ever meet who'll come close to the Devil's level.

Now, I have work to do. Just because I think it, doesn't

mean I'll act on my thoughts. I'm not a killer; I'm not a sword of anger — only in defense. I'm a spectator, not a doer. That might have to change though.

New plan: convince Soppy I'm on her side by fulfilling her less harmful orders, when they become too disastrous, I'll disappear without a trace. I don't care about this stupid war between the spies — let them kill each other for all I care. I just want a normal life. Victa was wrong; a normal life will never be gained by becoming a spy.

I double-check my outfit's on correctly and make my way back to the kitchen. There are fewer people than before, but what looks to be the head chef is still working. Hopefully, my work at the Devil's house is adequate enough for these dishes — and people.

The lady doesn't even look in my direction as I situate myself in front of the sink. There's a nice, new pair of yellow rubber gloves — they must be for me. The Devil never supplied me with any gloves; my hands always got burned. My skin has finally healed since the burned parts peeled a month ago. These people are so good at taking care of their employees — I don't see a good reason for Soppy to want to destroy them. Yeah, she's evil, but destroying the Royal Family would do nothing for her. She'll probably anger the people and have massive retaliations.

The kitchen people know how to make it super easy to clean dishes — they let all of the ones with crust and such on the sides soak in water! All I have to do is take the spritzer to remove the rest of the food down the drain. My first dish is spotless and dry in less than 5 minutes. The use of dish soap makes the sink smell like lavender.

It takes me about 30 minutes to finish an eighth of the pile, there didn't look to be this many when I started. The palace isn't that big; why are there so many dishes?

Even through the gloves, after the first hour my hands start to hurt from all of the hot water — more like scalding. I wish I could open the window in front of me; I'm really starting to overheat. But the chef is still preparing dishes and she might get mad if I open the window without asking. I'd ask, but she seems so busy and maybe she likes to work in a warm environment?

...

After about two hours, I hear the chef's pace and actions change. After I finish drying a pan, I look over my shoulder. Her counter's empty and she has taken her hat off and placed it on a hook near the door. She leaves without even glancing in my direction. Of course, I'm just the lowly dishwasher, but it would've been nice if she had said "bye". Well, it's better that she left instead of scrutinizing my work. I'm trying my best, but the palace may be too spiffy for my humble means of learning to clean dishes.

I'm only halfway done with the original pile, but I'm feeling really sick due to all the heat — they have the best water heater; the Devil's went cold after an hour straight — and my hands really hurt. It'd be nice to take a break or even call it a day, but I don't want them to think my work is inadequate and fire me after the first day! I must push on through my uncomfortableness and pain; I can't let my new plan be foiled.

By the time I finish the rest of the pile, the sun's way lower in the sky than when I started. It's not night yet, but it is afternoon. I take off the gloves and reveal the tragic aftermath of scrubbing dishes in scalding water for hours straight.

I immediately close my eyes and make a squeamish noise. They're totally peeling, are redder than a tomato, and in so much pain. They look like I have burns from a fire. They look crumpled and disgusting. I was wearing gloves; how's it way worse than at the Devil's house with no gloves? This is going to take more than a month to heal. Why is trying to find a normal life so much worse seeming than torture by the Devil? I think he might've actually gone easy on me. I mean, you can't help who you are and he just likes to torture people. He never once did any permanent damage or kill me — even though it was more than ten years of constant pain.

Before I can make my way back to my room, I notice a second sink tucked into a corner, piled with even more dishes than the one before. One of them must be the backup sink. Seriously?! How come nobody seems to have any idea of how to wash dishes?! Couldn't they have just done one or two each, so that I don't have to do so many and completely destroy my hands? Why are people so inconsiderate?

Whatever, I've no choice in order not to get fired. I find a new pair of dry yellow rubber gloves under the first sink and get to work. The water stays the constant, scalding temperature as before.

When I finally finish both sinks and all the dishes are spotless and dry, warily, I look around to make sure there's not a third sink that I missed. Luckily, there are only two. I feel completely exhausted; my hands are so bad off that I can't even feel them anymore. I slide down to the floor and don't even bother to remove the gloves.

...

I hear the door open like twenty minutes later. For the first time in hours, I look out the window. It's officially nighttime — maybe it's a guard on his rounds. I don't do anything except keep on breathing and ignore the numbing pain in my hands — they're starting to tingle. I didn't know what I signed up for. Is this how many dishes there'll be every day? My hands are always going to be ruined. Little deformities make society despise people; if my hands never have a chance to heal, I'll never be able to live a normal life.

I hear the person looking around, leave, and the door open back up again. Hurried footsteps approach. "Roma, what happened?" It's Trus. I have no energy to hide my personality; I find that I'm cradling my hands and feel tears making their way down my face.

Trus bends down and looks at my eyes first — to see if

I'm unconscious? Then he notices my hands and removes the gloves. "What did you do?"

"I did my job. There are no dirty dishes in the vicinity." All that's in my voice is exhaustion. Hopefully, my voice doesn't sound like Jezebel's — I'm surprised he hasn't caught on yet; he knows my voice. He's good enough to be protecting The Royal Family, so, how is he so easily fooled?

"You weren't supposed to do all of them. Nobody's washed them for a week, you had a few days to get caught up. We don't usually have so many dishes; we've had a busy week with visitors. Can I help you?" I nod my head and he helps me to my feet.

He walks me back to my room, has me sit down on the toilet in the bathroom, and opens up the mirror. There's a whole storage space behind it with lots of medical equipment — they must've dug into the wall because the mirror's as thin as can be. If he hadn't done that, I never would've known it was there.

He rummages through it. For a while, he can't seem to find what he's looking for. I'd protest that he's doing me no good, but all I can think about is the pain of my hands. It has now spread to my arms. Why does it hurt so much?! Did I permanently damage them? Will I never be able to wash another dish in my life?!

He stops throwing bottles around, closes the mirror, and turns around. There's a squeeze tube in his hands — it's yellow and has a very tiny script. "It might sting a little." Should I be worried that he's going to put more poison into my system? He seems so nice, but appearances can be deceiving. He has done nothing ill towards me, he's just brainwashed by The Circle.

If I object or act rude and ungrateful, I might get fired. Hopefully, he's merciful enough to kill me quickly.

"All done. Your hands will be sore for a few days, but no damage will arise. You'll have to apply this once daily until fully healed." He twists the lid on, places the tube next to me, and goes to leave. "I'll have them give you different assignments tomorrow — ones that won't be too taxing for your hands."

"Thank you." He gives me a quizzical, considering look before nodding and retreating.

I wait, hear no sounds other than my own, grab the tube, and make my way back to the bedroom.

I sit down on the bed and almost let sleep take me. Wait, what? I jump up and land on my feet. There's a bed?! I hadn't noticed, but I now have a fully-furnished bedroom.

Wow...yep, I'm definitely working for a Royal Family. This room didn't appear so big before — it has turned into a studio flat! There's a living room section, a bedroom section, and a kitchen. I so did not see a kitchen before.

They even hung up a tapestry on the wall containing the family's crest. The furniture is a mix of modern and beech wood. Oh...My...God! There's a gigantic, full bookcase!!! It even has nice glass doors. The books won't fall out, but I can still see the beautiful bindings and covers.

I open the doors and run my fingers along the bindings of a row of books. All of a sudden, my hand stops on a random book. Carefully, I pull it out. There's nothing too remarkable about it; it shows it has seen a good number of years, but there's no title or anything.

I flip a few pages and find the symbol for The Circle. Is this a history of the spy organization? Do they know that I'm Jezebel?! This isn't good! Soppy's going to kill me. No, first she'll beat me up, then she'll torture me. She won't kill me until she's satisfied with my suffering.

I can't breathe. There's no air; the walls are closing in. I can't see! Is the room spinning?! Not again!

Are they killing me? The blackness wants me. How do I deny it? I don't want to die! Please, Mother, Drew, anybody! Don't let me die! I promise I'll make the world right.

My fingers lose their grip on the book and I feel a collision before succumbing to the darkness.

CHAPTER
TWENTY-SIX

Victa

Who killed the king? All these books and no answers. What a waste of an hour. If I do not solve the nineteen-year mystery/investigation, then I will not be able to fully infiltrate The Circle.

If not with answers, then how else do I convince them of my value? Maybe my friendship with Theo is my way in.

But once he goes missing, I would be considered their first suspect. I wish Gevan was here; he can rapidly find everything important in a book. It would be nice to have someone helping me, but mother only trusts me — barely — with the most secretive and crucial missions.

Who knows, we might have a Royal Family sympathizer in our midst. He or she would alert the palace of a threatened kidnapping; The Circle would tighten their security. I do not like the idea of kidnapping Theo, but mother has a plan. When mother's plans are not followed through....it is never good for Man-Kind.

I will have better luck going to The Red List's headquarters. My "foster family" might make up a reason for my return. It has been a few years since my evil-containment mission. How old was I....15? Some years ago, mother cut off all ties with them as a punishment — this could work in my favor. They frequent a safe house outside of Baker St...and residents are allowed to bring in guests!

All I need is a disguise that mother has never seen before.

I know the culprit was a Red List Agent; I need a way to gain access to their records. All spy organizations keep proof of their missions and accomplishments. The documentation for the king's murder is probably on a wall of fame somewhere.

Looks like it is time to go shopping. Wait, with what money? Is it time to use my inheritance from my unknown father? It is the only account that mother cannot monitor. But I must not be caught on the main bank's cameras. Back to Potter's Town, I guess. Looks like I might actually use all five uses that I paid for.

I make sure that the device and my subway ticket are in my purse, grab the most promising book and stuff it into my purse — without anyone or the cameras noticing. Great, my mother is meaner than I thought; making me do illegal actions without all my cards. I do not even have my ID! How am I supposed to collect my inheritance? If I am able to get it, hopefully, I can withdraw cash.

The cool breeze hints at an evening rainstorm. I hail a taxi to take me to the subway — the fewer people who spot me, the less of a chance my mother will know my every move.

She probably has trackers in my clothes, but they only give location instead of actions. "Where to, miss?" I dig around my pockets for my cash.

"Nearest subway entrance, please." He pulls away from the curb and enters the traffic. I keep my features hidden from an outsider's view. The trip should have only taken ten minutes, but traffic is always thick. A car behind us honks its horn while we wait for pedestrians to stop crossing so that we can turn right.

Well, twenty minutes is not too bad — it would have gone faster if I had walked, but I could not take the risk. I pay him the cash and hurry into the subway while keeping my face masked.

I scan my ticket and go to the track to Potter's Town. I just made it, the train leaves in two minutes; the next one does not come until ten minutes and I have already wasted so much time.

As soon as we arrive, I rush to get my ticket punched. I am on my way to the new bank in no time. The town is almost unrecognizable. Nice housing, apartment buildings, and businesses line every street. Theo is doing a good job — he has a bright future ahead of him. Musalin has an innovative possible future; hopefully, Theo's kidnapping does not go south. I want to see what can come of this country.

The Newmond Bank is located where the landfill used to be. There are absolutely no traces left — not even the stench. I do not see any cameras on the outside; there is a security firm truck in the parking lot — they just started their work, good for me. Mother should not be able to view their live feeds until after everything is set up.

There are more people waiting than one would expect for such a new establishment. Where does one go for inheritance? There are so many different lines; I cannot waste time trying them all. I need to go after Iris. I go to the customer service desk — the only one that is labeled and secluded away from the others — and get into line behind three people.

To make the time go faster, I survey my surroundings. Nothing out of the ordinary in the front of the building. My eye catches a figure in the farthest corner from the door. His eyes are fixed on me, the hair on the back of my neck is standing up, and he seems to have a bloodstained red tint to his skin.

"Next." The customer service person flags me over. I look back at the corner, but the man is gone.

"Where do I collect my inheritance?" The corner was in shadow; I am just seeing things — nobody has bloodstained skin.

"Do you have an account with us?"

"Yes."

"Over there." She points to an empty cluster of chairs in front of an office.

"Thank you." As soon as I sit down, a lady comes out of the office. She is dressed all professionally in a dark blue blazer and suit.

"Hello, are you here to claim an inheritance?"

"Yes."

"Come on in." She turns around and goes back into her office. She closes the door behind me and goes to stand behind her desk. "I'm Bertha." She shakes my hand. Her grip is firm, mine is clammy.

"Victorious."

"Shall we get to business?" She sits down and fixes her suit. I sit down in one of the two chairs in front of her desk. "Last name?" She opens a new tab on her computer.

"Atributous." Her fingers fly across the keyboard.

"A-t-r-i-b-u-t-o-u-s?"

"Yes." Why did she not ask me before she typed it?

"There are no Atributouses in our system. I do have a Victorious Apollyon." I nod my head. This bank is only found in Musalin for spies and their families; I am the only Victorious. Wait — did she say Apollyon? As in the Keerg word for Satan/The Devil? Why is my name listed as that?

Is that my father's last name? Is he Keerg? Why is his last name so evil? As far as I have gathered, he was a Red List nobody who used my mother to try and gain power. He did not achieve any power and left.

"It looks to be £20,000. Do you want to withdraw it all?"

"No, can I have cash and put some on a Debit Card?"

"Yes. For identification, all I need is your fingerprint." She picks up the fingerprint scanner, puts it in front of me, and connects it wirelessly to her computer. I put my finger on it...it keeps its red color — maybe that is not my father after all? "No, honey. Your left pinky, not right index finger." I switch fingers and this time the scanner turns green.

She motions for me to take my finger off, puts the scanner back in its place, and does some actions on her computer. "How much in cash and on the card?" That is a good question. How long will this illegal — according to my mother's standards — mission last? Who knows when I will next be able to take out money without my mother knowing. I cannot take out the whole 20,000.

"450 in cash, and put 6,000 on the Debit Card."

"I'll need a pin for the card — make sure it is one you shall not forget." She turns the computer screen towards me and places a wireless keyboard in front of me.

It cannot be one, two, three, four...How about a mix of Gevan and Roxie's birthdays? Gevan was born in Maye and Roxie in Lithe — so zero, five, zero, three. I type it in and hand the keyboard back to Bertha. She types in a few more things on the computer, gets up, and leaves the room.

It only takes her a few minutes to collect everything. She hands me the £450 in an equal distribution of small and largely-summed bills. She gives me the Debit Card and a pen.

As I sign the card, she puts a bunch of documents into a folder and places her business card in a little slot on the pocket of the folder.

"Have a nice day!" I put everything into my purse and scramble from her office. She seemed friendly at first...but when she came back, she had changed. There was a forced and calculating air about her. I should have known better — my mother knows everything that happens; she has her talons in every situation.

Money, check. But there are still so many objectives: buy a disguise, locate the Shanas, infiltrate the Red List's Headquarters, find the king's killer, track down Iris, and figure out how to kidnap Theo. All in a day's work.

I exit Potter's Town via the bus and finish my trek to Lilith Square — Musalin's shopping district — using the subway. I must not use any shops that all of the spies use; luckily, most of the time, disguises are ordered via an online catalog. Spies do not waste their precious time shopping. They prefer to gather intel for missions. I never understood; shopping is wonderful. It makes one get lost in trying to find new styles and different combinations of clothes. When I get stuck trying to figure out a problem in a mission, I go shopping. After a stress-free shopping spree, I have new eyes with which to fix the problem.

I should use popular stores instead of ones that do not see

much activity. It will be easier to hide amongst all the shoppers. Also, I will be one face out of hundreds — with nothing special setting me apart from the mass.

I need face plaster, colored eye contacts, clothes, body padding, and a wig. I enter Oohoob first. I buy a body pillow, a plus-sized floral dress, and see-through high heels; a bunny backpack, neon pink cat ears attached to a headband, neon cupcake dangly earrings; a lavender fuzzy cardigan, floral tights, and a sparkly unicorn bracelet.

Next up is Chintel. I find a neon purple wig and sparkly gray-colored eye contacts.

My final shopping destination is Sienna Makeup. My final purchases are 2 packs of full face plaster and a unicorn eyeshadow pallet.

I make my way to a public restroom, make sure nobody is in there, and lock the door behind me. So far, so good. Mother will never recognize me in this disguise. It is so girly and ridiculous that I could puke.

I turn myself into a plus-sized girl who just hit puberty. I was even able to mould a few pimples. I put my purse in the backpack and hide my clothes in the paper towel dispenser. I step back out into the world as a completely different person.

I hail a taxi. "Huntington and Fraiser, please." I pitch my voice high and squeaky. Once we arrive at the intersection, I pay the driver and step onto the sidewalk. I wait for him to drive away before going in search of the safe house.

"125, 126, 127, 128...which side of the street was it on?" I mumble as a way to avoid thinking. Thinking is dangerous. Thinking leads to worrying. Worrying leads to turmoil. Turmoil leads to vulnerability. Turmoil distracts you, it lets your guard down. Turmoil allows people to view who you really are, and what your intentions really are.

"There it is!" Number 135: a red brick plantation house — a reminder of Musalin's history — with a balcony overlooking the street. It looks different than I remember. The vegetation has not been kept up and has started to take over the house.

It looks to be in disrepair. Hopefully, the Shanas relocated here. Maybe, when my mother let them go, they lost their funding for emergency housing.

I check the street before ascending the steps. I knock on the door...it opens before my fist finishes. I enter the grand hall and close the door behind me. It gives a fight before succumbing with a loud click.

Nobody is waiting to welcome me. I hear no sounds or movements from inside the house...but I feel eyes upon me.

"Hullo?" No response. I whistle a jolly tune. "Jolly Rancher comes a calling." I hear rustling; nobody steps out. "Rancher's stock went berserk and he seeks help from Skittens." No more rustling. Footsteps sound from upstairs. They echo — as did my voice — as if the house is void of furniture. Still, no faces appear. The footsteps end at the top of the stairs. I look up, but cannot make anything out. All but the front door is engulfed by darkness.

They should recognize the code. We came up with it in case I ever needed protection from mother. Maybe they do not want to show themselves because they do not recognize my voice. But, I cannot break my disguise.

"Cherries are blossoms bards do cherish."

A cough. "Skittens 'hamlet is far. Mayhap stock will find pie in Ottish." The house is under surveillance by mother.

"Sorry. Wrong Kershit. Listen, big turn, mop." I leave out the front door and continue walking down the street, pretending to search for the right house. At the corner — out of sight of the house — I hail a taxi.

"Chestnut and Hoovershim." It takes twenty minutes. Many twists and turns later, we arrive at the intersection. I get out and walk to Chestnut Park. I walk deep into the forest until I stumble upon a little clearing. A little picnic bench inside a beautiful gazebo becomes my perch for the next 30 minutes.

The first shadow that looms over the table belongs to a black-haired middle-aged man wearing glasses. He sits down across from me and watches as a red-haired woman makes her way across the clearing. She sits next to the man.

Twenty minutes later, a young man and woman cross the clearing holding hands. The woman sits next to me while the man leans against the table. He stands close to his father — of which he is the spitting image.

Once everyone is settled, a pen with a blinking light is placed in the middle of the table. After it emits a beep, it is as if a shadow has been ripped away.

"Victa, dear. How are you?" The woman reaches across the table to take my right hand in her left one. Her voice is as rich as the red of her hair.

"Fine." I drop the girlish accent and remove my hand from hers.

"Soppy has been watching us for months. Her rein has gotten tighter the past few days. That was very dangerous. You shouldn't have contacted us directly." Arturo's voice is as gruff as his appearance. He has always been one to get straight to the point.

"I am disguised. Would you have recognized me without our code?"

"It's a very clever disguise. As much as father would say otherwise. Soppy has him on edge. You look good, Vic." Dunner always was a charmer. My heart skips a beat as it remembers that he was my first fancy and kiss.

"But you subconsciously fidget with your nails. Some habits never change and will always give one away," Tenna has lost her shyness and speaks with a sure, mature voice. I look down at my hands and instantly stop fidgeting.

The twins are so grown up. I never thought I would see them reach adulthood. They look great for 19 years in a spy family. I definitely looked more stressed, tired, and on edge when I was 19.

It took me years to stop wishing I was a Shana. They love each other and look out for one another. When I finished my mission, I fought to stay with them. So what if they were a part of the Red List? They are the kindest people I know. My mother never loved me. With the Shanas, I felt like I belonged.

"What brings you back?" Cherise was the mother I never had.

"I need help infiltrating the Red List's Headquarters. It is time things changed." Once upon a time, I overheard them planning to take down Soppy. They wanted to replace her dictatorship with a democracy. I cannot have them thinking I just want to use them. I shall turn them in after they help me. Soppy installed in me that loyalty costs everything. Nobody must come between mother and daughter.

She will find out about this meeting eventually. I will tell her that I was ferreting out her traitors. A little sacrifice for the good of mankind — hopefully, they will understand in time.

Iris is key...I need to find Iris.

"So, it has officially started?" Arturo strokes his beard while interrupting my inner rant.

"Yes."

"Meet us a Strugart missile inks." Midnight at the docks. On the dot or not at all.

"Bye." I give Tenna a hug and whisper a message into her ear before departing.

I turn my cheerful, girlish appearance/air back on and leave to catch the subway.

I barely catch the train as it heads in the direction of Musalin's Town Centre. I find a seat on its own and block the camera's eyesight with my back.

First things first, I must locate Iris. I have about 3 hours until I have to be at the Docks. Hopefully, that is enough time. A day is never long enough for a spy's long list of things to do. I cannot let mother corrupt Iris. I fear it is too late for me. But Iris still has a chance.

When nobody is looking in my direction, I pull out the Traitor's Gadget. That is strange. The dot is not showing up anywhere...it is as if she has fallen off of the face of the Earth.

I press the home button, find the settings, and refresh the gadget. When that does not change anything, I shake the daylights out of it. It finally reboots and the dot appears.

Wait, is that...the palace? Why is Iris at the palace? Well, that kills two birds with one stone: I can sweep the best area to take Theo out by and see what Iris is up to.

Within the hour, I arrive at the station and make my way toward the palace. With a lot of traffic and people going in every direction, Musalin definitely earned its place in the Top Ten Busiest Cities of the World List. We get so many tourists and immigrants every year — last year I believe it was ten thousand. We are one of the last monarchy-ruled territories; the palace even hosts tours every day of the week except for Monday.

It is a good thing that today is in fact, a Monday. Not many people are about the palace; only a few tourists are taking photos. The gates are closed...but that is actually a good thing — it is not like I can enter and leave by way of the front gate while kidnapping Theo.

There must be a good amount of cameras, I will need to find a blindspot. I make my way around the perimeter. If there are any blindspots, the guards patrolling the roof and balconies will surely spot me. I will have to come back when it is pitch black and find an ideal spot then.

Iris will have to wait. The guards will never let me in looking like this until tomorrow. I must not dispose of my disguise until I find out who killed the king.

Back to the library? Ugh! Books are so dull and research is very tiring without much intel. Oh, well. I should have at least an hour available.

Back at the library, I find myself at a table on the opposite side of the room to my earlier one. I have grabbed books full of anything spy-related and a few containing family trees.

I pick up the Royal Family Tree book, find Prince Theo, and trace back up to the first known monarch. Many people I have heard of...but there is a branch off of the main one that does not sound familiar.

Maybe the librarian will know; she has worked here long before I was born. I find her putting books back on shelves in a secluded, dark alcove.

"Excuse me, miss?"

"Yes?" She turns to face me. She has acquired glasses since the last time I saw her; there is more silver in her raven hair.

"Whatever happened to this branch? Why have I never heard of it?" I show her the book. She squints at it for a few seconds.

"He was the youngest son to our first Queen and King. He disappeared when he was 3 and wasn't found until his 21st birthday. He never revealed what happened during his missing years. He arrived devoid of spirit and never lived a happy day. But the person who started this book went and discovered what happened." She shelves more books and goes to leave. I put a hand out to stop her.

"Wait, what happened?"

She turns back around. "Do you really wish to know?" I nod. "Follow me. My old bones can't take as much as they used to." She does not look a day over sixty, but I know she worked here even before Aunt Linris was born — probably since my grandma was a teenager.

I follow her back to her office. She closes the door, pours two cups of tea, and collapses into a chair facing the fireplace. I sit down on the chair next to hers and take a cup from the table between us.

"Victorious, this affects you and all you've ever known."

"But how?"

"Your disguise could never fool these ancient eyes. The youngest Prince was taken by 2 foxes. He was playing in the palace's gardens when 2 unique foxes came through a break in the walls. These were not ordinary foxes, they seemed otherworldly. They spoke in his head and he followed them. They delivered him to a healer who was visiting from many kingdoms away. She had no idea why a toddler was alone with 2 foxes, but she decided to take him home with her and raise him.

"Some say she bewitched the foxes, but all she made were potions from worldly ingredients. She raised the Prince in Ottishire — a country that was destroyed 200 years ago. He grew up a healer's son and made greater potions than she. She had a habit of taking in strays and raising them; he was raised alongside a girl named Eya. They grew up without the influence of other children. They were friends, accomplices, and soul mates; they were each other's first kiss and love. They got married at the age of 17. On Eya's 18th birthday, the Prince went to the closest village — 30 miles away — to get her a gift of great thought to express his love. When he got to the village, he saw a missing poster of a Prince who had not been seen in almost 15 years. There was a portrait that looked exactly like he did as a youngling. He ripped down the poster, shoved it into his rucksack, and went in search of the perfect gift. He couldn't find anything but useless baubles and trinkets that Eya wouldn't like. He professed that he wouldn't go home until he found the perfect, meaningful gift — he didn't want to disappoint Eya with empty hands.

"He stayed for a month. He spent his days searching until he collapsed from tiredness. He wore himself down to the bone. On the last day of the month, he stumbled down an alley and found a table. Its wares had an air about them; instantly, he knew he would find the perfect gift on that table. Carefully, he examined every item; his eyes were drawn to a necklace. The necklace contained a spyglass pendant. Spyglasses would not be invented until 60 years later...but the Prince knew exactly what it was. He and Eya dreamed of traveling the world; they had discussed an object similar to the pendant. They agreed that it would be easier to buy a boat and have an object that allowed them to see great distances. They could view towns and sightsee without wasting money on every little thing such as inns and transportation everywhere they went.

"The lady who owned the table stepped up and waited for payment. The Prince reached into his pockets and discovered he had no money left; therefore, nothing with which to pay the woman. She offered him the necklace and said her price was not money — she could take something else in exchange. The Prince had no idea what she meant, but he took the necklace because he knew there was no gift more perfect.

"He rode back home to the healer's cottage faster than the wind. But, when he got back, Eya was nowhere to be found. He waited for her. And waited, and waited. He waited for more than a year and came to the conclusion that she was never returning. He didn't know if she had found another or if she died. He blamed his stupid yearning to buy her a gift and regretted the whole month he wasted. He threw the necklace into the fireplace, packed up his belongings, and returned to his kingdom. He never let his heart be given to another. He never forsook his wedding vows." She stops to drink her tea. She acts as if she is done telling the tale, but, there has to be more than that.

"Then how does he have a branch? It does not appear to have stopped with him; he must have had children." She puts down her cup and looks into the fireplace. She watches the flames dance before continuing. I take another sip of my tea. It is awfully hot in here. The fireplace should not be needed this time of year.

"What he did not see was a little hand reach out and grab the necklace out of the fire. Eya didn't go anywhere; she was with him in the cottage the whole time. The price for the necklace turned out to be a high one. Their love was turned against them. Some say that true love is blinding; in this case, it truly was. One was oblivious to the other and they literally couldn't see each other.

"In the first year that the Prince waited for her, Eya gave birth to twins. The girl, Stellia, grabbed the necklace out of the fireplace. She burned her hand while her brother, Ivor, looked on. He jumped into action and tried to protect her when she cried out. He forgot he was only a baby and could do nothing to help his sister as he fell face-first onto the stone floor. Eya came in from collecting herbs to find her children howling in pain. She immediately made potions and poultices to heal her children. She m—"

"I am sorry, but can you speed things up?" I can not be late for my meeting!

"The children grew up to make brilliant potions that rivaled their father's. Stellia's line stayed in Ottishire until it was destroyed. But 150 years ago, some of Ivor's line made it to Musalin. You might find a surprise if you finish tracing that branch until you reach today's descendants. Goodbye."

"Thank you, bye." I rush out of her office while stuffing the book into my bag. If I run, I should be able to make it — barely.

CHAPTER TWENTY-SEVEN

Jezebel

I come to with the worst pain I've ever felt — and that's saying something. My head feels like it's on fire; with every breath that I take, I feel shards of pain.

A hand brushes my forehead and causes ripples of unbearable pain; a whimper forces its way out. My face contorts in pain and I clench my teeth.

"Roma, open your eyes." Roma...why is somebody calling me Roma? Who's Roma? "Jezebel?" Weakly, I open my eyes. "I thought so. How ever did you get here?" Where is here? Who is this guy? Wait...didn't I serve him dinner a little while ago? How did he convince the Devil to let him help me? Did the Devil beat me so hard that I almost died?!

I try to sit up, but the pain stops me. "Jezebel, stop. You'll only make it worse. Let me fix it, just rest. I will have to remove the plaster, though." He's the best healer I've ever been allowed — I'm usually forced to bear the pain until the wound heals on its own. Is the Devil going to kill him for being so nice to me? I hope not...

CHAPTER TWENTY-EIGHT

Victa

I arrive a second before the clock strikes midnight. Why would they want to meet here? The docks are at the opposite end of town from the Red List's Headquarters. As soon as I step closer to the boats, shadows come out of the darkness. They sweep me up and place me on a boat. The shadows are wearing cloaks; I cannot see their faces.

Not until the boat is a good distance from the docks, do they take further action. A cloak is flung my way and a couple of shadows unmask themselves. Arturo is at the wheel and Tenna was the one who grabbed my arms. The rest stay as shadows. Despite the promise of a storm, the night is peaceful and calm. The mist of the ocean feels good on my face, it cools the heat that my rushing caused.

We travel without light and go slowly; the boat barely makes a sound as it rides the waves. I pull the hood of my cloak up and wait. Who will I find at the end of the tree? Why will it surprise me? Is it me? Am I royalty?! No...mother never would have kept that a secret — right? And she would be next in succession if something were to happen to Theo. She would have killed Theo after his father was taken out — she wishes to control the world.

I sigh. A very ambitious goal, one that I hope never comes to pass. My mother is ruthless in leading the Unknown; the world would die under her rule. Besides, she only wants me to kidnap Theo — she never mentioned anything about killing him. If she really was next in line, she would not have waited this long to take control of Musalin. Well, then, who else could it be?

Gevan? No, he would live at the palace. And...he would not have married me. Instead, he would have married somebody more fit to be royalty. All members of the Royal Family have power; he would never have allowed my mother to treat him the way that she does.

I have never met a stranger who contained the Air of Royalty. At a young age, I was forced to memorize all types of royalty from the past two-hundred years. It must be somebody who is worldly...somebody who knows their place. I have no idea whatsoever as to who it is.

On to other matters: who killed the king? Will I have to kill them for it — in order to prove my loyalty? I am not comfortable with doing that. Yes, they committed a huge — unnecessary — crime, but I sincerely do not wish to kill somebody for my own gain. I prefer to look at the bigger picture, and not just at myself.

Who could be so power-hungry, selfish, and cruel as to kill a nice, good king in cold blood? I try to think long and hard if I know of such a person but am having trouble even picturing that kind of person. What do they even look like? Do they emit evil, or are they normal looking? Is such evil able to be contained under a normal façade? How do I meet them without causing them suspicion? Hopefully, just finding a name is enough to increase my ranking in The Circle. As of yet, I am not allowed to go near Theo at the palace.

Great, I am out of things to ponder and we are no closer to the headquarters than we were five minutes ago. Actually, is not the building located in the other direction? We should be heading toward land, not out into the vast ocean. The ship is pointed to open waters. Where are they taking me? Did they turn me in? The Shanas?! No...they would never. I have their loyalty; there is no way that they know about my plans — nobody but myself knows of them.

Should I ask Tenna? Everybody has been silent since I boarded — I assumed that they thought mother was following me. Do they not trust me? I know that it has been six years, but I really have not changed since then. I am still the same person; I still have the same ideals. Really, the only differences are Gevan, Iris, and this new as-of-yet-to-be-named organization — absolutely nothing that changes who I am.

A cup is thrust in front of my face. I remove my right hand from the rail, grab the cup, check for poison, and gulp it down. The ale warms me up from the inside out; my goosebumps vanish.

My head feels heavy. All the excitement of today must have exhausted me. I turn to ask Tenna if I may retire...all I am met with are blurry shapes. I can no longer discern the shadows from the dark of the night. The heaviness of my head is taking a toll on my feet — I no longer feel them; they have gone numb. My mouth feels full of cotton balls. What...is...happening?

They did **not** betray me. They trust me. They did **not**—

Made in United States
North Haven, CT
11 March 2023

33924699R00161